The Tropical Ticket

SWEET ROMANCE & WOMEN'S FRIENDSHIP FICTION

HILTON HEAD ISLAND
BOOK FIVE

ELANA JOHNSON

feel good fiction

ELANA JOHNSON

ISBN-13: 978-1-63876-256-0

Chapter One

B essie Clifton shook her head as one of her best friends held the blow dryer over it. She scrubbed her fingers along her scalp, because she'd been sitting with the bleach and dye on it for what felt like a long time now, and she needed relief.

Behind her, Sage laughed, the sound barely registering over the blowing of the dryer. Bessie had been getting her hair cut and colored by Sage for several years now, since they'd met and started attending Supper Club together.

That life felt like it belonged to someone else. Certainly not Bessie, who'd been married and raising a teenager when she'd first gone to the initial meeting for a Supper Club in Sweet Water Falls, a small town along the Coastal Bend of Texas.

She was currently divorced and lived with her adult daughter on Hilton Head Island, in South Carolina, and the only thing that even remotely resembled the life she'd had a decade ago was the Supper Club.

Not even the women who belonged to and attended the Club. Just the fact that the Supper Club still existed. And to Bessie, that was significant, because for a year or so there, she'd thought they'd disband and go their separate ways.

A new kind of relief filled her when she thought about how they'd saved their Supper Club. Her and Sage. Because they'd realized that if they didn't make the move to Hilton Head, the monthly dinners would have to end.

Bessie usually held her tongue and didn't make close friendships with very many people. Those she did tended to be very close—like her Supper Club ladies—but she wasn't very confrontational. She knew a lot of people on the surface, and she recognized people who came into the bread shop where she worked.

People had come and gone in her lifetime. Friends for a season. There, then gone. She knew that once common interests were lost or too many miles separated two people that it became harder to stay friends. Harder to stay in touch. Easier to focus on those closer, or those who shared new common interests.

And, as she'd watched her friends lose husbands, go through divorces, become empty nesters and widows and reinvent themselves, she hadn't wanted to lose her connection to them. She hadn't wanted to watch Bea, Cass, Lauren, or Joy walk out of her life, never to be heard from again.

Or, if she did hear from them, it was a lame social media

message after a few years, stating how they'd "lost touch," and wanted to catch up.

No, that wasn't good enough for Bessie, and it hadn't been good enough for Sage either. They'd gotten together, and they'd made plans to move to Hilton Head too, each with a loved one, so they could keep and continue their relationships.

Bessie lived with her adult daughter, and Wynona made dinner almost every night. Bessie didn't much care to spend time in the kitchen if it wasn't to bake something golden and delicious, and Wyn could put together something simple in a matter of minutes. Sage lived with her sister, Thelma, and the two of them got into so much trouble together, even now that Sage was in her early fifties.

Sage switched off the hair dryer and asked, "Well? How do you like it?" Her hair bore the same color as freshly churned earth, but it looked a little washed out to Bessie today. Sage insisted that she never dyed it, but Bessie wasn't always sure she believed her.

Bessie reached up, shaking her hands loose of the drape she wore buttoned tightly around her neck, and ran her fingers through her hair. "It's really blonde," she said.

"The dark smudge offsets it," Sage said, fingering a lock of hair. "I think that turned out great. It might be my new favorite thing to do." She smiled at Bessie in the mirror, and she really was the best colorist Bessie had ever met.

"I love it too." She grinned back at her friend. "Thank you, Sage."

"You're gonna be the talk of the island, what with your

sexy new 'do and your new bread bakery opening up." She switched on the blow dryer again and blew it over Bessie's shoulders and down her back to dislodge any errant hairs. Then she silenced it, holstered it in the compartment at her station, and unsnapped the drape.

Bessie sighed as she got to her feet, the chemically smell of the salon one of her very favorite things. It meant she was taking time for herself, doing something that made her feel good, and spending time with a friend. She stepped into Sage's arms and hugged her. "You'll be at the grand opening on Saturday, right?"

"I'm not even going to answer that," Sage said. All of her friends had promised and re-promised to be there. Bessie wasn't sure why she was asking. Probably because her guts writhed at the thought of truly doing what she'd been dreaming of doing for the past four years: Opening her own bakery.

Not just any bakery. She wasn't making double-fudge brownies or eclairs, raspberry pistachio tarts or birthday cakes. All Bessie wanted to make was bread. Loaves of bread in all shapes and sizes. Rolls and croissants for parties, family functions, and the holidays.

She and Wynona had been back and forth about the name of their joint-venture bread bakery since the moment they'd started discussing it. They'd narrowed it down to two —Flour Power or Bread & Butter—and Bessie still hadn't told her friends what the name of the shop would be.

"See you Saturday," Bessie said after she'd checked out and booked her next appointment, and she left the high-end salon that seemed to be made of glass, metal, and light in a strip mall near the beach. She loved the beaches here in Hilton Head, as she visited them far more often than she had in Sweet Water Falls.

When she pulled up to the shop, she smiled fondly at her daughter's sedan parked out front. She took a moment to imagine a line of eager bread lovers extending out the double-glass doors. They currently hid behind a painter's cloth that covered the name of the bakery.

Wynona had bought into the business as the business-woman working behind Bessie's beautiful bread. She'd come up with the idea to reveal the name of the shop at the grand opening, and she'd put out all of the press releases to the local papers, online forums, and social media groups. She'd passed out flyers and visited with other small businesses and managers of local interest around the island, including the various Country Clubs, the public library, and other non-competitive businesses who might be able to simply put a stack of flyers about their grand opening on the checkout counter.

Bessie had stopped keeping track after the library, the restaurants, the historical lighthouse, the quilting and yarn shops, and the bigger outdoor malls had agreed to shelve their event flyers. Even the owner of Gourmet Goods—a direct competitor for croissants had gushed over the fact that there'd be a new bread bakery in town, and grumpy Oliver Blackhurst had also agreed to put some on the counters of The Mad Mango. Bessie had sent Wyn to do all of that community outreach and education alone.

She ducked under the drape and into the shop to find Wyn sitting at one of the front tables. She'd wanted to go in the French direction, as so many people equated good bread with France. But she didn't want to be kitschy or outdated too fast. She didn't want people to assume she only made baguettes or that they wouldn't find their favorite regional bread in her store. Because they would. They absolutely would, as Bessie had handmade bagels on her menu every day of the week, along with a German pretzel recipe that wowed every person who'd ever tried it.

She'd recently perfected arepas from Venezuela. She usually made hers straight up to be savored with coffee, but she'd been known to stuff them with meat and cheese too. She adored pitas from the Middle East—if someone had never tried a homemade pita, the way she scored it into a grid and then baked it... They hadn't lived yet—in Bessie's opinion.

Her mouth watered every time she thought of her Egyptian bread recipes, as well as the naan she'd been working on for a while too.

"Hey, sissy," she said to her daughter. They could've decorated the shop in any number of styles, from French or European to Moroccan or Middle Eastern. In the end, they'd gone with classic, beautiful tables with a muted metal frame and pure wood tops made from planks—almost mirroring some of the seasoned wood planks Bessie had been cooking on for years.

The tables held two or four and had chairs that matched in frame and wood. They'd bought restaurant-standard napkin holders and equipped each table with a container of plastic knives for butter and jam spreading.

At her old job at the Bread Boy in Texas, a friend had made jams and brought them into the shop. Wyn had been working on a partnership with a local farm to provide and feature their jams instead, and Bessie only bought the best butter from an Amish community in Pennsylvania she'd gotten to know through her connections in Texas.

The quality of a loaf of bread came partly from the ingredients, so Bessie paid close attention to those. The rest came as the dough got worked with the hands of a master, and Bessie went by her daughter and into the kitchen. "When is the final staff meeting?" she called.

"Two hours," Wyn answered.

Bessie whipped an apron from the hook by the back door that led into the narrow parking lot behind the shop. Her new bakery sat second-down in a row of little shops, and she loved the location. Only a couple of blocks from the beach, she shared the row with a kite shop, a bistro that only served dinner on weekdays and lunch and dinner on weekends, and a wig shop down on the other end.

It sat about six blocks from the place she'd looked at beside The Mad Mango a few months ago, and only one and a half miles from the house she and Wyn were renting together. She'd wanted to be close to her commercial space and feel like it was in a safe spot, because she'd arrive early in the morning and probably work for hours in the strip shop alone, before any other employee showed up, including her daughter.

Two hours was enough to get something going that would be ready by the end of the final staff meeting. They'd hired eight people to help them run the shop, and that included one custodian, an assistant baker, and six people to man the cash register from the hours of six-thirty am. to three p.m.

Bessie's adrenaline kicked in, and by the time the meeting started, she had a batch of quick-yeast dinner rolls ready to go into the oven. She slid the tray with all the dough balls pressed together into the waiting oven, set a timer in her phone, and went to join her daughter in the front of the shop.

Everyone else had arrived, and someone had brought coffee. Bessie took the last remaining cup—the one with her name on it—and sat down at the table with Wyn and all of her papers.

She leaned over and said something to a man named Winslow, who would be their custodian in the shop. He'd come in close to noon and work for several hours, staying after the storefront closed to get the trashcans emptied, the floors and counters cleaned and ready for the next day, and any maintenance on her ovens and mixers that might arise.

"How's Darla?" she asked.

His face lit up. "She's doing so much better," he said. "Claire is thrilled with the progress, and she's eating more." Their Pomeranian had just had puppies, and the fourth one had been born late. His wife had thought they might lose it, especially when the little pup wouldn't eat.

"I'm seriously considering taking one of them," she said.

"She's only sold two, so we have a couple more," he said.

"All right, everyone," Wyn said. "Let's get started. I've got a game plan for the grand opening in a couple of days, and I want to go through it and make sure there are no questions." She stood in the middle of the grouping of tables but moved over to where Bessie sat and collected a thin stack of papers.

Bessie knew the game plan already, and she pulled Wyn's yellow lined notepad closer and started making a list of the breads she needed to make tomorrow for the following day's grand opening.

Four hours of a grand opening. A name reveal. One ribbon-cutting ceremony. A tiny, short speech. Coupons. Samples. An email list. Special orders. And any sales they could rustle up.

Bessie had decided to start with what most people loved —sourdough, whole wheat, classic French white, croissants, dinner rolls, and her signature salted honey whole wheat.

She couldn't wait to come in at three a.m. tomorrow morning and start baking.

Chapter Two

B essie stood next to Wynona, both of them wearing nearly identical outfits. They'd wanted to come across as casual but professional, and they'd chosen black slacks or jeans, along with a pretty blouse they felt comfortable in, with their baking apron tied around their waist.

The sun had already heated the entire island, despite the grand opening being at nine o'clock in the morning. Bessie couldn't believe how many people had shown up for the grand opening and the name reveal of the shop, and more people kept gathering. The clock ticked to time, and Bessie glanced over to her. "Should we begin?"

Bessie did a quick check—Bea and Grant had arrived, as had Cass and Harrison. Lauren and Blake had been here since seven, helping Bessie put the bread into the display cases and onto the shelves, as well as printing and cutting the one-time-use coupons.

Joy and Scott had taken all the trash out this morning,

and they'd helped Bessie clean the kitchen after she'd made several more loaves of bread this morning. No bread bakery worth its salt didn't smell like something golden and delicious had just come out of the oven, so while Bessie had done the bulk of her baking yesterday, she couldn't have this grand opening without the scent of yeast, milk, and butter hanging in the air.

Sage stood front and center with her sister, and Bessie didn't recognize a lot of the other faces. Tyler Barker, who'd helped her find this place, stood off to her left, and she nodded to him. He smiled like he attended all of his clients' functions, and perhaps he did. She didn't know him well enough to know.

"Mom?"

She nodded, and Wynona put her movie star smile on her face. Bessie's stomach swooped, and when she blinked, the whole world went black, despite the brightness of the sun. Her vision cleared quickly, and her eyes landed on a dark-haired man that shouldn't have accelerated her pulse quite the way he did.

Oliver Blackhurst had been dipped in all the best gene pools, and Bessie sure did like the sweep of his thick, dark hair across his forehead. The way his nearly black eyes zeroed in on her, and that slight, arrogant curl of his lips as he smiled.

Oh, the man was dangerous to her health, as her stomach dropped to her knees and her heartbeat accelerated. Again.

She gave her head a small shake, and Oliver cocked his

right eyebrow. She hadn't realized she hadn't looked away from him before moving, as she hadn't meant to communicate with him. She'd been telling herself *no*. A very solid, very loud, *No*.

She wasn't interested in Oliver Blackhurst. Not only was he one of the grumpiest men she'd met on this island, but she didn't have room in her life for a boyfriend. Especially not one as hot as the surface of the sun.

"Welcome everyone," Wynona said, and Bessie tore her attention from the gorgeous Mister Blackhurst. Why was he here anyway? "My mother and I have had a dream of opening a bread bakery for a few years now." She glowed as she looked over to Bessie, her smile genuine and pure and oh-so-good.

"We're excited to have found this perfect shop, on this perfect island in South Carolina, and we're first going to reveal the perfect name." She look up and to her left, where she lifted her hand and gripped the drop cloth still covering the sign.

"Without further ado, I give you...Flour Power!" She tugged on the cloth and it came down just as she'd rehearsed. The gorgeous logo Bessie had commissioned from Lauren, which was a bright pink daisy with a perfectly golden-yellow center—in the shape of a loaf of bread.

Applause broke out and filled the air surrounding the new shop, then the whole parking lot. The dropping of the cloth was the cue for their employees inside the shop, and they spilled out onto the sidewalk. Bessie and Wynona parted and both gestured to the held-open doors, and Sage and Thelma were the first to surge inside.

"Hello," Bessie said to the woman who followed them. "Thank you for coming. Good to see you. Thank you. Hello." She greeted everyone who streamed past her, and soon enough, the crowd had filled the shop and more remained on the sidewalk in front of the shop.

Thankfully, Wyn's game plan had anticipated this, and before Bessie could say "Hello," again, one of her employees, Rachel, handed her a silver tray full of samples. Wyn got one too, and then the three of them started walking around the crowd still mingling outside.

Just her luck, Oliver stood on her side, and she couldn't avoid him. "Bessie," he said. "This is fantastic." He seemed perfectly pleasant today, but he couldn't very well act like Oscar the Grouch in public. Many of these people were probably his customers too.

"Thank you," she said. "This is my salted honey whole wheat, but Wynona has the French white, and Rachel has the sourdough."

He didn't look away from her as he said, "I'd like this." He reached for a sample, which already had a toothpick speared through it.

"There's butter and jam on the tables," she said, wondering if he'd started to melt out here too. That was the reason her skin felt seared, and not because Oliver still hadn't looked away from her.

She forced herself to turn toward someone else, but

Oliver said, "Wait." Bessie turned back to him, her eyebrows lifting into a silent, *Well?*

"There's a small business...thing here on the island. For locals who own small businesses." He reached up and pulled at his collar, then quickly dropped his hand. He stuffed the bite-size sample of bread into his mouth, those handsome eyes widening. "Bessie, this is fantastic."

"And you didn't even have it with butter," she said with a smile. "There's nothing better than bread with butter, you know."

"Oh, I can think of a few things," he said, and Bessie felt sure her eyes had started to see red, for Oliver was blushing. *Blushing.* He cleared his throat. "The Island Collective meets every month, and I think you'd benefit from attending." He held out a card.

Bessie wanted to toss the sample tray and take the card, then devour the words on it. Instead, she blinked at it and then Oliver. He smiled, and wow, he shouldn't be allowed to do that in public.

"We meet this coming week, and we'll be talking about the upcoming Heritage Festival."

"The Heritage Festival?"

"It's a huge celebration in late August, right before the tourists leave," he said. "We have booths for each of our businesses, and the city gives those of us who are in the Island Collective better placement, special consideration, and the first chance at sponsorships."

Bessie was a long way from sponsoring anything but

paying her own rent, but she took the card from his fingers. "Thank you, Oliver."

He nodded, kept that glorious smile on his face, and said, "Now, I need to go buy a whole loaf of this salted honey whole wheat bread." He dodged through the crowd and managed to get inside the shop, all while Bessie stood there and watched.

WEDNESDAY MORNING, BESSIE HUNG HER APRON on the hook by the back door. "Hillie, I'm headed to a meeting, okay?"

"No problem, Miss Bessie," she said, her hands working the dough on the board in front of her without looking. She'd grown up out in rural South Carolina, and she'd been baking since the age of five. Bessie had loved listening to her talk about her mammy and grammy, and the interview had been more storytelling than questioning.

Bessie had also hired her at the end of that, and she'd been happy she had. They'd been baking together for about three weeks now, as Wyn interviewed and hired the rest of the staff, as the tables and chairs and napkins holders had come in.

She went out the back door and over to her SUV, her hands feeling too hot and everything else suddenly too cold. The overheated interior of the vehicle made breathing difficult, and Bessie got the engine started and the air conditioning vents blowing right on her face.

By the time she arrived at the community center where the Island Connection meeting was set to take place, she felt like throwing up. Bessie didn't normally eat breakfast, except for a couple of bites of croissant and the coffee Wyn brought her when the shop opened. She hadn't eaten more than that now, but maybe she should've.

She looked toward the entrance, but she couldn't make herself get out of the car. A couple of women who were dressed like they might be on their way to the meeting went by and inside, and Bessie took a deep breath.

"You can do it, girl," she told herself. She hadn't seen Oliver yet, and she didn't want him to find her sitting in her car, too scared to go inside. She told herself she'd left work early for this meeting. She told herself she wanted this opportunity. She told herself it would be good for her to meet other locals who also owned small businesses.

None of those got her out of the car, and Bessie found herself kneading the steering wheel though she then wouldn't be setting it to rise the way she did her flawless dinner rolls.

"Come on, Bessie," she moaned the words as she leaned her head back against the rest. Her eyes drifted closed, and a twinge of exhaustion stole through her. She'd been getting up in the middle of the night for years, so she wasn't really tired yet.

The grand opening had gone so well, and they'd had a steady stream of customers in the four days since. Word seemed to be spreading, as Wyn had been having their cashiers ask how people had heard about Flour Power when they came in to buy.

She and Hillie had sold through all of their inventory every day so far, and Bessie told herself these things as motivators to get herself inside the community center. It still didn't work, and she told herself she didn't want to leave the air-conditioned interior of her car and step out into the near-July heat and humidity.

The fact that the community center also had air conditioning didn't weigh on her decision, because she couldn't let it.

A sharp knock met her ears, and Bessie yelped as she shot forward. She jerked her attention to the side window as her adrenaline spiraled up into her brain and down into her toes. She tingled, and not in a good way.

Oliver stood there, and he backed up with both hands up. Amusement rode in his expression, and Bessie pressed the on-off button and practically pushed the door open into his body.

He chuckled and said, "I'm sorry. I didn't realize you were taking a nap."

"I wasn't taking a nap." Bessie turned back to the car and pulled out her purse. It was really more the size of a small carryon, and the only reason she could carry it around was because she had some pretty impressive arm and shoulder muscles from all the kneading.

She slammed her door, and they fell into step beside one another as she started toward the community center. "You're late, you know."

"You were sitting in your car, apparently asleep." He didn't even look over to her as he said it. When they reached the door, he opened it and lifted his eyebrows to usher her through it. A blast of the blessed AC hit her in the face, and she went into it willingly.

She didn't know which way to go after that, and Oliver put his hand on the small of her back and said, "To the right. Down that skinny hallway there."

"You call hallways narrow, not skinny," she hissed at him as she started that way. Now she had to deal with her irritation with Oliver Blackhurst as well as the queasy feelings of walking into a meeting with complete strangers.

"Next doorway," he said from behind her, and Bessie didn't break stride as she made the turn and entered the room. Unfortunately, they were late, and that meant a whole room of local business owners turning to take them in.

Men and women, and several of them broke out into smiles. "Ollie," a woman said, and that nearly made Bessie roll her eyes. The room was small, but Bessie hadn't anticipated it being so full.

Only two chairs remained, and she edged over to one, only to have Oliver's perfectly cologned body drop into the one beside her, trapping her on the row between his sexy Versace scent and a woman wearing more foodstuff on her clothes than Bessie ever wanted to see outside of a kitchen.

She gave the woman a tight smile and tried to inch a little closer to her. That was a mistake, as the scent of stale oven cleaner met her nose.

"All right," the woman up front said. "So as I was

saying." She shot a look toward the corner where Oliver and Bessie sat, but it didn't feel like her eyes roamed anywhere near Oliver. "We'll need to be in pairs for this year's Heritage Festival, and you'll be working closely with that person to advertise the festival, come up with marketing ideas, and this year, you'll be able to cross-promote each other's businesses in a whole new way."

She acted like these things were so amazing, but Bessie had no idea what she was talking about. Oliver had said that they'd be talking about the Heritage Festival, and Bessie did want to be involved in that. She simply thought it would be an introductory meeting. She cut a glance at her phone and saw that they'd only been eight minutes late.

The whole intro to an entire Heritage Festival couldn't have happened that fast, could it?

She didn't dare look over to Oliver, as he'd been through this before. Maybe she could ask him a question or two if she got partnered with someone who acted like she should already know everything about this island and its traditions.

The woman up front talked for a few more minutes, and then she said, "We'd like to welcome any new members." She zeroed in on Bessie again, and she managed to put a smile on her face before she added, "You guys missed the sign-ups, so Oliver, would you be willing to introduce the woman you brought and be her partner for the festival this year?"

Bessie gaped at the woman, then switched her attention to Oliver. "We missed that much?" She faced the front again, barely able to bear the load of all the eyes in the room which had landed on her. "We were eight minutes late."

"*Thirty*-eight," the woman said, and Bessie's heartbeat flailed behind the bars of her ribs.

She turned more fully to Oliver. "Thirty-eight minutes late?"

He actually lifted his arm to the back of her chair like he might fold her into his side. He smiled at her and then up to the woman standing in front of everyone. "I totally forgot we switched the time for our summer meetings," he said easily. "I apologize, Amy." He looked at Bessie, who blinked at him like he'd gone crazy.

His smile slipped a little, and he shifted on his chair though he still broadcasted the picture of ease. "This is Bessie Clifton," he said. "She just opened the best bread bakery on the island—Flour Power." He leaned closer to her, and Bessie's first inclination was to do the same to him.

But she had no idea what game he was playing, being snarky and throwing banter her way as they walked in— thirty-eight minutes late—and then turning into Mister Nice Guy Oozing Charm for this meeting. So she didn't move a single inch.

"And sure, I'd love to partner with Bessie for the Heritage Festival this year."

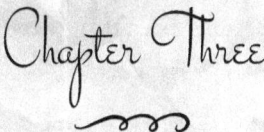

Chapter Three

Oliver Blackhurst couldn't help finding a little bit of humor in the way Bessie's mouth turned into an O and her eyes rounded even more.

"Great," Amy said from the front of the room. "I've got your sponsorship packets up here at the front, and remember, you do need to sponsor as a pair this year. Hilton Head wants to focus on the concept of a double, as we now have a pair of twins as the Mayor and the Fire Chief."

She beamed like this was just so cute, and Oliver seethed inside. He did not care one whit who the mayor or the fire chief were, and he certainly wouldn't plan island festivals around such a thing.

"Our platinum sponsorship is only open today," Amy said. "And we only have three spots for pairs, for a total of six platinum businesses." She glanced over to Oliver, who didn't move. He'd always sponsored the Heritage Festival at a high level, because that gave him better booth placement, bigger ads in all the printables for the festival—both before it began, during, and after—and he'd seen noticeable increases in customers and profit for months after the event.

The other business owners in the room started to stand, the chatter between them breaking out as they waited to get closer to Amy to get their packets.

Next to him, the gorgeous Bessie Clifton sat ramrod straight, the tension radiating from her. "You need to relax," he said quietly.

That earned him a glare, and she quickly switched her gaze back up front. "Should we get a packet?"

"We can do it online." Oliver pulled out his phone and tapped on the icon to load his web browser. "I'm going to sponsor at the platinum level."

"You're kidding."

Oliver raised his eyes from his phone to Bessie's. They were the kind of blue that made Oliver sigh. The kind of blue that the late spring sky held for days. Not too rich. Not brilliant or bright. But so beautiful, Oliver's thoughts scattered.

He gathered them all back together and said, "I'm not kidding. With pairs this year, that's six businesses who'll get the most exposure."

Bessie leaned closer to him, her blonde hair falling forward over her shoulder. He couldn't stop himself from looking at it, his imagination kicking into gear about what it would be like to slide his fingers through those golden locks.

He swallowed and leaned toward her too. "What's the problem?"

"I don't know what platinum costs, but I can guarantee I can't pay for it."

Oliver's lips twitched as the scent of butter and oranges met his nose. This woman was going to be the death of his no-dating rule. The death of his aversion to trying to find someone to spend his life with. The death of him as Oliver Blackhurst.

All of his walls re-erected themselves at the thought of losing himself simply so he could fall in love with someone. He'd done that before, and it had ended with him standing on the side of the road—literally—wondering who he was and how to find his way home.

He'd worked for every inch of his life since then. He'd clawed his way back from the version of himself he'd been just to be with Helena.

He'd found himself, rediscovered his own passions and what made him happy, and had everything he could ever want. It had cost him a lot, and he wasn't going to throw it away for a beautiful woman, even if she called to him in a way no one had in a while.

Besides, he *almost* had everything he wanted.

He blinked at Bessie, at those pink lips and worried cornflower blue eyes, and thought again, *Almost*.

"I can cover you," he said.

"No." She shook her head, the action getting faster and more violent with every passing moment. "No. No, thank you."

"We have to sponsor at the same level," he said, looking back at his phone. He tapped on platinum at the top of the sponsor screen and found all three spots were still available.

Several others had their phones out too, and Oliver ignored Bessie's protest as he quickly filled out the form and submitted it. The number that came up made his heartbeat pause for a moment, and then he tapped the big yellow button to pay it.

"Oliver," Bessie hissed at him. She did a lot of hissing, in his opinion. Or maybe that was just how she spoke to him. He hadn't noticed her talking like that to anyone else.

Not that you know, he told himself as he entered his business credit card. It wasn't like he'd spent a lot of time with Bessie, a fact he'd been lamenting and trying to figure out how to rectify since he'd spilled smoothie down the front of her daughter, months ago.

He'd caged his feelings for her until he knew for sure she'd be moving here. He didn't want a long-distance relationship the way Scott had done with Joy. Even Grant and Bea and Harrison and Cass had dealt with flights back and forth from Hilton Head to Texas.

Oliver had marveled at that at the same time he'd vowed he wouldn't do it. Hundreds of thousands of tourists came to the island every summer, and sure, Oliver had enjoyed a fling or two over the years.

More than he wanted to admit out loud. But he'd grown up and matured since then. He'd only been dating women who lived on the twelve-mile-long island or a neighboring community off the barrier island, but even Charleston was too far away for him.

He could drive there in an hour, but an hour spent behind the wheel was an hour he wasn't spending at The Mad Mango, growing his business or training the ever-revolving cast of employees he had.

The site reloaded, his payment complete, and he pressed the power button to make his phone go dark. He stood and tucked it in his pocket. "Come on," he said, glancing around the room. It was too small and stifling, and Oliver couldn't breathe in here, let alone think.

Bessie stood too, and she clutched her oversized purse like she'd use it against anyone who got too close. Oliver took a moment to wonder what she had in there that she absolutely had to carry with her at all times.

He didn't ask, and he wouldn't. But he'd love to go through the bag when she wasn't around, just to see what she had.

"Do you have time for lunch?" he asked.

"It's ten-twenty," Bessie said.

Oliver's smoothie shop didn't open until eleven, but Bessie had left her bread bakery to attend this meeting. A thread of guilt pulled through him that he'd gotten the time wrong, and he pressed his lips together so he wouldn't grovel.

"Breakfast then," he said. "I know a great place that won't be so loud." His skin crawled, especially as a few people started looking his way.

Bessie studied his face, and he had no idea what she was looking for.

"Ollie," Samantha said, and Oliver put his business-smile

on his face as he looked past the beautiful blonde he wanted to spend time with to another one he didn't.

"Hey, Sam." He moved by Bessie and kissed both of Sam's cheeks. "Who did you partner with? Wait." He held up one hand. "Let me guess."

He didn't have to look more than two feet to her right. "Cast-Iron Creations." He beamed at the man at Sam's side and extended his hand for Stanley MacDonald to shake.

"It's a good pairing," Sam said, looking over to the man who probably had ten years on both her and Oliver.

"You do meal kits," Oliver said. "He has the wares to cook them. It's brilliant."

Sam nodded to Bessie, who'd turned toward them but hadn't joined their threesome. Oliver backed up a step to give her room to slide into the huddle, but she didn't move. Frustration filled him, and he reached for her hand and pulled her forward.

Her feet seemed glued to the carpet, but she finally managed to take the couple of steps to join them.

"Bread and smoothies," Sam said as her eyebrows went up. "What's your strategy there?"

"Well," Bessie said. "My strategy would've been to be on time so I could find a partner who makes sense, but." She hit the T hard and gave Oliver a pointed look.

"Oh-ho, boy," Stanley said, his voice mostly made of a laugh. "I like you, Bessie. I'm Stanley MacDonald. Do you ever bake bread in cast-iron?"

"I have, yes." Bessie gave him a bright, kind smile, and

instant jealousy spiked through Oliver. She'd never looked at him like that, and wow, he wanted her to.

He heard his name in a voice he absolutely did not want to engage with, and he took Bessie's hand again. "We have to jet. Sorry. Good to see you guys."

Oliver started for the door, but Bessie didn't come with him. He turned to glare at her. "We have to meet privately," he said.

"Our platinum spots are sold out!" Amy crowed from the front of the room.

Bessie squeezed his hand, but not in a romantic way. Then she tried to yank her hand back.

Oliver steadfastly held on. "Please," he said through clenched teeth as Kamille's eyes locked onto him. She nodded to her friend, and Oliver had to leave. Now.

He released Bessie's hand and said, "I'll meet you outside." He hightailed it out of there, his heartbeat thrashing against his sternum and sending frantic blood through his veins.

Maybe he hadn't forgotten about their earlier summer meetings times. Maybe he'd subconsciously known he better not be on time, or he might be paired with an absolute nightmare of a partner.

"You didn't even know it would be a partnership this year," he grumbled to himself as he strode down the *narrow* hallway.

He burst out into the open area at the community center, the high ceilings and larger space allowing more air to enter his lungs. *You're fine*, he told himself. Bessie had never done the Heritage Festival before, and Oliver had. Many times. He could do the whole thing without having to speak to her again.

A tight, pinching loss eased through his stomach and up into his lungs and throat.

Sunshine poured in through the front windows and doors, and Oliver turned that way. If he couldn't take Bessie to a late breakfast or an early lunch, he might as well get to work. He could start planning his booth in his office at The Mad Mango.

He hadn't gotten his feet to move before Bessie asked, "Why are you just standing there?"

She actually glared as she went in front of him, curving around him on her way toward the doors. His attraction to her arced through the air, and she had to feel that.

"Are we going to breakfast, or what?" Bessie tossed over her shoulder as she headed away from him, and Oliver's heartbeat boomed at him to *go with her, you idiot. Don't just stand there!*

He cleared his throat and straightened the collar on his polo. Then he hurried after Bessie, that *almost* echoing dangerously in his head.

Chapter Four

B essie hadn't been out with a man on a first date in a very long time. Almost twenty-five years now.

As she eased herself into the passenger seat of Oliver's expensive SUV and settled her purse on the floor, she tried to catalog everything at once.

The interior of the car smelled like Oliver's cologne and something sweet. She spied a pastry bag lilting lazily in the cupholder, and she assumed he'd eaten something fried and frosted for breakfast. His first breakfast.

That, or he bathed in ocean water, chocolate frosting, and male goodness.

He'd opened her door for her, and she had time to glance into the back seat before he joined her in the car. She immediately swung her head back to him, her brain somehow cataloguing that he'd been a gentleman by helping her into the car first. "Your car is really clean."

"You sound surprised."

ELANA JOHNSON

Bessie faced the front again, every muscle in her body drawn tight. "Let's just get this over with." She was surprised, though she wasn't sure why. She didn't know Oliver Blackhurst, and she had no reason to think he'd be a slob. Every time she'd seen him, he'd actually told her something different with the pressed slacks he wore and the wrinkle-free polos.

He wore such clothes now and combined with that dark hair being swept so perfectly, and the scent of everything man-amazing in her nose, Bessie had very few defenses against him.

"I have a couple of things I'd like to discuss first," he said. Even his voice tickled something inside her in a pleasant way.

Bessie's eyebrows shot up. She glared at him again. "A couple of things?"

Oliver's mouth curved upward into that delicious smile, and Bessie told herself to stop staring at his mouth. She couldn't do it and ended up closing her eyes instead.

"One," Oliver said. "I've done this for over a decade. I always want new ideas, and I'll seriously consider what you say. But I'd like some sort of agreement that you'll trust me to make good decisions for both of us."

"Trust you?" Bessie's eyes flew open as she scoffed, her blood so hot in her veins. Despite the air conditioning blowing in the car, her body felt like she'd stepped into a sauna. "I don't even know you."

"Trust my business experience with this, then," he said, his voice low.

34

Bessie wanted to argue with him, but she folded her arms and looked out the windshield. "I will try," she said stiffly.

"Great," Oliver said easily. Bessie wished his voice didn't rumble quite so perfectly in her ears, and then down into her chest.

"Second," he said. "You have to promise not to fall in love with me."

A strangled yelp flew from her mouth, and every cell in her body burned with pure fire as she faced him again. He wore a wide smile on that handsome face, his dark eyes flaming with the same energy Bessie felt in every corner of her being.

The problem was, she wasn't sure if the heat inside her came from irritation or attraction. Or both.

She forced a laugh out of her mouth. "That's a promise I can make, Mister Blackhurst."

He laughed too, and Bessie suddenly wondered if he'd been joking. Probably. "Then I think we'll be great partners for the Heritage Festival." He put the car in reverse and backed out of the stall. "Have you been to Circle Tree?"

Bessie shook her head, not sure she trusted her voice.

"I'm not going to murder you and bury you in the bayou," Oliver said with a chuckle.

Bessie tossed him a glare. "I know that."

"You're so...tight," he said.

"Thank you," she threw back at him.

He laughed lightly again, the sound almost under his breath, trapped behind his tongue.

BESSIE IMAGINED THE HANDSOME FACE OF OLIVER in the bread dough beneath her palms. She folded it over and punched it down, her heart rate still elevated though their "brunch date" had ended hours ago.

"Mom." Wyn moved to her side. "What are you doing here?"

Punch, punch, punch. "Making bread."

"But...why?" Wyn sounded genuinely confused, and that caused Bessie to come out of her frustrated-filled cloud and look at her daughter. Wyn searched her face. "Everyone's been calling and texting you."

Bessie's brain had gone on vacation the moment she'd hung up her apron to go to that blasted Island Collective meeting.

She looked around the kitchen in the back of the bakery. "I don't know where my phone is."

Wyn frowned, her expression part concern and part irritation. "Hillie's made everything we need for tomorrow's pick-up orders, and Bea finally called me to say you hadn't shown up for their afternoon tea."

Wyn held up her phone. "I've called you and texted you a million times."

Everything held tight inside Bessie fell. "I'm so sorry." She dusted her hands on her apron and stepped away from the dough she'd been kneading. "What time is it?"

"Four-thirty."

Bessie needed a hot shower and a comfortable couch and

maybe something she'd seen a bunch of times playing on the TV in front of her. She wouldn't be watching it, but it would be like a friend in the room, filling the silence so her mind couldn't revolve around and around thoughts of Oliver.

She went into the small office she and Wyn shared, a feeling of being trapped and smothered covering her. She didn't live alone. She couldn't just escape anytime she wanted. Her purse sat on the chair in front of her desk, and she rummaged around in the big front pocket until her fingers touched her phone.

She pulled it out and sighed as she looked at it. Sure enough, she'd missed nine calls and twice that many texts. Instant overwhelm hit her, and since she already knew what the messages were about, she didn't tap to read or listen to them.

At the bottom of the thread for her Supper Club friends, she simply typed, *I had a terrible day, and I spaced out on our midweek tea time. I'm sorry. Rain check?*

Her friends would forgive her, Bessie knew. The real problem was they'd also want to know why her day had been bad and what they could do to help her.

Wyn filled the doorway of the office, and Bessie looked up at Her. "I was late to the Island Collective meeting and had to be partnered up with Oliver for the Heritage Festival. That man is...he insisted on taking me to breakfast and then bossing me around for hours."

Wyn's expression changed the moment Bessie had mentioned Oliver. "You have to be his partner?"

"If I want to be in the Heritage Festival, and you said it would be really good for us."

Her daughter's jaw set. "I can handle Oliver Blackhurst." Wyn had handled almost all of the marketing and promotional opportunities for the grand opening. She *should* probably handle all of this.

"Mom, you bake the bread," Wyn said. "You don't have to do this too." She came closer and drew Bessie into a hug. "This is why I'm here."

"I know," Bessie whispered against her shoulder. "I just wonder if I should be able to know and do what you do." She stepped back, her emotions quivering so close to the surface. "What if you move on to something else one day? I have to know how to do more than bake bread."

Bessie hated that her skills extended to baking and not much else, and she shook her head. "We're new to this, and Oliver isn't. I can learn a lot from him."

"But at what price?" Wyn asked. "I can take this on, and I can keep you updated."

Bessie nodded, because that sounded good. At the same time, part of her really wanted to spend more time with Oliver. She'd thought of a few good comebacks for some of the things he'd said today while she'd been measuring yeast and flour.

She wanted to best him at his own game, and he wasn't hard on the eyes. He smelled incredible, and he'd taken her to a quiet, off-the-beaten-path, quaint diner for breakfast that had served the best buttermilk pancakes Bessie had ever tasted.

She sighed, because while she'd rather only see him when she had something fiery and perfect to throw at him, she also felt some strange attraction to him.

She could never let Wyn or her friends know, and she lifted her head to look at her daughter. "He's an expert on Hilton Head Island. The tourism in the summer. The Festival. The people who live here and those just visiting. I could learn a lot from him." She let the words hang there, and Wyn nodded, giving them validity.

Well, she thought. Now she had a reason to keep seeing Oliver Blackhurst—and it most certainly wasn't because she wanted to be the one to straighten that cocky smile from his face...by kissing him.

Chapter Five

B essie pulled up to Cassandra Tate's house, noting all the cars that had already been parked in the circular driveway. She hadn't been able to get out of the tea with her friends, as she'd forgotten that Cass had organized it so they could go over their Supper Club schedule for the summer. Everyone had activities in the summer, and both Cass and Bea had college-age kids coming to stay with them.

Bea's husband, Grant, had a daughter who lived with him full-time every June, July, and August too, and there were a couple of holidays to work around as well.

Bessie had just opened Flour Power, and Lauren owned and operated a private marketing firm as well. It hadn't been open very long, and she was still actively trying to build her clientele.

Bessie sighed as she put her SUV in park and then reached for the giant bowl of bread dough. She could've just thrown it away, but she could also bake it off here and they could have fresh bread with their tea. She couldn't quite get it and get out of the car, so she left it on the passenger seat and rounded the vehicle to get it.

Her back ached, and she felt about to pop out of this blouse. She may have put on a bit of weight this year as she prepped to leave Texas and strike out on her own in a new state, with a new business she'd never owned herself. Plus, she never baked in anything but well-worn T-shirts, usually with some cowboy or Texan saying on them.

She'd need to go shopping around Hilton Head Island to find something that would fit in to the community here.

Bessie turned toward the house only to find all five of her best friends standing on the front porch. "Oh, boy," she whispered to herself. "Sorry," she called to them as she started toward the group. "I just…"

Bea came down the steps, and she'd started to grow out the pixie cut she'd been sporting for a handful of years now. Her blonde hair framed her face now, almost wisping as she moved.

She had bright blue eyes while Bessie's were definitely more washed out. They sparkled as she took Bessie's big bowl of bread. "Something major must've happened to make you start punching dough." She lifted her eyebrows in a silent yet incredibly loud question.

Bessie wiped her hair back off her forehead. She wanted to take her secret crush on the grumpy Oliver Blackhurst to the grave. Her friends all knew about the smoothie incident, as well as everything he'd said to her while she peered through the window at the shop next to The Mad Mango.

She could trust them with this too.

"Yeah," she said. "I'll tell you about it inside." She went up the steps behind Bea and sank into Sage's embrace.

She held her tightly for a moment then asked, "A rain check? Really?" She pulled away, her smile residing on her face and in her eyes. "That alone was code for 'I have so much to tell you guys, but I don't want to.'"

"Plus, you forgot about *tea*," Lauren said. She too had dark hair and eyes, and Bessie had celebrated plenty when she'd married Blake Williams, as Lauren had never been married and desperately wanted to have the opportunity.

"You love tea time," Lauren said.

"It usually signals the end of my day," Bessie admitted, because she did boil water and make tea most afternoons. If she had anything leftover from the bakery, she'd dunk it in the tea and just enjoy the afternoon.

At least that had been her life in Sweet Water Falls, Texas. Here in Hilton Head, she and Wyn often sat down together in the afternoon and talked business. Bessie didn't hate it, but she missed leaving work at work, that much was for sure.

"Let's go inside," she said as the other five women continued to look at her. "I'm not saying anything about my no-good day in this heat." She led the way inside, where blessed air conditioning had filled Cass's house with cool air.

The table in the dining room held six teacups and plates, only one of which hadn't been used. Bessie sat there, trying to decide what to say.

When Bea had come to Hilton Head to rejuvenate and live out her "love list," she'd met Grant Turner. They'd fallen in love quickly, and Bea had been the first to make the move from Texas to South Carolina.

She'd told everyone about Grant the day she'd met him, and they'd brainstormed together about whether Grant had asked her out or if he was just being friendly.

Back and forth they'd gone, and Bea had quickly learned that Grant was interested in her.

Surely Oliver wasn't...

"All right," Cass said, her voice full of authority. "We've given you plenty of time, Bessie." She poured hot water into Bessie's teacup, and Bessie reached for her spoon. "Time to spill the tea." She grinned as she sat beside her. Cass did everything with grace and fluidity, including stir her own tea and then lift the delicate cup to her lips. She raised her eyebrows and set her cup down with a soft sigh.

"Okay," Bessie said, still searching for the right words. This was why she baked. Measuring flour and soda and salt didn't require her to sift through her thoughts and find the right thing to say. When she'd sparred with Oliver today, the words had just been there—at least some of them. The comebacks she'd stored up since then would be ready for next time.

"It started this morning when Oliver got the time for the meeting wrong. We were a half-hour late—more, because I couldn't get myself out of the car." She shook her head. She didn't need to outline her anxieties for these women. They knew her almost better than she knew herself.

"Anyway." She blew out her breath and continued the story, ending with, "And the most ridiculous thing he said today?" She scoffed, her eyes out the floor-to-ceiling back windows. Surprisingly, no one had interrupted her and asked any questions as she'd told them about getting paired with Oliver, his insistence that they go to breakfast, and the platinum sponsorship she couldn't afford.

"You have to promise not to fall in love with me." Bessie shook her head, the sound of Oliver's voice still lodged in her head. Heck, she'd probably fall asleep with the deep rumbling of it in her eardrums.

She drew a deep breath and then blew it out. "So, yeah. I was imagining his face while I kneaded bread this afternoon." She got to her feet. "Oh, the dough."

"I put it in the fridge," Bea said. Her cup clinked as she set it back on her saucer. "You didn't even notice."

"She's a little hot under the collar about Oliver," Lauren said.

"Mm." Joy hadn't said hardly anything up to this point, and Bessie blinked and met her eye.

"I—" She didn't know what to say. "He's incredibly annoying."

"And incredibly good-looking," Bea said lightly.

Bessie's attention whipped to her. "Bea."

"I'm just saying."

"I'm not interested in him," Bessie said, stating it explicitly. Maybe then it would be true. Maybe then, her pulse would stop rioting at her. "I'm going to learn all I can about the island, the tourism, and the Heritage Festival. That's all. He's just a—a—a necessary evil so I can—he's knowledgeable. That's all." She looked around at everyone, and they all wore some form of a smile.

She didn't like Cass's knowing one, or Bea's bright grin. Joy nodded along with her smile, like she totally agreed with Bessie, but Bessie knew she didn't. And Lauren grinned like the Cheshire Cat—like she'd just eaten all of the cake and only she knew where more was hidden.

"What?" Bessie asked.

"You like him," Cass said.

"No," Bessie said. "He's arrogant and obnoxious."

"He's got that dark hair you like," Lauren said. "You two are like night and day."

"He told me I'm too tight," Bessie said.

Joy gave a loud gasp, which was entirely fake. She grinned afterward, and then laughed.

Bessie's chest tightened, despite her extreme desire for it not to. She got up and cleared her dishes. "I have to get going," she said.

"Bess," Joy said. "I didn't mean to laugh. I'm not laughing *at* you."

"Sure, you are," Bessie said. And she didn't appreciate it. She wasn't a child. She also hadn't felt anything for a man in a long time. As she rinsed out her teacup and then picked up the one Lauren put in the sink next to it, she paused.

She looked at the brunette who hadn't moved from her side. Lauren gazed back at her. "It's okay to like him."

"I *don't* like him," Bessie said. "He *is* obnoxious and arrogant."

"But you still like him." Cass joined them, but she stood

on the other side of the island. She stretched her hand toward the sink, and Bessie took her teacup.

Their eyes met, and Cass offered her a kind smile this time.

"It's...this weird attraction," Bessie admitted. "There's this electricity between us. There has been since the first time I met him outside that shop. But he's...infuriating."

"Maybe he likes you too," Joy suggested.

Bessie scoffed again. "Men like Oliver Blackhurst aren't interested in women like me."

"Why not?" Sage asked, the last to arrive around the sink.

Bessie put her head down and focused on washing the dishes. "Because he's gorgeous, and gorgeous men don't concern themselves with middle-aged, non-gorgeous women."

"Bessie, you *are* gorgeous," Lauren said as she put her arm around her. "Now, no talk like that. Let's make a plan for how you can get Oliver-the-Grouch to take his grump down a notch. Then we'll know if he likes you, or if he's really not worth it."

Bessie looked over to her, then to Bea. She nodded encouragingly, and Bessie didn't know how to argue this point.

"I suppose I live here now," she said. "So that's one obstacle out of the way."

"He's friends with Grant," Bea said, her voice back to the light, falsely nonchalant tone.

"No." Bessie shook her head, her voice as strong now as

it had been this morning when she'd tried to deny Oliver the platinum sponsorship. She still didn't know how much that would set her back. "Don't you dare talk to Grant about him." She pinned Cass with a look. "Or Harrison."

She gave Lauren a glare. "Or Blake. I know they're all friends, and just—no."

"Then you're going to have to do all the questioning," Cass said.

"Fine," Bessie said. "Believe it or not, I dated enough to get married once." She looked around at her friends, these women who loved her so well, and whom she loved with everything she had.

"This is stupid," she said quietly. "I'm not going to fall in love with him."

Joy put her arm around Bessie on her left side. "But, sweetie, what if you could?"

"He's already made me promise not to," Bessie said. "And he'll be insufferable if I do." She shook her head, the fantasies of kissing his curved lips straight drying up. "No, I'm not going to let him break my heart." She nodded like that was that.

Bessie gazed evenly at each woman gathered around her. "I'm not strong like some of you. I can't—" She shook her head. "I'm doing great with Wyn and the bakery. I'm not going to let a handsome face ruin things for me. I'm not."

She wasn't. She'd already had her heart pulped and juiced and handed back to her after nineteen years of marriage. She wasn't even sure she wanted to enter into holy matrimony again.

She could admit one thing. "I am a little lonely," she said.

"Oh, Bessie." Bea reached out and covered her hand.

"It makes no sense, I know." Bessie's eyes burned, but she would not cry. "I live with Wyn. I literally thought earlier today that I'm never alone, and I miss that."

Bessie backed away from the sink and picked up a towel to dry her hands. "I'm not making any sense. Today was just a confusing day." She'd get some sleep, and then she'd look at things in the light of a new day.

"Okay," Cass said brightly. "I don't mean to kick you out, but Harry's been smoking sausage all day, and he promised me a hot date night." Her words broke up the rendezvous at the sink, and Bessie was able to fade into the background of her friends, the way she usually did. She felt comfortable in that place, and she hugged Cass before following everyone out of the house.

Her friends could be relentless, but tonight, they simply hugged good-bye, and Bessie went back to the house she shared with Wyn.

The shower ran, and Bessie decided to walk right back outside. The house sat a block from the beach, and Bessie's feet ate up the distance effortlessly.

Relief sank through her the moment the sidewalk gave way to sand, and Bessie went down the path between rolling sand dunes with grasses growing out of them to the beach.

Summertime in Hilton Head brought thousands of tourists, and the beach certainly wasn't empty, despite it being close to suppertime. Families lounged under umbrellas and on blankets and towels. Teens threw footballs and Frisbees. Couples walked down where the water washed the golden sand. Singles ran, either alone or with a dog.

Bessie breathed it all in, her mind finally calming in a way only sunshine and yeast could accomplish. She loosened, her shoulders and back relaxing for the first time since she'd left the bread bakery that morning.

"You're okay," she whispered to herself, glad the wind and the waves had a voice far louder than hers. "You've got this."

Her bread bakery was off to a great start, and she had an incredible mentor here on the island. She'd figure out how to handle Oliver soon enough, and she'd learn what she could from him in the meantime.

"Do you come here often?" a man asked, and Bessie couldn't believe the pick-up line from her younger days.

Worse, when she finally tore her gaze from the ocean and turned toward the man, she found the gorgeous Oliver Blackhurst grinning back at her.

Chapter Six

O liver felt the no-dating rule he'd implemented for himself grow wings and fly away with the other birds on the beach this evening. He also wanted to kick himself in the teeth for what he'd asked Bessie.

He drew in a deep breath. "We sure seem to end up in the same places a lot," he said when she didn't respond to his cheesy pick-up line from yesteryear. He'd never used it in his twenties, and he didn't understand why he'd thought saying it in his forties would be a good idea.

"I just came, because..." Bessie trailed off, and Oliver wanted to thread his fingers through hers, so she'd know she wasn't alone. His throat shriveled, narrowing as he let his hand swing out, trying to find hers. His fingers brushed hers, and in less time than it took to breathe in, he slipped his hand into hers.

"I came, because the shop is driving me nuts tonight," he

said. "And I was late to this important meeting this morning, and then I was too bossy when I took this beautiful woman to brunch, and I don't know." He exhaled, wishing some of the summer light would go out with the force of his breath. It didn't, leaving him completely exposed. "I guess I just need a do-over."

Bessie's gaze landed on the side of his face, but Oliver didn't turn toward her. The electricity snapped between them, and his ears filled with the crackling energy of it until it covered the roaring of the ocean a hundred yards away.

He finally couldn't hold off any longer, and he turned his body toward her. Her body still faced the water, but she looked at him fully. "A do-over, huh? Do those happen outside of video games and movies?"

Oliver smiled, because Bessie wore one in her expression. It did not curve her lips, but the longer he let her voice linger in his ears, the more he detected a smile in her tone too. "If they don't, they should."

"What else would you do over?"

"Oh, boy." He took another big breath and faced the beach again. "That's a hard question to answer."

"Just today, then?"

His mind fractured, so many of his mistakes coming to the forefront. "I dated one of my managers once," he admitted. "If I had a do-over power, I'd definitely make sure I didn't do that." He cut a look out of the corner of his eye to Bessie, and she'd gone back to people-watching too. "You?"

"My daughter made me try this pizza," she said. "It was

laden with mushrooms, but she said they were good." Bessie actually shivered right there on the beach. In the summer. "They were not good. I'd do-over that whole meal. None of that pizza was good."

"How disappointing," Oliver teased. "Pizza is the one food I didn't know you could ruin."

"Well, you can." She nodded, clearly having spoken on the subject. Her gaze flitted over to his again, darting away just as quickly. Her hand in his tightened, and that only made Oliver's blood heat further. Much more, and he might burst into flames.

She moved her hand, and he released it, and a keen sense of loss flowed through him as the spaces between his fingers emptied. "What about that?" she whispered. "Would you do that over?"

"Hold your hand?" he asked, his voice just as low as hers. "Yeah, I'd do that again. No regrets."

She faced him too, and Oliver searched her face. Surely she felt this...thing between them. Didn't she?

He sure did, but he didn't know what to say. He didn't normally find himself tongue-tied around women—even the pretty ones—but he'd already allowed his inner grump to surface with Bessie. She knew more about him than women usually did at this stage of the relationship, and he felt like he'd blasted off to another planet and needed to find his footing.

"I'd go back to that day outside the shop," he said. "And be nicer to you and Wynona."

Her eyes widened the way they had at the meeting this morning. She stepped back, putting a bit of distance between them. "I should go," she said. "I have to get up early to bake."

Oliver nodded as frustration filled him. The words he'd said to her had been smooth, and they'd flowed easily from his mouth. No stuttering. No hiccups. He'd essentially told her she was beautiful, and he wished he'd been nicer. Oh, and he'd held her hand. Could he be any more obvious?

She didn't smile as she lifted her hand in a half-hearted wave, turned, and walked away.

"And, now she's leaving," he muttered to himself. This was why he shouldn't have even considered breaking his rule. He started toward the water, which had been his ultimate destination. He'd walk along the edge, where the water met the land, and let the relentless voice of the ocean steal his thoughts.

Then, he'd be able to return to The Mad Mango and fix whatever needed to be fixed. They closed in an hour, and Oliver sighed as he made it to the harder-packed sand. Then his feet didn't shift so much, and his arches stopped aching.

Bessie consumed his thoughts as he walked, the wind whipping in off the water and someone's music trying to break his concentration. When he reached the lifeguard tower, he knew he'd gone far enough. He turned and went back the way he'd come, some of his irritation starting to lie down.

Back at the shop, he put a customer-friendly smile on his

face and stepped into the fray. "You can go on break," he said to a twenty-year-old named Lydia. She gave him a grateful smile, with all the anxiety living in her eyes, and turned to leave.

He started taking orders, and when the clock moved to eight, he nodded to his Team Lead for the night, Jordan. He moved to lock the doors and flip the sign to closed. They still had a half-dozen people in line, and twice that many loitering at the tables in the shop, but with an hour, everyone would be headed home, Oliver included.

He had to come in early tomorrow to do a couple of interviews, but he rose with the sun anyway. He loved watching it come up over the horizon in the east, and dawn often found him back on the beach he'd just visited.

As he took the last few remaining orders, he wondered how Bessie would've finished her sentence. *I just came, because...*

He wondered if she lived near the beach where he'd found her.

He wondered if she'd say anything about him holding her hand to any of her friends. His heartbeat tapped quickly for a moment, because some of his best friends were married to her best friends. Word spread quickly on Hilton Head, even if there were thousands of tourists here for the summer.

He wondered if they'd all sit together for the Fourth of July this weekend, as they had for the past several years. That really got his smile to move up a notch, and he started filling the last order after he took it.

With everyone checked out and sipping or leaving, Oliver started the clean-up procedures. Plenty of sunlight remained in the evening, which was why Oliver closed at eight. He wanted his people to be able to enjoy their summer nights too, and he'd been in business long enough to know that staying open for an extra hour rarely paid off.

Sure, every now and then, he'd get a big group of people that would make it worth it, but for the most part, the traffic at The Mad Mango slowed considerably after eight p.m.

The shop got cleaned; everyone left; Oliver drove the few blocks home. He sat in his SUV in the garage and tapped on his phone to unlock the door. He'd had a new security system installed a few months ago—both at The Mad Mango and here at home—as he did most of his shopping online and therefore, had packages delivered all the time.

He didn't live in a ritzy beachfront community like Cass and Harrison, but he could easily walk to the beach in a few minutes. His community didn't have a gate, and they did have a private walkway to get to the sand and surf.

Inside the house, Oliver let the door slam closed behind him. Then he just stopped and listened. The house said nothing back to him, as only silence filled the air. He ran a fan at night, but he meticulously turned it off before he headed out for the day.

"You should leave the TV on," he muttered to himself, though he'd never be able to do it. But if he could waste that much energy, he'd at least come home to a friend.

He reached for the remote and flipped on the TV now.

Noise filled the air, and that calmed Oliver's nerves. A television couldn't truly compensate for a companion, for having someone to come home to, but right now, it was all Oliver had.

After he'd washed his hands, he put together a quick dinner of pizza and salad, and he took it all into the living room. He bit off the point of his supreme pizza, thinking it decent for frozen food, and picked up his phone.

He wasn't sure who would be the friendliest with Bessie. All of the women in that Supper Club seemed close, and Oliver stared at Grant's name, then Harrison's, and then Blake's. Scott, Joy's new fiancé, likely wouldn't know as much, as he worked more than Oliver did, especially in the summer.

Grant would ask too many questions.

Harrison didn't pay attention to gossip.

So he tapped on Blake's name, took another bite of pizza to settle the raging waves in his stomach, and typed, *Talk to me about Bessie Clifton.*

It only took Blake ten seconds to respond. *What does that mean?*

Oliver shouldn't have to spell things out so bluntly, not at his age. He only had to ask Blake one question for his friend to get it, but he hesitated to do so. He finished a couple of slices of pizza first, his nerves firing at him with every passing moment.

Is she single? he finally sent.

His phone rang, and Oliver heaved a great sigh. Still,

Blake obviously knew Oliver had his phone, so he couldn't just ignore the call. He swiped it on and said, "Yeah, hey, Blake."

"Is she single?" he repeated, and Oliver could see the high eyebrows and the buggy eyes. "I thought you weren't dating right now."

"I'm *not* dating right now," Oliver said. "I'm single. I'm wondering if—" He cleared his throat. "If Bessie is also single."

"She is," Lauren called from somewhere on the other end of the line. Great. Oliver hadn't truly expected Blake to keep this conversation from his wife, but he also hadn't expected her to be on speakerphone.

Still, he'd come this far... "Would she go out with me if I asked?"

Jostling happened, along with some scratching, across Blake's speaker. "I just want to talk to him," Lauren said crossly, and he imagined her wresting the phone away from Blake. The image made Oliver smile as he waited.

"Okay," Lauren said, her voice loud. She'd obviously taken him off speaker. "Here's the deal, Oliver."

His eyebrows went up. Of course he knew who Lauren was, but he wouldn't call them best friends. They'd hung out on beach days last summer while she dated Blake, and he brought her and his son in for smoothies often.

"Okay," he said when she didn't go on.

"You've been...a little short with Bessie," she said. "But I think if you backtracked and made up for that, she'd go out with you."

"She did just open her bakery," he said, fishing for a reason Bessie would reject him. "Maybe she's too busy." His fingers flexed where they'd touched hers, and Oliver didn't want the "I'm too busy" excuse to come out of Bessie's mouth.

"She's usually done baking by noon," Lauren said. "She's a lunch person, not a dinner person."

"This is good intel," he said.

She sucked in a breath. "No." She moaned. "I can't be giving you intel. Forget I said that. Forget I said anything. We didn't call you!" She ended the call before Oliver could say another word, and he blinked at the screen that clearly showed, yes, she'd hung up on him.

"Unbelievable," he muttered to himself.

Sorry, Blake said. *Lauren doesn't want to feed you "intel" on Bessie. She says to ask her out and figure it out yourself.*

"How helpful," he said to the home improvement show blaring on his TV. Still, he'd gotten one little nugget from the conversation, and he tapped over to the text thread he had with Bessie. Could he text-invite her to lunch tomorrow? Or to sit by him at the Fourth of July fireworks?

He navigated back to Blake's messages and asked, *Are we all sitting together for the fireworks?*

Planning on it, Blake said.

Maybe he should just wait until then to see Bessie again. He knew he wouldn't run into her on the beach in the morning, as she'd be baking. "You *are* out of bread," he mused.

Even as he planned to go into Flour Power tomorrow

and get some of her salted honey whole wheat bread, he shot a message through cyberspace too.

Now, he just had to hope she hadn't gone to bed yet and wouldn't keep him waiting until morning for an answer.

Chapter Seven

B essie held her phone above her head and read the
message from Oliver for a second time, because surely
her eyes hadn't been working the first time.

*If I could do something over from tonight on the beach, it
would be to ask you to lunch for tomorrow. Want to?*

She sat up, her heart thumping against her spine. Her
pulse settled back into its regular place, but Bessie still didn't
know how to answer him. Every cell in her body sang, but
she wasn't sure if the notes rang with fear or with excitement. Or both.

"This can't be happening," she whispered to herself.
She'd listened to her friends talk about Oliver Blackhurst at
teatime that day, and more than one of them had speculated
that he liked her.

But there was *no way* he liked her. She'd seen the glares,
remembered the argument from months ago, and could still

hear him telling her she couldn't argue with him all the time about the Heritage Festival.

"He did hold your hand tonight." She thought he'd done that, because he could tell how lost she felt. Then, he'd put his hand in hers, anchoring her to the ground, to Hilton Head, to him. She hadn't held hands with a man in so long, and the gesture was as hot as it was tender.

Business or pleasure? she tapped out and sent.

Pleasure. No qualifier. No extra declarations of love. No flirty *maybe a little of both.* Oliver didn't strike her as a flirty type of man, but Bessie wasn't entirely sure.

He had called her beautiful at the beach too, something Bessie hadn't truly heard until she'd been halfway home. Her feet had frozen to the sidewalk, and she'd twisted back to the beach to see if he'd followed her. He hadn't, and she'd walked away from him after he'd told her he regretted how he'd acted the first time they met.

He wasn't as grumpy as she'd thought. Or rather, he was, but he didn't mean to be? Something.

Bessie shook her head and focused on her phone. *I can go about one,* she said, feeling irrational and wild. What would she tell Wyn? How could she explain this to her friends?

Great, Oliver said. *Should I pick you up at home or at the bakery or...?*

A small smile formed on her face at his use of the ellipses and then the question mark. Her suspicions about him being formal down to the core seemed accurate, and she couldn't wait to find out more about him.

Home, she said, and then she listed her address.

You live three blocks from me, he said, following it with a smiley face. *We're practically neighbors.*

Bessie looked up and toward the window, as if he'd be standing right there, texting. He wasn't, of course, and she focused on her phone as it buzzed again. That sound had originally gotten her to roll over and check her device in the first place. She normally put her phone on silent when she went to bed, but tonight, she'd forgotten.

Her friends knew not to call or text after eight if it wasn't an emergency, but she hadn't given that memo to Oliver yet. It wasn't too terribly past eight o'clock yet, and she felt nowhere near sleep, especially now, as she read his text.

If you could do-over one thing from today, what would it be?

Bessie thought about how she'd been late all day today. Late to the Island Collective meeting. Late to tea with her friends. Late getting home and having to answer Wyn's questions.

I wouldn't have run late all day, she texted him.

Some of that was my fault, he said. *I feel really bad about the meeting.*

You wanted to leave something fierce, she said, remembering how he'd practically dragged her out of the Island Collective meeting. Then, when she wouldn't go, he'd abandoned her there with complete strangers. *What was that about?*

In the relationship do-over department, I wouldn't have gone out with Kamille Burr.

Bessie smiled to his message. *I sense you have a lot of interesting dating stories. I can't wait to hear about all of them.*

That is not happening.

I was married for almost twenty years, she typed out, her chest feeling puffy in one moment and fragile in the next. *I haven't dated since my divorce several years ago.*

She stared at the words, wondering if she was giving away too much, too soon. She added, *So I could use some interesting dating stories, especially for what NOT to do.*

Before she let her fear rule her, she sent the text. She settled back down into bed, already typing out that the witching hour had come, and if she didn't get to sleep very soon, she'd have to cancel their lunch tomorrow.

All right, he said. *I'll hold off on all the stories until then. Good-night, Bessie.*

"Good-night, Oliver," she whispered to the room, and she silenced her phone and put it face-down on her night-stand. Her smile accompanied her into her sleep, and Bessie dreamt of being swept away by the handsome Smoothie King and into a life of luxury.

She knew better than that, but it was still a nice fantasy, and she fell asleep with thoughts of Oliver dancing through her head.

TIME HAD A WAY OF MOVING REALLY FAST WHEN she didn't want it to, or dragging its feet when Bessie wished it would hurry. Intellectually, she knew a second was a second was a second, but it felt like the minutes weren't ticking by as she baked the next morning.

Hillie kept her entertained with stories of her children and grandchildren, and Bessie's eyes roamed to the clock over and over again. Finally, she pulled the last loaf of bread out of the oven, brushed it down with the highest quality olive oil and sprinkled the dry herbs over it.

"All right," she said with a sigh, noting that the clock had ticked to twelve-fifteen. She lived only a few minutes from the bread bakery, but she needed time to freshen up. Or freak out. Probably both. "You're okay here?"

"Just finishin' up these rolls for this afternoon's rush," Hillie said, her smile as wide as the ocean.

Bessie relaxed just being in the room with her, and she paused. "Thank you, Hillie. You've been a Godsend."

"You're welcome, Miss Bessie." She molded the rolls without even looking at them. "Y'all are invited to our Lowcountry Boil," she drawled. "I told Wyn about it."

"When is it?" Bessie asked, the thought of adding one more thing to her already bulging calendar making her tired. Of course, she'd added a lunch date with Oliver, and he'd not texted her since. She wasn't sure if she should wear shorts and a T-shirt, a skirt, or something else.

It's lunch, she told herself, trying to reassure herself that she knew how to dress for a lunch date though she hadn't been on one in ages.

"Sunday afternoon," Hillie said. "Every Sunday afternoon." She hummed afterward, and Bessie really wanted to go.

"I'll talk to Wyn and get the details," she said. She didn't want to work seven days a week, and she couldn't ask her daughter or any of her employees to do that. So she and Wyn had talked to a few people at the Hilton Head Island Commerce office, and learned that a lot of local businesses closed two days a week in the middle of the week.

The summertime was an exception, but Bessie had just opened Flour Power. She didn't have the personnel to operate seven days a week right now. She and Wyn wanted beach days with their friends. Non-baking days with each other. Time to enjoy this new place they'd moved to, go on Lowcountry tours, sample all the local restaurants.

Just thinking about a life outside of the bread bakery made the tightness in Bessie's shoulders evaporate. She and Wyn had decided to close on Tuesdays and Wednesdays, but that started next week.

She'd wanted to put in a full week at the shop before the Independence Day holiday, and then they could relax. Take stock of how the grand opening had gone. Go through feedback forms from customers and employees alike. Rest.

After hanging up her apron, Bessie stepped into the office. Wyn sat at the computer, and Bessie cleared her throat. Her daughter looked up at her. "Taking off?"

"Yes," she said as Wyn's gaze moved back to the screen. "I don't want—" She didn't know how to continue. She ran a dry hand through her ponytail, feeling the weight and thickness of it. She'd always hated how hot her hair made her in the summer, but now she panicked that she should've left it down for her lunch date.

"Wyn," she said, and her daughter's gaze drifted back to hers. "I'm going to lunch with Oliver."

Her daughter blinked, alarm entering her expression. "Again? He can't give you one day off? What could there be to talk about already? Weren't you going to provide for him a menu for the Festival?"

Bessie shook her head, her chest vibrating strangely. "It's not for the Festival. It's…"

Wyn frowned, her confusion evident. "Not for the Festival?"

"He asked me out."

Her eyes grew into full moons, and the chair she sat in scraped as she stood. "He asked you out? And you said yes?" A smile started to form on her face, and Bessie didn't like the sight of it. All of the Supper Club ladies would wear similar know-it-all grins, and Bessie pressed her eyes closed in a long blink.

"I don't want to talk about it."

"He wasn't even very nice to you."

"We've texted a little," Bessie said. "He's…layered."

"Mom." Wyn came around the desk and took Bessie by the shoulders. "You deserve someone who treats you like a queen."

Bessie couldn't swallow the lump in her throat. "I know." But she didn't know. She hadn't had the knight in shining armor. She hadn't known a man to drop his own interests and rearrange his schedule to accommodate her. *She'd* been the one to do that for Wendell, and it still hadn't been enough.

"Maybe he will," Bessie said.

"He threw smoothie at me," Wyn said.

"You've said for months that it was an accident," Bessie challenged. "Are you changing your mind on that?"

"You ranted and raved about him just yesterday," Wyn said, gesturing toward the kitchen. "I found you here after hours, punching in bread while imagining his face was on it."

"I never said that."

Wyn folded her arms. "Are you going to deny it?"

"No." The fight left Bessie's limbs and lungs, leaving her feeling limp all over. "We ran into each other on the beach last night. He asked me out. I figured...I figured I'd at least try. One date. How bad can one date be?"

Wyn snorted. "The first date is always the worst, Mom." Her smile touched her mouth then, and Bessie quickly returned it.

"It's lunch," she said. "I'll be home in a couple of hours, okay? We can dissect it all."

Wyn turned and went back to the computer. "Yeah, sure."

They wouldn't dissect it all, Bessie knew. Wyn knew too, which was why she'd answered the way she had. "Okay," Bessie said. "I'll see you later." With that, she collected her purse and went back to the rental she and Wyn shared.

Doing so had allowed both of them to move here when

neither of them would've been able to otherwise. Wyn had needed to leave the farm in Oklahoma where she'd been working, and Bessie had desperately wanted to maintain her friendships with Bea, Cass, Lauren, and Joy.

She'd never dreamed in a million years that she'd find someone to fall in love with the way they had. Even as she quickly changed her clothes and spritzed lavender water over her shoulders and chest, she told herself, "This is just a first date."

Oliver wouldn't be proposing by suppertime.

She pulled her hair out of the ponytail, glad when she discovered it hadn't bumped too badly, and she swept on a pale pink lip gloss before stepping into a casual pair of sandals to go with her dark blue shorts and white T-shirt with an anchor on it.

She wasn't fashionable and classy like Cass. She couldn't remember the last time someone had called her "cute," the way they did Bea. She wasn't stunningly gorgeous like Lauren, and she didn't have nearly the refinement that Joy did.

She knew how to work hard, and she did her best to look good and feel comfortable when she went out with her friends and family. This would have to be enough for Oliver. As the doorbell rang, Bessie's pulse lodged in the back of her throat, and she knew without a doubt that she was indeed not good enough for Oliver.

"Just go open the door," she coached herself. She did, and she found him standing there, head down, looking at something in his hand. Her eyes dropped there too, and she found him holding what appeared to be a couple of tickets.

Only his eyes moved upward as he looked at her, and the pounding of Bessie's pulse deafened her. He looked like he'd been polished and poised just-so on her porch. He wore a black pair of slacks, a pair of stylish wingtips where the shoes were blue and the cutouts black, and a golf shirt the exact same shade of blue.

With all that dark hair, and those delicious, dreamy eyes the color of the night sky, Bessie had to mentally tell herself to take a deep breath in, and then release it.

"You look great," he said as he raised his head fully. The tickets came up too. "I'm wondering how you feel about seafood…"

Chapter Eight

Oliver hadn't felt this alive for a while. Months. Maybe longer. He reminded himself that he always had these zings and zaps at the beginning of a new relationship. He'd know by the end of this date if there was anything for him to pursue, though he'd been getting deeper into relationships before figuring out they weren't a good fit.

Thus, the no-dating rule he'd implemented for himself.

"Seafood?" Bessie asked as she looked at the tickets and then back to him. "We need tickets to eat at a seafood restaurant?"

"These are behind-the-door passes to the fish market." Oliver loved going to the fish market. "Do you cook?"

"Do you?"

"I can," he said. "Yes. I love going behind-the-scenes at the fish market, picking out the freshest stuff, and then seeing what I can make with it."

Bessie came out onto the porch, crowding into his space.

He didn't back up at all, the scent of yeast and hairspray mingling in his nose. He never would've put those two together and found them attractive, but on the blonde, he took a long, deep breath and committed the scent to memory.

"So this *is* like a working date," she said.

"I'll cook for you," he said.

She wore a dubious look, but said, "Okay."

Victory washed through Oliver, and he turned to lead her down the few steps that had gone up to her porch. "Great," he said. "We get thirty minutes behind the door. We can buy whatever we want, but we have to be in and out in thirty minutes."

"Sounds intense," she said. "I didn't realize fish markets had such strict rules."

"Wait'll you see this one," he said, glancing over to her. "Have you been to the fresh fish market here in Hilton Head?"

"Why would I do that?"

He grinned at her sass, though when those cornflower blue eyes met his, she didn't carry any attitude in her expression. "For fun," he said.

She scoffed as she walked along the passenger side of his car. "Oliver, if you think shopping at a fish market is fun, you need to get out more."

"Oh-ho," he said, half-laughing. "Tell me the last social activity you did, Miss Thing."

"I had tea with my friends just yesterday," she said.

"That so doesn't count." He opened her door for her and glared at her.

"Why doesn't that count?" She turned toward him, plenty of fire blazing in those eyes now. "It so counts. What did *you* do yesterday afternoon?"

"I walked on the beach."

"That is not social," she said.

"Hanging out with your friends doesn't count," he shot back. "I meant like...like what festival or party or movie or event did you go to?"

"And you think walking on the beach counts as an event?"

Oliver swallowed, the words he wanted to spew from his mouth right there. So close. "It does when I hold a pretty woman's hand."

Bessie opened her mouth to say something, then snapped it shut. "Thank you," she said with plenty of diplomacy. "For saying I'm pretty." With that, she sank into the passenger seat, plucked the tickets from his hands, and added, "Let me see these."

He chuckled as she started to study the behind-the-door passes. Those didn't come for free, but Oliver kept that to himself as he rounded the SUV and got behind the wheel.

"We have to be there in twenty minutes," she said.

"It's ten away."

"These were twenty bucks."

"I got them from a friend." He cut a look over to her as he backed out of her driveway. "Did Ty help you and Wynona find this place?"

She handed him the tickets, which he put in the cupholder between them. "Yeah," she said. "We'll see about buying something. Maybe."

He wasn't sure why they wouldn't, but he didn't ask. "I got your last loaf of salted wheat bread today," he said. "Things seem to be going well at the bakery."

She looked over to him, but Oliver kept his gaze on the road. "You like my bread?"

"I love that salted wheat bread," he admitted. "I can't stop eating it." He chuckled, finally feeling brave enough to look over to her. "Why is that so surprising?"

She quickly faced the front again. "I don't know."

Oliver would much rather trade jabs with her, comments flying back and forth between them, than sit in this angsty silence. He told himself that real relationships weren't built on sarcasm and quick wit, and he had to leave room for real discussions about real things.

"So," he said, clearing his throat. "I went out with Kami, oh, I don't know. Last year? Last spring, maybe. Anyway." He told himself not to grind his vocal cords again. He wasn't nervous, not really. He just didn't want the silence to seep into the SUV any more than it already had.

"We were eating at this great place on the water—Iron Anchor? Have you been there?"

Bessie shook her head, and Oliver plowed forward. "It's great. Local cuisine, cooked well. Anyway."

He cursed himself for using that word again. He was usually much more eloquent than this, and he squeezed the steering wheel like the right thing to say would then bleed from it. "We're there, and Kami gets up to go to the restroom. We'd been dating for a few weeks. It certainly wasn't our first date. I've known her from the Island Collective for a while at this point."

"So you do mix business and pleasure." Bessie wasn't asking, and Oliver wouldn't answer even if she was. He had done that in the past, and it had never ended well for him.

"She owns this leather jewelry shop," he said. "We never would've partnered up for the Heritage Festival. I heard she paired up with Cherise from Gems-R-Us."

Bessie faced him again. "There's a place called Gems-R-Us?"

Oliver laughed, and it felt so good to do it. He honestly couldn't remember the last time he'd really laughed. "No," he said, still chuckling. "But Cherise has all these crystal towers and whatever-whatever stones. I think they're just kind of silly."

"I guess gems and jewelry go together."

"I guess," he said.

"Better than bread and smoothies."

"No way." He glanced over to her. "We have the perfect pairing, Bessie. I told you that yesterday."

They both had food-based businesses, and who didn't want a sample of bread and smoothie before buying one of each?

"It's going to be great," he said.

"If you say so," she said.

"I do."

She exhaled louder than she had before, and Oliver

decided to move on. "Anyway, so she gets up and goes to the restroom, and when she comes back, she sits down at the table in front of me. There was another dark-haired man sitting there, and she started talking and talking and *talking*."

"She didn't realize it wasn't you?"

"She did not." A pinch brought two of his ribs closer together, making him twitch and shift in his seat. "For at least a minute. Maybe more. Finally, the man turned around and looked at me—all while Kami kept talking and talking."

"So you don't like women who talk."

"Of course I do," he said. "When they have something good to say."

"You did not just say that."

"She talked to him as if he were me and didn't even realize he wasn't," Oliver said. "You can't be mad that I thought that was ridiculous."

"Is that why you broke up?"

"Yes." Oliver kneaded the wheel again. "The other man said to her, 'I think your boyfriend is over there,' and I stood up. I said, 'well, he was.' Then I left."

That deafening silence roared into the vehicle, and Oliver's first instinct was to cover it up with more talking.

Bessie looked out her window, then the windshield. She eventually looked at him, but Oliver refused to return her gaze. "You just left her there?"

"No," he said just as quietly as she had. "I drove her home first. I guess we broke up on her front porch."

"Any do-overs from that relationship?"

"Be more unique?" he guessed.

Bessie reached over and took one of his tight-tight hands off the wheel, easing it into hers. "You're plenty unique," she said. "You're allowed to be who you are."

Oliver hadn't realized how much the experience with Kami had shaped him in the past year. He hadn't realized that his identity had taken such a big hit that night. He hadn't realized that he needed someone to tell him that he was okay just how he was.

He cleared his throat—blast it all—and said, "Okay, we're here." He pulled into the parking lot at the fish market, and he had to use both hands to steer. He wondered if he could easily slip his fingers between Bessie's once they got out of the car too, but she didn't wait for him to come open her door.

As she stepped to his side at the hood, she shaded her eyes and read the sign out loud. "Barrier Reef Fish Market." She looked up to him. "Is there a barrier reef here?"

"No," he said. "But Hilton Head is a barrier island. That's where the name came from." He nodded toward the market and said, "Follow me." He carried the tickets as he walked between cars, Bessie on his heels. When they finally emerged closer to the building, she fell into step beside him.

Oliver loved the display cases of fish in ice. He'd grown up in Alabama, and he'd been eating barbecue or seafood since his baby teeth had come in. "Mahi-mahi," he said. "Red snapper." He did like both of those. "King mackerel. Black sea bass."

"You don't have to name them off for me," Bessie griped. "I can read."

Oliver only smiled at her. "Did you eat a lot of fish in the Coastal Bend?"

Her eyes flitted away from him as she took in the huge, ice-filled case that held equally as large cobia. "I've never seen these before."

"They migrate along the coast here in the spring and summer."

"They're massive."

"They're good too," he said.

She looked up at him. "You just buy a whole one? It's like the size of a whale."

Oliver burst out laughing again, and he hoped that Bessie didn't find him manic. "A whale, Bessie? You've seen whales, right?"

She folded her arms. "Of course I've seen a whale...on TV."

That got him to quiet down quickly. "Wait a second. You've never seen a whale in real life?"

"I'm not very outdoorsy." She sounded like she'd swallowed bricks and would be spitting them into a ten-foot wall if she spoke again.

"But...you've never been to SeaWorld or anything like that?"

She shook her head, her mouth tight.

"Well, that settles it," he said. "Our next date will be a whale-watching tour." He turned toward the double-doors several yards away. They resembled the kind that waiters and waitresses pushed through to get into the kitchen in a restaurant, but these led back into the fish monger's lair. "We're over here."

"Our next date?" Bessie asked as she lurched to keep up with him.

Oliver cut a look to her out of the corner of his eye. "Sure," he said.

"You're assuming I'll want to go out with you after this."

"Yes, I am."

"You're making me shop for my own lunch, and then I have to wait for you to cook it too."

He paused, turning his back fully on the behind-the-door entrance. "Are you not having fun?" he challenged.

"I might've eaten a little before you picked me up," she said. "If I'd known I wasn't going to eat for hours." She gave a one-shouldered shrug. "That's all."

It was a fair point, but Oliver didn't want to concede it. "Do you like sushi?" he asked.

The way her nose wrinkled up set his hormones on fire —and also answered his question. He chuckled and shook his head. "I can't believe you grew up near the Gulf of Mexico and don't like sushi." He turned to join the group now gathering to go through the double-doors.

"Not all of us have led lives of luxury."

"Whoa," he said. His anticipation for getting behind the doors changed to alarm. "Lives of luxury? What does that mean?"

"Never mind."

"No," he said slowly. "That's not fair."

She lifted her chin. "I want a do-over, and it's that I didn't say that." Her eyes searched his, a hint of desperation filling them the longer he searched.

He finally acquiesced and said, "Okay, Bessie. I'll give you a do-over on that."

"Thank you," she whispered. "I think we're about to miss our tour."

Oliver spun toward the black doors, and everyone else had already gone it. "Yep." He strode forward and held out his tickets for the man standing there. "Howdy, Howard."

"Ollie, you're back today."

He suddenly wished the cement would fracture and swallow him whole. He said, "Yeah," and picked up one of the black baskets for his catch-of-the-day.

"You know the drill," Howard said, and he nodded Oliver and Bessie through the doors.

Oliver stepped inside the back room and paused, really taking it all in. The fish back here weren't in perfectly heaped mounds of ice. They might not even be the best specimens. The variety exceeded that of the main market, and he became aware of Bessie's body heat as she inched closer to him.

"It's freezing back here," she said.

"Yes," he said with plenty of glee. "Isn't this great?" He took a look at her, and no, she didn't think this was great. "You can pick anything you want, sweetheart. Okay? Pick something, and let me cook it for you."

She met his eye, and she did a fair bit of searching herself. Oliver could admit they'd already been up and down a few times in the past thirty minutes. His emotions rose and dipped just as quickly, and sometimes his tongue ran away from him.

She neared, rising up onto her toes. "I don't want you to call me *sweetheart*."

He blinked as she settled back to her normal height and then stepped away from him. "Sheepshead? I've never heard of this."

Oliver's heartbeat hammered at him, and so many things flew through his mind. He lunged after Bessie. "What do you want me to call you?"

She barely flicked a glance in his direction. "I don't know," she said. "Not sweetheart. My ex-husband called me that, and it always felt a little condescending."

Oliver could barely swallow. "I apologize. That'll be my do-over from this date, okay?"

She nodded without saying anything, her hair falling over her shoulder as she leaned down to look at a pile of snapper. She straightened and looked at him. "Would you hate me if I just wanted something safe?"

"You choose," he said, meaning it with everything inside him.

She nodded again and moved past the pile of vermilion and red snapper. She went past the fish heads without comment, which Oliver found amusing at the same time he found her strong and full of wisdom.

"I use those to make fish stock," he said. "It's great for shrimp scampi or gumbo or paella."

"And you said you only cook a little."

"No, I said I can cook."

She faced him at the end of the aisle. "Most people don't even know what paella is, Mister Blackhurst."

"I don't want you to call me Mister Blackhurst." The words exploded from his mouth before he could censor them.

Bessie's eyes widened at the same time Oliver's did. "I mean—"

"No, it's okay," she said. "I'm sorry." She went around the aisle, and Oliver trailed behind her like a lovesick puppy. "Crab? Lobster?" She glanced over to him, but neither was his favorite. He tried not to give anything away, and he did need to make something to eat that didn't need to simmer and bubble and blend flavors for the next five hours.

Or maybe he could do something like that, and keep Bessie with him for longer...

He banished the thought as she came upon the Atlantic salmon. "A fish I know," she said.

"Those are farmed," he said.

"Oh, so not good enough for you?" She gave him a knowing smile and moved on. The back room wasn't that big, and several people had made their selections already. "I hate to say it, but I'm still thinking snapper."

"Snapper I can work with," he said, moving back to the refrigerated case with the snapper. He picked up two of them, put them in the basket, and then headed for the back wall, Bessie in tow. He had plenty of seasonings at home, but lunch would go so much faster with a couple of homemade sides.

"Let's see…" He scanned the case there. "Collard greens, spinach and garlic, or asparagus?"

"How about you pick the sides?" she asked.

"They make these in-house," he said. "They're home-made." Why he'd repeated himself, Oliver didn't know. Bessie made him nervous in a way he couldn't describe. He picked up a plastic container of the spinach and garlic. Then he added a bottle of the cilantro lime sauce, and a lemon and herb quinoa. Those were all heat-and-eat, and the only thing he'd have to do was butcher and cook the fish.

"Ready," he said just as the bell sounded.

Bessie jumped, alarm pulling across her face. "What was that?"

"Ten-minute warning," he said. "Let's go. I'm starving." He checked out, and the air warmed considerably as they left the back room. He sighed, because he loved the fish market.

Now, he just had to make it through cooking for Bessie in his own home, and this date might not be full of do-overs.

Chapter Nine

"I just can't believe it," Bessie said, swiping up the last piece of perfectly flaky fish and dragging it through the bright green cilantro and lime sauce. "It's *so* good."

Oliver smiled at her from across the table-for-two in his house. He'd filleted and pan-seared the fish in only a few minutes, and while it had finished cooking in the oven, he'd heated up all of the sides in the microwave.

She'd been with him for ninety minutes, and her belly was now full and she didn't want to gouge out her eyes.

Quite the opposite, in fact, which unsettled her more than she'd like it to.

"You can't believe it's good, or you can't believe I cooked it?"

"Both," she said as she forked up her last bite of spinach and quinoa. "And the fact that I'm...having a good time."

"Did you expect to not have a good time?"

"I mean..." She let the words hang there, and it was clear

Oliver didn't like them. "You have to admit we didn't exactly hit it off."

His dark eyes continued to watch her, but he'd already finished his lunch. He'd wiped that strong mouth with a napkin and everything, and he'd been watching her eat for the past couple of minutes.

He did not admit they hadn't exactly hit it off, and Bessie wondered how to get him to open up. "Who taught you to cook?"

"Who says someone had to teach me?"

She felt the cold front radiating off of him. "Why are you being like this?" She stood up and took her plate into his kitchen. She rinsed it off and placed it in the dishwasher while he sat there, unmoving, silent.

"I'll call a ride," she said.

Finally, his chair scraped against the tile in his kitchen as he stood. "No, don't do that."

She didn't look up from her phone, where she was searching for the ride share app.

"Bessie," he said as he put his plate in the sink too. He didn't flip on the water to rinse it. "I'm sorry."

She did look up at him now. "I don't know what just happened. You flipped a switch on me."

He nodded. "I did."

"Why?"

He'd flipped a lot in the past several days, actually. Hot, cold, hot, cold. She didn't know what to do about it, but she didn't want to constantly be juggling his moods. She'd lived through a marriage like that already, and it hadn't been fun.

"I—I made a no-dating rule for myself," he said. "It's... you're making it hard for me to keep it."

Surprise coursed through Bessie. "A no-dating rule?"

He nodded and gently took her phone from her.

"Why did you ask me out then?"

"Come on," he said almost under his breath. "I'll take you home." He led the way out of his kitchen and right on out of his house, still holding her phone in his hand. Bessie scrambled to find her purse and shoulder it, then she followed him.

"Oliver," she called as she stepped outside, but he waited at the top of the steps.

He passed her phone back to her. "I'd like to break my rule with you," he said. "It's just... I find myself wanting to open up and tell you things about my life—like it was my aunt who taught me how to cook—but then I remember that I'm really bad at dating, so I better not say anything that might bring us too close."

Bessie wondered who'd hurt him so completely. He hadn't even been able to tell her about his aunt teaching him to cook, so she shelved the question. For now. Instead, she slipped her hand into his.

"I don't think our next date should be whale watching," she said.

He exhaled heavily. "Let me guess. You don't want to see me again."

Bessie watched the heat waves shimmer in the air above the road in front of his house. "I do," she whispered. "But I understand if I'm not special enough for you to break your rule." She pulled her hand away and went down the steps.

"Bessie," he said again, his voice that same begging, yearning tone he'd used inside. He caught up to her quickly. "What do you want our next date to be?"

"Fireworks," she said. He reached past her to open the passenger door, and Bessie found herself facing him again. "I don't know what happened in your dating past." She reached out and cradled his face in her hand, and he leaned into the touch there, almost like he craved it.

Her heart filled with compassion for him, despite the fact that he'd taken her on quite a ride today. "I don't know why you have a no-dating rule. I don't know what will flip you from hot to cold and back again. But if you asked me out again...I'd say yes."

"Fireworks?" he asked. "Like, our own private show or the big celebration in the park?"

She smiled at him, because he had to be close to her age, but the hope in his eyes spoke of a young boy ready to open exactly what he'd wished for on Christmas morning. "The fireworks are in two days. I know you'll be there with everyone."

"Yes," he whispered.

"I will be too. It can be a low-key, group date." She dropped her hand. "And you can decide if you're really interested."

"I don't need to decide that," he said. "I am."

Which only made his behavior more of a mystery. "Well, then, I look forward to more dating stories," she said. "And more delicious meals together. And maybe a walk on the beach, or a whale watching expedition."

With that, she got in his SUV, and when he didn't close the door, she reached out and pulled it closed. She felt certain he'd change his mind in the time it took him to go around to the driver's door.

She wasn't special. Certainly not special enough to make a good-looking, successful man like Oliver break a self-imposed no-dating rule. The very idea was insane.

But he slid behind the wheel and said, "What if I wanted our next date to be at this run-down gas station that has the best boiled peanuts in the state?"

Bessie stared at him. "Boiled peanuts?"

"Me and you. Tomorrow night." His eyebrows went up, a clear question mark on his statement.

"Again, *boiled peanuts*?"

His stoic demeanor finally broke, and his eyes crinkled as he smiled. "You'll love them, I promise."

"I'm not usually very adventurous with my food," she said.

He shook his head as he started the car. "That's ridiculous. I've seen the different kinds of breads you make. They're from all over the world." He raised his eyebrows now as a challenge.

She wanted to swipe them back into their proper position as a flash of irritation stroked through her. "That's bread. It's different."

"So I'll pick you up at six?"

Bessie turned her smile to the passenger window, where

she could only see the faintest image of it. "All right," she said. "Six is fine." She turned back to him. "But how far is this run-down gas station? I have to go to bed at eight."

"I will have you back on time," he promised. "Don't you worry about that."

No, what Bessie had to worry about was explaining this date to her daughter and her friends. Then, she had to sort through all of the back-and-forth they'd had today, including the fact that she liked spending time with Oliver. She liked that he wasn't an open book, and that she might have to work to get to the bottom of who he was.

People were complex beings, and while she didn't know everything about him, and he certainly didn't know everything about her, she was willing to stay on the ride for a little bit longer.

And oh, she liked that he reached over and held her hand for the three-block ride back to her house.

BESSIE LOOKED OUT THE WINDSHIELD AT THE HUT on the side of the highway. "We're buying *food* from this place?" Surely Oliver was joking. The building in front of her spanned several car lengths, and it had been painted blue at some point in the past. A single set of wooden steps led up to a porch that ran the length of the convenience store, but only one door allowed people in and out.

"It's great," Oliver said, some measure of joy in his voice. He almost seemed like Oscar the Grouch, reveling in the stink and trash of his can. Or someone from the Addams Family, who loved the macabre or dark things of the world.

Oliver actually grinned at her. "Come on. They have the best boiled peanuts in the world." He opened his door and got out of the car, but Bessie stayed seated. She wanted to see if the roof would collapse on him when he dared to put any weight on the steps.

Unfortunately, he didn't go up the steps without her, and when he turned back to her, an expectant and boyish look on his face, Bessie couldn't refuse him. She sighed as she got out of his SUV and joined him.

He took her hand, and Bessie let him lead by half a step as they went up the steps. They bore their combined weight, and part of her started to calm. "I'll even let you get some candy."

Bessie's first reaction was to roll her eyes. She did, but the smile that touched her face felt very soft and very real. She wasn't sure what Oliver saw when he looked on her, but he smiled too.

He opened the door and waited for her to enter first. She did, sort of ducking her head as if to protect herself from the certain roof collapse. When it didn't come, she looked around the shop. It held a little bit of everything, from a couple of aisles of groceries, to the usual candy, chips, snacks, and soda pops.

The far corner to her left held plaques and wall hangings, along with T-shirts and mugs and keychains. A gift shop of sorts. Bessie found the whole thing quaint and wonderful, and she relaxed fully.

"The peanuts are over here." Oliver spoke in a quiet, almost reverent voice, and Bessie decided to play his game. She let him show her the pot of boiled peanuts, and she leaned over and smelled them as if he'd presented her with a big bouquet of red roses.

"They have the regular ones," he said. "I recommend those if you've never had boiled peanuts." He indicated the next couple of cauldrons down the counter. "But they have these Cajun ones too. I love them."

"You like the spice, huh?" she asked.

"From time to time." He picked up a cardboard cup and started spooning in regular, salted, boiled peanuts. He handed it to her and then got himself some Cajun-flavored ones. "Do you want to try the barbecue ones?"

"Not particularly," she said. "I think this is great." She turned away from the counter to scan the rest of the store. "I am so getting some candy." She moved that way, trying to decide if she wanted something fruity or something chocolatey.

She picked something of both and met Oliver at the register. She put her peanut butter cups and her sour gummy bears on the counter. His eyebrows rose, but he said nothing as he plucked his wallet from his back pocket and presented the cashier with his debit card.

"What would you get?" she asked him as he waved off the receipt and picked up her candy. "You can tell a lot about a person by their choice of candy."

"Can you?" He carried their peanuts as he left the store, and Bessie scurried after him. He didn't answer her question while they got re-situated in the car, and then he looked over to her.

"I'm not into the fruity candy at all," he said.

"Fascinating."

He opened his mouth to say something, but it fell closed a moment later. Stunned silence filled the car for a beat before he asked, "Why is that fascinating?"

"You own a smoothie shop," she pointed out as if he didn't know. "It's *all* fruit."

Oliver looked like she'd stumped him mightily, and then he chuckled. His shoulders relaxed out of their boxed position, and he said, "I guess you're right."

"It would be like me saying I didn't like waffles or muffins. They're in the same family."

"I want a caramel Twix all day, every day," he said, his smile blindingly white and beautiful. "Now, I didn't mention this part, but..."

Bessie's chest tightened right up again.

He nodded down the parking lot a little. "There's a little trailhead there, and we can take our snacks out to the beach."

Bessie followed his gaze, but she couldn't see a "little trailhead" anywhere in the copse of trees. "You brought me on a *hike*?" She faced him again. "After I specifically said I wasn't outdoorsy?"

"It's a great spot," he said. "Flat walk through the woods —trees." He swallowed, and Bessie looked back down the parking lot. Indecision raged inside her.

"It's maybe a quarter-mile," he said, his voice growing

softer. "And there's a little beach where we can enjoy the sunshine, and the peanuts, and those gummy worms."

"First off," Bessie said, bringing her attention right back to him. "They're gummy *bears*. Not worms."

Oliver grinned as wide as the sky. "My mistake." When she didn't go on, he said, "And secondly?"

"Secondly," she said, imitating him. "I don't believe it's only a quarter mile to the beach. We left the island and drove for at least ten minutes."

"The coast is a mystery," he said. Then he got out of the car, taking the peanuts with him. Bessie couldn't really just sit in the car while he walked away with the food. She grabbed her candy—she wasn't going to leave her peanut butter and chocolate to melt—and went after him.

"If this is one step past a quarter of a mile, this is the last date we'll go on."

Oliver simply looked over his shoulder at her and kept walking. She had to jog-walk to catch him, and when she did, he slowed. He said nothing, and he found the slimmest spot to walk between two trees and ducked through it.

Bessie's heart pounded against her eardrums. The woods —*trees*—had just swallowed him whole.

"Come on, sunshine," he said from somewhere behind the leaves and limbs. The term of endearment made her smile—it was far better than *sweetheart*—and Bessie found herself ducking her head and pushing through the branches too.

Oliver stood a couple of paces down the path, and he smiled at her. "See? Not hard." He continued on, and Bessie followed him. The path wasn't steep or even slanted at all. It had been walked on plenty, and it had been wet at some point in the past. Little cracks and divots ran throughout it, but she had no problem keeping up with Oliver, despite the fact that she'd worn sandals with her cute white shorts and a pink-and-white striped tank top she'd gotten advice about from Cass.

She'd just started to wonder when the beach would appear when all at once, the trees stopped, and the ocean started. "Oh," she said, the word falling out of her mouth.

Oliver came to a stop, and she eased into the spot beside him. The water stretched in front of her, the wind flying across it, and the sound of the waves somewhere below her.

"This is incredible," she said.

He moved to his left, and she went with him. A bench stood there, and not another soul was in sight. Oliver sighed as he sat, and Bessie felt heavy with wonder as she joined him. He handed her the cup of salted boiled peanuts, and she picked one up and peeled the soft shell back, popping the meat of the nut into her mouth.

Salt exploded, and she smiled. "These are good."

Oliver chuckled. "Are you admitting that I was right?"

Bessie wanted to deny it. Heaven knew the man had a head as big as the sky. But she glanced over to him and said, "*Sunshine* is better than *sweetheart*."

"Noted." He slid his hand along her waist and cupped his fingers at her hip.

She leaned into him, and she didn't need to say out loud that he was right. That this was the perfect spot to come enjoy the peace and tranquility of the water. They just sat together, them and the breeze, and ate their peanuts.

Bessie couldn't imagine a better way to spend her evening, and she prayed this man would be able to give her a lot more experiences like this one here in Hilton Head.

Chapter Ten

auren Williams let her husband set up their chairs, noting that he put hers way out of the way of the sun. She'd gotten a little crispy at the beach yesterday, and she currently wore a long-sleeved blouse that showed the red and white stripes of her tank top through the gauzy fabric.

"Have you seen Bessie?" she asked Bea, who handed her step-daughter a package of gum.

"She said she was coming with Oliver." Bea looked down the sidewalk they all had to walk on to get to this part of the park.

"Ready," Blake said, beaming at Lauren. He swept a kiss along her cheek as he reached for the bag she carried. "Do you want me to set up your little table?"

"Yes, please." She ran her fingers down his arm, her way of telling him she appreciated how he took care of her. She sat while he set up the tiny table between their chairs, then put her 44-ounce soda cup on it and turned to help his son with something.

Lauren basked in the warm South Carolina sun, though she sat in the shade. She loved everything about the big, leafy trees in this park, and the emerald green grass that ran seemingly forever in front of her.

She and her Supper Club friends had been gathering here for the Fourth of July fireworks for five years. This was the sixth summer celebration since Bea had come for a ten-day vacation, fallen in love, and disrupted all of their lives.

Lauren wasn't complaining. She no longer had a job in Texas, and she'd dated a lot without any success in finding her One True Love. Turned out, he'd been living in Hilton Head all these years, and now they shared a quaint little house on a quiet street here on the island, and his fifteen-year-old son lived with them.

"They're late," Lauren said, her eyes glued to the sidewalk.

"Don't make a big deal out of it when they get here," Cass said from the other side of Bea. "Bessie won't like that."

"Not three days ago, she sat at teatime and complained about Oliver," Lauren said. "I get to ask some questions."

"Just be nice," Joy said. "Can't it just be...nice that they're exploring something between them?"

"I think it's great," Sage said as she crossed in front of Lauren. She'd braided her dark hair back into a thick rope that fell just past her shoulders. "Thelma and I would take a strong, dashing man, wouldn't we?"

Her sister laughed as she spread a blanket on the ground.

Thelma was definitely several years younger than Lauren, but she couldn't imagine getting down on the ground to watch the fireworks. To do anything, actually. Her knees and back hurt just thinking about it.

But Thelma dropped to the ground and opened a picnic basket. She offered chips and fruit to everyone, but Lauren passed on all of it. She, Blake, and Tommy had gotten shrimp tacos from the best food truck in town only a half-hour ago.

Chatter surrounded her, and it filled the park as more people kept coming. A band would start playing soon enough, and the last couple of hours of daylight would dwindle away on this perfect summer day.

Lauren really wanted to relax, but she couldn't. Not when Bessie was the only one of them still not here. Her daughter hadn't arrived either, and while a few of Grant's friends crowded around him and Bea, and a couple of Harrison's construction guys set up chairs down by him and Cass, she still didn't see Oliver or Bessie.

"I'm going crazy," she murmured.

"Stop stressing over it," Blake said. "Would you have wanted everyone staring at us?"

"She totally wanted that," Joy said in a deadpan. "She held your hand as she came around the corner, this fiercely determined look on her face."

"I did not," Lauren said.

"You did too." Joy leaned forward and looked past Tommy and Blake to Lauren. "You were practically daring any of us to say anything."

"There they are," Bea said, and Lauren whipped her attention away from Joy. So she was probably right about the summer Lauren and Blake had shown up to these very fireworks together. She didn't have to admit it out loud.

Bessie walked in the middle of Wyn and Oliver, her hands holding that oversized purse she took everywhere with her and a bulky water bottle. Oliver carried all three of their chairs, and Bessie grinned at her daughter and said something.

She looked over to Oliver, and he gave her a smooth smile too. Lauren could admit he was good-looking—perfect for Bessie, that was for sure. She had blonde hair with that dark root, and those medium-blue eyes. Oliver was dark from head to toe, and wearing that white button-up shirt open at the throat...

"He has *three* buttons undone," she said to Blake.

"Scandalous," her husband said.

She could see Oliver's chest from those undone buttons, and he wasn't hard to look at. He certainly seemed to push all the right buttons for Bessie, and she slowed as they arrived.

"Right here," Lauren said. "You can sit in front of me and Bea."

Bessie looked there, but she shook her head. "I don't want to turn around all night."

Lauren stood and backed her chair up, creating more of an arch. "Then here. We'll make the row more circular."

Bessie and Wyn moved into the created space, and Oliver started unfolding their chairs. Bea and Grant switched spots in all the movement, and Oliver sat next to him. Bessie took the seat next to Oliver, and Wyn sat between her mother and Lauren.

It wasn't right where Lauren wanted Bessie, but it felt close enough. She watched as Oliver took her purse and shoved it between their chairs, and then he reached into it and pulled out a bag of candy.

He handed it to her even as he engaged in a conversation with Grant.

"Stop staring," Bessie hissed, and Lauren managed to blink.

"How's the bread bakery, Wyn?" she asked, tearing her eyes from Bessie and Oliver.

The younger woman grinned and sighed simultaneously. "It's great. We made it through to our first break."

"You're taking the rest of the weekend off, right?"

"Tomorrow," Wyn said. "We'll be open on Monday, but then yes. We're closed Tuesdays and Wednesdays."

Before Lauren could come up with a plan for a beach day or suggest lunch on one of those days, Bea said, "Supper Club is going to be so amazing, you guys." She started gushing about a new recipe she'd found in one of her online groups. "I've already tested it on Grant and Shelby, and they both loved it."

Lauren usually ordered food when it was her turn to host Supper Club. Cass did the same thing, so she didn't feel bad about it. She could cook; it just wasn't her favorite thing to do. Unless she had a problem to work out, or she wanted to avoid another unpleasant task. Then she could put together soups and stews and all kinds of delicious things.

Blake reached over and threaded his fingers between hers, and Lauren switched her attention to him while keeping one ear on the conversation her friends were having about Bea's Supper Club.

He closed his eyes as he sank further into his chair. "You okay, baby?" She reached over and brushed his hair off his forehead.

"Just tired," he said. "I'm glad we get a holiday on Monday too." Blake ran a busy insurance office, and Lauren gave him a quiet smile.

"You can close anytime you want."

"Yeah." But he wouldn't. Having Tommy out of school for the summer caused extra strain too, because Blake wanted to keep him busy, and he wasn't quite old enough to have a summer job yet.

"I have a date announcement too," Joy said. She actually stood up, a box of doughnuts in her hand. "Scott and I want to get married before my daughter-in-law has her baby in September." She glanced over to her fiancée, who smiled up at her like she was made of starlight. Lauren loved the look on his face, because Joy deserved a man who thought she'd hung the moon.

"So we're going to get married right before school starts in August."

"That's less than two months," Cass said.

"Yes, I own a calendar too," Joy said dryly. "It's not going to be a big thing."

Lauren watched Cass, who frowned. She loved all things gold and silver and sparkly. Everything for Cass was a big thing, and she liked nice, expensive things. Lauren did too, and she'd stopped apologizing for it several years ago.

Her wedding had been a massive affair, and she met Cass's eyes. "Hey, you probably won't have to pay for her venue."

"We're getting married on the beach," Joy said. "It's free."

"The beach?" Cass asked like Joy had just said they'd find a way into a penitentiary to tie the knot. "It's so windy on the beach."

"You'll die when I tell you where I'm getting my dress." Joy wore a smile full of sunshine and mega-wattage, and Lauren couldn't stop herself from smiling too.

"Where?" Bea and Bessie asked at the same time.

"Online," Joy said nonchalantly. "Then, I'm going to work on jazzing it up myself."

"Lots of people buy their dresses online," Cass said.

"You want to see it?" Joy asked, already swiping on her phone. She held it out to Lauren, who leaned over to take it.

She sucked in a breath when she saw the dress. Or rather, costume. "You're kidding," she said. The amount of shock in her voice alerted the others, and Bea practically snatched the phone out of Lauren's hand.

"Hey," Sage said. "I wanted to see it."

"This is not a wedding dress," Bea said, her voice pitching up higher with every word she said. She looked up from the device, dumbfounded. "It's a Halloween costume."

"A what?" Cass took the phone, and her face actually turned white. "It's a Bride of Frankenstein dress." Her hand went limp, and she stared at Joy.

Joy, who laughed. Bessie took a good look at the phone and passed it to Sage, all of them then staring at Joy.

"It'll be fine," she said as she reached to take her phone from Sage. "I'm just using it as a guide."

"A guide for what?" Bessie asked, and Lauren thought that was a very good question.

"I'm going to sew my own dress," Joy said. "And you're all invited to the beach that day." She pinned a look on Lauren. "So bring sunscreen. We'll probably be out there for twenty minutes. Then we'll eat, and that'll be that."

She looked down at the dog at her feet as Ghost stood up. She picked up his leash to keep him close as a family walked by in front of them with a dog of their own. They went by, and Ghost settled back at Gypsy's side. Sage reached over and patted her huge, black dog, who hadn't cared one whit about the one walking by.

Bea and Cass both had dogs too, but neither of them had brought them to the fireworks. Bea said Fresco cowered in her bedroom while the booming fireworks filled the night sky with color, and Cass never brought Beryl to events. No explanation, not that Lauren needed one.

She herself had two cats, but they obviously didn't get leashed and led around the park on Independence Day. They'd probably claw her eyes out if she tried.

She looked over to Bessie, and they exchanged a glance, the silent conversation clearly about the Halloween-costume-wedding-dress. Joy was talented with a sewing machine, and she leaned closer to her and said, "If anyone can pull it off, she can."

"If we have to go emergency wedding dress shopping two days before the wedding..." Bessie let the threat hang there, but Lauren knew they'd both drop everything to do that if they needed to.

Lauren had had to do that, and they'd taken precious time from their Supper Club to watch her try on new dresses when her first choice hadn't been able to get altered in time. She reached over and squeezed Bessie's hand. "I'm so glad the bakery is going well."

"Thank you," Bessie said. "What are you doing Tuesday? We should go to lunch."

Lauren hadn't even had time to consider her schedule before Oliver said, "You can't go to lunch on Tuesday, sunshine. You and I are meeting with the builders of our booth that day. Eleven-fifteen."

Bessie swung her attention to him, but Lauren was still hung up on the word "sunshine." She even mouthed it to Wyn, who only smiled like she'd swallowed the sun. Lauren leaned closer to her. "Is this weird? Your mom dating?"

Wyn looked over to Bessie and Oliver, who were both bent over her phone, discussing her calendar and how long it would take to meet with the builders of their booth for the Heritage Festival. Oliver had done the small-island festival many times; this year was Bessie's first one.

"I don't think it's weird," Wyn said. "Look how happy she is. It's really kind of sweet."

Lauren agreed, and she nodded. "What about you? I bet we can find a super-cute guy in his twenties on this island."

Wyn laughed and shook her head. But she said, "If you can find me someone, Lauren, I'd go out with him."

Now given the task, Lauren started watching the people streaming by more intently. There was nothing she liked more than setting someone up, and she said, "I'll see what I can do," right before the band started to play.

Chapter Eleven

Beatrice Turner reached for her phone as it rang. Her son's name sat there, and she quickly swiped on the call from Ted. "Hey, baby."

"Mama," he said, his Texan twang so dang cute. "Did I get you at a good time?"

Bea surveyed the various ingredients in front of her. She hadn't started combining the dry ingredients with the wet yet, so she had time. "Sure," she said. "How are the wedding plans coming? Still getting married?"

"Yes," he said. "Ten days. I can't wait."

Bea smiled, because she wanted her son to be blissfully in love with his wife. He cleared his throat, and that made her grin falter. "What's up?" she asked.

"Daddy said he can only contribute five hundred dollars to the wedding luncheon."

Bea frowned now, turning her back on the ingredients spread across her kitchen counter. "No," she said slowly. She didn't want to argue about her ex-husband with her son. "I'll call him."

"I don't want you to do that," Ted said. "I know you hate it, and it's not your job anymore."

"You're our son," she said. "I can handle your father."

Ted sighed, and that made Bea's mother heart unhappy. "Don't worry about me, Teddy," she said quietly.

He still said nothing, and she appreciated her contemplative, studious middle child. He'd always been quieter than her younger son, and he was wildly different than her oldest —a daughter who'd graduated in piano performance a few years ago.

Bea had several trips to Texas planned this year, first for Ted and Courtney's wedding, and then to visit her only daughter and granddaughter. Meredith and Stewart had had a little girl they'd named Willow at the end of May, and Bea had spent two weeks in Texas, only to return to Hilton Head in time for the June Supper Club.

"Court and I just wanted to let you know that we're going to give back some of the money you gave us," he said.

"No," Bea said firmly, blinking as the landscape outside her window came into view. "That's not necessary, Ted. And I can pay more for the wedding luncheon too. Whatever you need." What she didn't say was—*whatever your father won't.*

She wasn't sure what Ted heard when Bea said things like that. He'd been grown and out of the house when Norton had cheated and their marriage had dissolved.

"Teddy," she said when he remained silent. "Send me the bill, okay? No questions asked. You hopefully only get married once, and I want you and Courtney to have everything you want."

He drew a breath sharply enough for Bea to hear. "Mama."

"I don't want to argue with you," she said with plenty of power in her voice. She turned back to the biscuit dough she'd been about to put together. "Now, I'm making a big Southern seafood feast for Supper Club tonight, and I need to get these biscuits in the oven. Is that all you had?"

"Yes," he whispered.

"Put whatever you need to on the American Express," she said. "I'll be there in a week. I can't wait." Bea really couldn't either. She, Shelby, and Grant were going to Texas for this wedding, and she didn't even care if she ran into Norton. The man had made his bed, and he was the one who had to sleep in it.

She didn't. Not anymore.

"I love you, Teddy," she said.

"I love you too."

The call ended, and Bea kneaded her worries into the biscuit dough. Then she added a couple of handfuls of cheese and mixed it all up again. She cut out perfect rounds, placed them on a sheet tray, and slid it into the oven.

She had more dough to get through, but she set it aside for now and focused on the hot crab dip she was serving with crostini for an appetizer. She loved working in the kitchen, and the hours passed as more biscuits got baked, as the crab dip melted and warmed, as the grits boiled and softened.

She took the shrimp to just-right and not a moment over the flame more. She seasoned the Lowcountry Boil with the precise amount of Old Bay. Her little beach cottage filled with all of the scents of sausage, seafood, and baked bread.

Even Bea could admit some things were better bought, and she'd purchased a creamy cole slaw and a tart key lime pie to complete their feast for that evening. She had bottled lemonade in a variety of fruity flavors, and she'd just set a pitcher of sweet iced tea on the counter when her front door opened.

"Hey-ho," Cass called, though Bea could see her just fine. Her kitchen, dining area, and living room was all one big room from front to back, and while the house was small, Bea didn't need more. For nine months out of the year, only she and Grant lived there. His daughter came to stay with them all summer, and Bea absolutely loved Shelby.

"Look who I found texting out front." Cass smiled over her shoulder to the near-adult as Shelby entered the house too.

"How was work?" Bea asked, noting that Shelby tucked her phone away in a flash.

"Good," Shelby said.

"How's Chase?" Bea asked, expertly moving her eyes back to the food in front of her. Shelby had a boyfriend back in Alabama, where she lived with her mother.

"He's good," Shelby said. "It smells amazing in here."

"You're coming, right?" Bea asked, daring to look up and meet the girl's eye.

"No, she's not," Grant said as he swept into the house too. "We have a hot date at the arcade tonight."

"Dad," Shelby whined as she rolled her eyes. "I'm eighteen years old."

"Yeah, but you still have a thing for Pac-Man." He grinned at her and pulled his shirt over his head. "I'm going to change, and then we'll go. I want one of those brisket sandwiches from Mike's!"

He left the room in a wake, and Shelby sighed. "He doesn't understand the concept of an indoor voice." She sat at the bar while Bea laughed. "Sorry about the peep show, Cass."

Cass grinned and waved away Shelby's apology. "I've seen Grant at the beach plenty of times." She joined the younger woman at the bar. "You're seeing a boy named Chase?"

Shelby nodded, but she didn't seem happy. Bea glanced at Cass, and her best friend nodded. "What's he like? He lives near you?"

"He graduated already," Shelby said, shooting a look at Bea. "I still have my senior year, but he does live in Lincoln Point."

Cass nodded, her smile friendly and kind. She had three adult children—a married daughter, a nomad daughter, and her younger son who lived with her in the summers. "What does he do?"

"He works at the tire shop." Shelby reached up and wiped her face. "I sure like him, but I don't know."

"What don't you know?" Bea asked before she could

stop herself. Shelby looked miserable, and Bea wanted to alleviate that from her life. She reminded herself that she couldn't fix someone else's problems, and she simply stirred the boil while she waited for her step-daughter to say something.

"He's great," she said slowly. "He's seriously the cutest boy ever. He treats me real well." When she spoke, sometimes Bea could hear the small-town South in her voice. She smiled, but she kept her head down.

"But he—he doesn't want to go to college. Says it scares him, and he wouldn't even know what to study. It's not like his daddy owns the hardware store or the movie theater and he'll take it over one day. He's literally rotating tires for a living, and I—don't—" Her eyes grew wide, and she snapped her mouth shut.

Cass and Bea both watched her, and while Bea told herself to look away, she couldn't make herself do it.

"It's okay to want more than that," Cass said quietly.

Shelby turned her head and stared at her. "He's a great guy. I don't mean to sound so judgmental."

"Oh, sweetie, you're not." Cass pulled her into a side-hug. "It's also okay to want a great guy who wants to leave the town where he grew up."

Bea nodded, trying to decide what to say. "Do you want to stay in Lincoln Point, Shelby?" Her mother had been there for the past few years, after a string of towns from north to south. Grant had finally told her she better pick somewhere for the duration of Shelby's high school career, or he was going to try to bring her back to Hilton Head to live with him full-time.

That had been about the time that Bea and Grant had gotten married, and his ex had settled in Alabama since then.

Shelby shook her head. "No," she said. "I don't have any strong ties to that place."

"Maybe you'll come back here," Bea said brightly. "Or go to college in Charleston."

"Or Atlanta," Cass said.

"Or anywhere," Bea added.

"All right," Grant bellowed as he returned to the main part of the house. "Who's ready to eat some ghosts?" He clapped his hands together and rubbed them vigorously.

Shelby rolled her eyes again, but she adored her father. Bea grinned at him, stepped into him to kiss him, and said, "I'll save plenty for you."

"Mm, you always do." He led the way out of the house, and they side-stepped someone coming in.

Thelma and Sage, who never seemed to go anywhere without the other since they'd moved to the island a couple of months ago. Together. Thelma had cats; Sage had an enormous dog. At first glance, Bea would've never named them sisters, but the more she got to know Thelma, the more she heard and saw Sage in her younger sister.

"Did you ladies meet anyone interesting at the Gardening Club?" Cass asked.

"Actually," Thelma said. "There was a nice man there. He showed us a thing or two about how to make sure our soil isn't too sandy for azaleas."

Bea's eyebrows went up. "Oh, okay."

"He wasn't a nice man," Sage said dryly. "He was a nice *gentle*man."

"Sage," Thelma said with a sigh.

"What?" her sister asked. "He was ninety if he was a day."

Thelma shook her head. "She's not wrong." A beat of silence followed, wherein only the pot on the stove could be heard boiling away. Then all four of them started to laugh.

"He did know a lot about soil," Sage said through her giggles.

"Soily and sexy," Thelma teased.

"I don't know what that means, and I'm actually afraid to ask."

Bea looked up and found Joy standing only a few feet away. Lauren came to her side and she asked, "What's so funny?"

"Nothing," Sage said quickly. She expanded the circle, as Bea didn't have enough barstools at her counter.

"Dinner's almost ready," Bea said. "Let me get out the appetizers." She flitted around then, getting the crostini out and arranging it around the baked crab dip. She put that in the middle of the table, and that got everyone to find a chair and sit.

Bea had borrowed a couple of chairs from the storage shed for the rental units she and Grant managed. It was a tight fit, but she'd managed to get all seven chairs around the table. She set a stack of plates next to Lauren, who started to pass them out.

"Napkins," she said, handing a stack of pressed white cloth napkins to Cass. "And I have shrimp and grits too."

She placed that dish on the table and glanced toward the door. "Where's Bessie?"

As if summoned by her question, the strawberry blonde walked in. Well, most of her strawberry had been colored over by regular blonde-from-a-bottle, but Bea still thought she looked like a million bucks.

Tonight, her face held a glow that made Bea smile, and she went to greet her as she turned to close the door behind her. "You started already?"

"We just barely moved over to the table," Bea said. "You're not late."

"I didn't think I was." She stepped into Bea and hugged her. She groaned and added, "Oh, I'm tired."

"First day back after your mid-week weekend is rough?" Bea asked.

Bessie had admitted as much on their group text. Her Thursdays were like Mondays, and she looked to already be dragging her feet. "It was rough getting up this morning, and then I had to stand in line forever at the city offices to get a permit to sell at the Heritage Festival."

She shook her head. "It's dumb. If I sign up to be a sponsor, that should come with the sales permit." She went toward the table, adding, "It smells great in here."

"Thanks," Bea said, wanting to ask more questions of Bessie. She hadn't said much about her and Oliver, nor the Heritage Festival on their group messages. Everything was about Wyn or the bakery. "You didn't invite Wyn?"

"She has a summer cold," Bessie said. "She was passed out, snoring, when I left." She gave Bea a warm, if tired, smile and took the last spot at the table. She didn't elbow her way in to get food. Lauren pushed the crab dip plate closer to her, and Bessie took it with a nod of acknowledgement.

She'd always been a steady force in Bea's life. When things had fallen apart for her, Bessie had not. She was rational and kind, hard-working and studious. She loved genealogy, old newspapers and photos, and out of all of them, only Bessie understood the joy that came from creating in the kitchen.

"All right," Bea said, pulling herself and her emotions back into a tight lace. "I think everything is ready, and I'm not going to serve you in courses tonight."

She moved to the counter beside the fridge and grabbed the stack of newspaper there. "I made a traditional Lowcountry boil, and I'm pretty sure I followed everything just right." She spread the newspaper down the middle of the table and went to the stove to get the stew.

It was potatoes, corn on the cob, sausage, and shrimp, and the recipe had said to dump it out down the middle of the table. Then people could eat it with the biscuits, the dip, the grits, or the creamy cole slaw.

Sage got up to help Bea put out the sides, and then they all looked at the mess of food in front of them. Bessie reached in first with the words, "I love corn on the cob," and then hands reached into the middle of the table and started picking out proteins and veggies.

Bea took a couple of potatoes, speared some shrimp, and

nabbed herself a long length of sausage as chatter started. Sometimes they went around and had announcements at their Supper Club. Sometimes they had to share something significant or new.

Tonight, they just talked and ate, and Bea counted each one of these women as a blessing in her life. A pure miracle.

"Okay," she said once they'd picked through the biscuits, the cole slaw, and the sweet tea. "Time for dessert, and I want a dish to go with it."

"Dish and dessert," Cass said as she rolled up the newspaper and tossed it in Bea's sink.

Bea put the pie in the middle of the table, along with a fresh stack of dessert plates. "You have to give us at least one sentence that's something we don't already know."

She looked around at everyone. "I'll go first. Curtis is going to be coming back here with me after Teddy's wedding." She grinned and sat down.

"That's great," Cass said, smiling. Similar sentiments moved through the group, and Bea rose back to her feet to cut herself a piece of pie. "No one else wants any? It's from Castleton's." The fresh, sharp citrus scent hit her right in the nose as she lifted a pristine piece of pie from the tin.

"I like Oliver Blackhurst," Bessie blurted out.

Bea blinked as she picked up a fork. Just like with Shelby, she didn't want to scare Bessie away by looking at her too quickly or for too long.

"That's not something we didn't already know," Lauren said into the silence.

Bea chanced looking over to her friend. Bessie's face held

the strawberry in it now, and she shook her head. "I didn't—like, we're *dating*."

"Yeah, honey," Cass said. "We know."

"You say nothing about him," Sage said.

"That's because..." Bessie trailed off, confusion covering her face. "I've been fighting against the tide, haven't I?" Everything in her expression cleared, and she heaved a great sigh as she reached for the knife to cut herself a piece of pie.

"Have you really not admitted that you like him until now?" Joy asked. "It's been a few weeks, hasn't it?"

"He has some flaws," Bessie said.

"What man doesn't?" Lauren asked. Bea threw her a sharp look, which Lauren ignored. "I mean, you should *see* the number of socks Blake has. And the real shocker is that none of them ever seem to have a match." She rolled her eyes as everyone gaped at her, Bea included.

They all burst out laughing again, but this time was so much better. Because this time, all of them were there, in person. In the flesh.

Not some of them on a video chat twelve hundred miles away.

But all of them, the whole Supper Club, together again.

"I thought you were going to say you'd kissed Oliver," Cass said as they quieted, and all eyes went to Bessie.

She didn't like that, but she didn't squirm either. She simply shook her head and said, "Not yet," with a devilish glint in her eye that had Joy tossing a bit of cheddar biscuit at her. That nearly started a food riot that thankfully, Joy put a quick stop to.

Bea met Cass's eye, but she only shrugged. "I don't have anything," she said. "I'm super boring."

"Fine," Bea said. "Have a piece of pie anyway." She didn't make anyone say anything else, and once they all had the tart key lime pie and a fork, she said, "I sure do love you guys."

"It's so much better in person, isn't it?" Lauren asked, to which everyone agreed.

"Okay," Sage said. "But I don't want Bessie waiting until August's Supper to tell us she's kissed Oliver. Night-of."

"Night-of?" Bessie shook her head. "No way. Besides, who says it'll be at night? I turn into a pumpkin before the sun goes down."

"Within twenty-four hours," Joy suggested, her eyebrows up in a silent question mark.

Bessie rolled her eyes, but she said, "Fine. I'll text you all within twenty-four hours, but I feel stupid even saying that."

Bea patted her hand, and the conversation moved on to something else. She'd had an eventful summer already, and it sure seemed like it would continue to bring unexpected surprises.

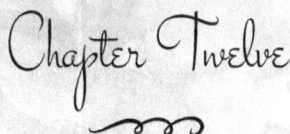

Chapter Twelve

Oliver kept his head down and his fingers flying over the keyboard as the shop opened. They didn't usually have a big rush in the morning, as eleven mostly found summer tourists getting to the beach. They'd either buy lunch there or pack something in.

His busy times were in the middle of the afternoon, after people had enjoyed their fill of the sun, sand, and surf. And the wind. Dear stars in heaven, the wind.

It never stopped, and that alone gave Oliver a headache today.

He finished the payroll and turned to his next task. His heartbeat bumped and thumped, because it was the final ad layout for the Heritage Festival, and he'd need to call and talk to Bessie to get it finalized.

At the same time, the fact that he had to call and talk to Bessie to get the ad layout finalized annoyed him. He couldn't wait to give Amy and her Heritage Festival Committee a piece of his mind on this partnership thing they'd done this year.

Sure, he hadn't minded partnering up with Bessie, but anyone else? He'd have ripped out all of his hair by now. She'd been easy-going so far, agreeing to almost everything he'd said and suggested. They'd designed their booth to have six open sides, because at the platinum level, they got priority placement that put them on the end cap between two aisles.

So he'd have six blenders there, two busily making smoothies on each side. It would take five employees to run the booth at the Festival, and it was a grueling twelve-hour day. He'd hired more people now, just to get them trained and ready for the Festival.

Bessie had decided to do her traditional breads and samples on one side, her ethnic and world-cuisine breads and samples on another, and then a butter and jam station on the third. She'd been busy trying to find a local artist to partner with on the jams, and she'd texted earlier this week to say perhaps she and Wyn would just make the jams and compound butters themselves. *It's something I've wanted to add to the bread bakery*, she'd told him. *I just haven't found the time.*

Time was definitely something that always marched against Oliver, a fact he got reminded of when he looked up at the sound of knocking on his door.

"Come," he called, and Bessie herself opened the door.

He instantly regretted the sharp tone he'd used, and he leapt to his feet.

"Hey, sunshine."

"Hey." She gave him a fleeting smile and let him hug her for a moment. Nothing for too long, and she felt extra-stiff today.

"What's up?"

She said nothing, and that added more fuel to the frustrated fire inside him. "I'm glad you're here," he said. "We have to submit our final ad copy and design by Friday, and I wanted to get your opinion and permission."

He had a lot of skills, but graphic design wasn't one of them. "I actually sent the concepts and ideas to Lauren, and she's sent back a few mock-ups." He bent to pull them from his bag, and he'd no sooner straightened to lay out the pages when Bessie sucked in a breath.

"I don't think I can do the Festival," she said in one steady stream of words.

Oliver blinked, sure he hadn't heard her right. If she didn't do the Heritage Festival, he couldn't either. He tried to find the source of her uneasiness, but he couldn't. "I've done almost all the work," he said slowly. "Why can't you do it?"

"You've done almost all of the work?" Her eyes shot flames at him. "I have been at your side every step of the way —and it's harder for me, because I have no idea what I'm doing. I've been learning and learning, and...you've done almost all of the work?"

She scoffed and shook her head. "I've already seen these, Oliver. Lauren showed them to me on Sunday. You don't corner the market on knowing things."

He leaned back in his chair, almost amused at her outburst. He wished it didn't turn up the attraction inside him, but it so did. He liked that she stood up for herself, though she seemed like the meek and mild type of woman who wouldn't.

"Why can't you do the Festival?" he asked. "If you saw these two days ago, then you know they're fantastic, and we're going to get a lot of increased business from this. Both of us."

He always wanted more business, and her bread bakery was brand new. She'd almost survived the first month, and he had no idea what her profit margins were. She hadn't paid him anything for the platinum sponsorship, and he hadn't asked her to.

She shook her head, a dangerous tremble in her bottom lip now. Looking away, she said, "I can't—I need so many people to work that booth. I don't have the employees to do it."

Ah, so it was a staffing issue. "It's selling bread. How hard can it be?"

Her shoulders boxed up, and she glared until he thought his face would melt off. "I'm going to pretend you didn't say that."

"I would like a do-over," he admitted.

"Mm hm." She took the glare down to simply a daggered look, and added, "It's not just the people in the booth, either. It's having enough inventory for three full days of selling at the festival. There's only two of us that bake, and we're barely keeping the shop stocked."

"Can you bake in advance?"

She shook her head. "No one wants to buy three-day old, frozen bread. Would you?"

"No." He folded his arms, not even bothering to sugarcoat his response.

"I just feel like maybe this was a mistake. I can't pay for the sponsorship. I can't staff the booth. I can't even *stock* the booth. I feel like a fool."

"Bessie—"

"I'm not a businesswoman," she said, exploding to her feet. "I'm good at baking. Why did I think I could open a bakery?"

He stood too and rounded the desk. He put his hands on her shoulders, recognizing the spiraling behavior. "Bessie," he said again. He normally didn't say her name at all, and he felt the weight of it against his tongue.

She stepped away from him, and his arms fell back to his sides. "I need a minute." She spun and left the office, pulling the door so hard it banged against the wall as she stalked away.

Away, not out, and Oliver frowned as he went to the doorway and watched her go to the end of the counter to order. He wished he had the right words to say. The precise thing to do to calm her down.

He left the office, his mind firing at him. Behind the

counter, he moved to Thad, one of his new boys. "Did she order the Surfer Boy?"

"Yes, sir," he said.

"I've got it." Oliver nodded at him and edged him away from the blender. He poured the smoothie into a cup, lidded it, and grabbed a straw while Bessie stood at the cash register. "Come on."

"I can pay for that."

"And I can go a day without eating your salted wheat bread. But I'm not going to, just like you're not paying for this." He stepped around the counter and handed it to her. "Go on now. Put your card away."

She slid it into the pocket of her black pants. "Fine," she said. "But I'm not doing it because you told me to."

"Of course not," he said.

She turned and walked away from him, once again leaving his mind in a froth. Did he follow her? Force her to talk to him? He sighed, annoyance heaping onto frustration and irritation. He did follow her when she stayed in the building and tucked herself into the very corner of the shop.

He pulled out the chair across from her and sat. "Bessie," he said again.

"You never say my name."

"Then you know it's serious."

She looked up at him while her head stayed down, her mouth bent over the straw of her smoothie. He really wanted to taste that Surfer Boy on her tongue, but he tore his eyes away from her mouth.

His mind had gone blank. Their eyes met, and he

opened his mouth. "I can help you find some people to sell bread."

"You don't have time to do that."

"Your friends would come do it for you," he said.

She shook her head. "I'm not going to ask them to do that."

"I can have my people run credit cards," he said. "Then, if you have people there to hand out the samples and bag the bread, it'll be fine."

Bessie looked away from him, toward the bank of windows at the front of the shop. The sense of unrest rose from her like steam, and Oliver didn't know how to cool it. In the past, he hadn't had time or patience for women less put together than him. But with Bessie, he couldn't walk away.

He didn't even want to.

She had done something incredibly hard, that he admired greatly. She'd moved here from several states away and opened her own bakery. So many people had dreams exactly like hers, and they never acted on them. They sat in wishes and "what-ifs," their ambitions gathering dust in the corners of their minds. But not her. She embraced the challenge, stepping boldly into the unknown—or rather, Hilton Head Island—and turning the ephemeral into something tangible.

Every day, she rose long before the sun, her hands kneading love into dough, her heart beating in rhythm with the hum of the oven. Each loaf of bread a testament to her dedication, an edible echo of her passion.

She transformed an ordinary storefront into a haven of heavenly aromas and heartwarming flavors, an oasis for the dreamers, the doers, and those caught in between. Her bakery was not merely a shop, but a symbol, a beacon reminding everyone that it was never too late to pursue their dreams, to shift from wishful thinking to meaningful action.

That was why Oliver admired her. In her, he saw not just a baker, but a dreamer, a fighter, a woman of remarkable strength and resolve. She was a shining example that dreams didn't have to remain as mere wishes and what-ifs. They could be lived, breathed, and tasted.

"Why did you open Flour Power?" he asked.

She glared and took another long draw on her straw. "I like baking."

"No, come on."

"I don't want to talk about this."

"How old are you?"

She eyed him warily. "Forty-five."

He allowed a brief smile to touch his lips. "I'm forty-six."

"Great," she said. "At least I know I'm not a cougar." She rolled her eyes, and while she was definitely the more chipper out of the pair of them, he recognized a bad mood she wanted to keep. He'd often been in that position, because it was easier to be and stay upset than to admit defeat.

"You left your home state at age forty-five," he said. "You packed up everything you own. Everything. And you moved it twelve hundred miles to South Carolina. Why?"

She started to settle right in front of him, and Oliver had

no idea where he was going with any of this. "You opened a bakery here. You work with a family member, and that can sometimes turn out to be a nightmare. And I want to know why." He folded his arms across his chest, keeping the table between them in case he needed to use it as a shield.

Not that he thought Bessie would be violent. Still, he couldn't take the chance.

As she stared at him, and he gazed right on back, he saw the moment she started to crumble. Oliver quickly abandoned his chair and squeezed onto the bench seat behind the table for two, further trapping her in the corner.

"Okay, don't cry," he whispered. "I didn't mean to make you cry. I was just..." He sighed as he turned his body so her tears wouldn't be broadcast to the whole smoothie shop. The noise inside had definitely started to pick up as the lunch crowd came in.

"I was simply trying to get you to see that you're stronger than you think." He ducked his head only to get his nose closer to her skin. Then he could breathe in the wonderfully citrus scent of her, catching notes of yeast and freshly baked bread too. Oh, he could die and go to heaven in that scent.

"I want you to see how much you've already done. Impossible things. Things other people don't do. So you need a few more people to help out in the booth for three days? Okay. No problem. We'll find them."

Bessie swiped at her eyes, though no tears had truly fallen. They'd only gathered in her lovely eyes, where she'd contained them.

"You're *so* strong," he whispered, all of his guards down now. "And so beautiful." He reached up and tilted up her chin so those gorgeous eyes would seek out his. "Why did you open the bakery?"

"My daughter had things go bad at her job in Oklahoma," Bessie whispered. "She needed something. I needed a change. My friends were here, and...I've dreamt of owning my own bakery since I was fourteen years old. It felt like it was time."

Oliver nodded at her just once, his eyes falling away from hers and landing on her mouth. His pulse boomed at him to absolutely not kiss her right now. Certainly not in his own smoothie shop, where anyone from the community, any of his employees, and a whole host of tourists could see him.

"You are the best bread baker I've ever met," he said. "We can do this Festival. You need something? You ask me."

She nodded, and he did too. "Okay? You ask me, sunshine."

"Okay." She sniffled as she curled into his chest. Oliver held her close, mentally adding another item to his to-do list. People. He knew how to hire people to do a job.

Bessie drew in a long breath and straightened. "Thank you, Oliver." She looked right at him, and he swore he opened every door for her. "You want to go look at the graphics?"

"No," he murmured.

"No?" Her eyebrows went up.

He leaned closer. "No," Oliver repeated. "I want to kiss you."

Something akin to panic flowed through her eyes, and oh, Oliver wanted that to go away. He wanted to promise she'd like it, though his own nerves at landing a really great first kiss reared up.

So it was probably for the best that someone said, "Mister Blackhurst? There's someone here for you."

"Who is it?" he asked without looking away from Bessie. She likewise kept her gaze on his, her eyes searching his.

"Someone named Wendy," the boy said. "She said she has an interview at eleven-thirty."

"Sure." Oliver moved back, scooted out, and stood. "Thanks, Jackson." He clapped the boy on the shoulder, and he turned and went back to work. Oliver faced Bessie again. "Do you want to sit in on the interview? I have all the people I need, but maybe we could—maybe *you* could use her."

He really needed to stop using the word "we" before it became something he desperately wanted.

Too late, he told himself, wondering how he'd gotten here in only a month. True, it had been longer than that. He'd been eyeing Bessie for a while now. When he lay down at night, and it was really dark, he could admit that to himself.

Bessie stood up and pressed into him. "I'll sit in," she said. "If we can pick up our conversation afterward."

A slow grin spread across his face. "Oh, were we *talking* about something?"

"Yes," she clipped out. "I believe the last thing you said was, 'I want to kiss you.'" She smiled sweetly at him, though an edge sat in those eyes. "I'd definitely like to respond to that."

"I look forward to it," he said as he gestured for her to go back to his office first. The sooner this interview ended, the sooner they could get back to their "conversation."

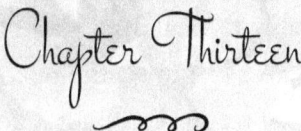

Chapter Thirteen

Bessie slid a tray with four loaves of sourdough bread into the waiting, hot oven. That done, she opened the one below it and took out four loaves of perfectly baked nine-grain bread—one of her personal favorites.

She loved a bit of chew in bread, and she hadn't found a seed better than a pumpkin seed. She loved the texture of it, and she wanted to slice right into the loaves, slather them with butter, and eat.

But bread needed to rest, so it didn't smash when sliced. Therefore, Bessie slid the hot loaves into a cooling rack and turned to clean up her work station and move on to the next item on her list. She'd no sooner done that—and started the dough of a quick bread recipe she'd then divide and flavor differently before baking—when Wyn walked in.

She lumbered, really, under the weight of a heavy box. "Mom," she grunted, and Bessie abandoned her baking to help.

"What is this?" she asked as she put her hands underneath it too. "Oh, it's heavy. How did you carry this?" They managed to stutter-step and get it on one of the tables.

Wyn grunted and exhaled, then wiped her hair out of her face. Bessie stared at her. "You dyed your hair."

"Yep." Wyn reached to open the box. "And, while I was picking up our new bread slicer, I got asked out." She enunciated every word with precision, and Bessie's eyes got wider with each one.

Her heartbeat raced around the track of her ribs, finally shooting back into the proper place. "What did you say?"

Wyn grinned, and Bessie hadn't realized that her daughter hadn't truly been smiling until now. Her heart ached then, and she moved into Wyn and took her into a hug. "You said yes."

"He was really cute," Wyn said with a laugh. "His name is Douglas Polletson, and he runs the warehouse for the restaurant supply store here on the island."

Bessie stepped back. "So he's a local."

"That he is." Wyn got the flaps of the box open and peered inside. "Here's the manual." She took it out and handed it to Bessie, who did love to look through a good manual for a new appliance. She flipped it open and said, "You got the nice one."

"I told you we should." Wyn threw a somewhat frazzled look over to Bessie. "We have the money to put back into the business."

"Okay," Bessie said airily. She and Wyn went over all the numbers for Flour Power every other week. It wasn't Bessie's strong suit, but Wyn sure seemed to know what she was doing.

"And we can hire two more people to help in the booth if you need them," she said as she started to lift the silver slicer from the box. "Grab that and get it out of the way, would you?"

Bessie hastened to move the box the slicer had come in, and Wyn groaned again as she held the weight of the appliance for a moment. Then it landed back on the table, and they both gazed at it.

"Now we can offer sliced bread loaves," Wyn said. "It literally takes ten seconds, and it's amazing." She turned toward the racks at the back of the bakery. "Do you have one we can test it with?"

"Sure do." Bessie went to retrieve a loaf of her salted whole wheat bread. "This is for Oliver, and he won't mind if it's sliced."

"Surely not," Wyn said. "Unless he likes to just rip it off with his hands." She laughed, and Bessie smiled. Oliver certainly wasn't the type to rip off hunks of anything and eat with his hands. He was Southern refinement, and Bessie had never really seen a hair out of place on him.

She hadn't kissed him yet either, despite his statement from a week or so ago. She'd told all the ladies about it, and they'd gone wild—until she said, *Then we got interrupted, and we've never revisited it.*

Well, revisit it! Bea had said. She was gone to Texas at the moment for her son's wedding, and Bessie expected a slew of pictures by that evening. Ted and Courtney were tying the knot today, and Bessie almost wished she were there.

She'd known Bea for almost twelve years now. Ted had been fifteen when the Supper Club started, and she'd given him money for his high school graduation and a little something when he finished college too.

But she couldn't get away from the bread bakery for a wedding in Texas at the moment. Not with August just around the corner, and the Heritage Festival nearly upon them. Not with her smooth, delectable, handsome boyfriend she'd be leaving behind here.

Cass and Harrison had gone to the wedding, as had Joy. She claimed she wanted to see what "brides were doing these days," though Bessie suspected Joy already had all the pieces of her wedding in place.

Bessie wondered what a second wedding would look like for her. She'd been divorced for longer than anyone in the group, and she'd actually grown quite fond of her solo routines. She sure did like it when Oliver picked her up after work, her favorite buttermilk pie in a small box, and a devious smile as he refused to tell her where they were going.

"Okay," Wyn said, taking the loaf of bread from Bessie and bringing her back to the situation at hand at the same time. "Let's see how this works." She fitted the loaf on the tray at the bottom of the slicer. It had all the blades up above, and Wyn removed the cover.

"Okay." She bent to plug it in, and then she looked at Bessie with wide-eyed wonder on her face. "Let's see if our money was well-spent."

She pressed the only button on the machine, and it did nothing. The excitement fizzled, but Bessie quickly grabbed the manual. "Maybe we missed a step."

"Missed a step?" Wyn grumbled. "You put the bread in, and it slices it." She picked up the whole wheat loaf. "There's nothing to it."

Bessie scanned quickly, reading the directions. It sure seemed like Wyn was right. "Oh," she said. "There's a safety catch you have to press." She moved next to her daughter. "So put the bread down again."

Wyn did, and Bessie looked up near the slicers. "Right there." She pointed to a white button. "You have to press that in."

Her daughter did that, and they both stepped back like they might be setting off fireworks. "Ready?" Wyn asked, looking at the book and then Bessie.

"Then it says you press the SLICE button, and the magic happens."

Wyn pressed the button again, and sure enough, the slicers lowered over the bread. Crumbs from the outer crust flew up a couple of inches, and within a few seconds, the slicers lifted again. A click filled the otherwise silent kitchen, and Bessie noted that the safety had engaged again.

"It's so you know you can then pick up the loaf and the knives won't come down and get you." She did just that, holding the now sliced loaf of bread in both hands. "This is incredible."

"Then we bag it up as usual." Wyn grabbed one of their regular-sized plastic bags—Bessie had them in long for

French loaves and baguettes, and round for her sourdoughs and pumpernickels.

A lot of her bread was just a regular loaf of bread, and she slipped it into the bag, all of the pieces simply sliding in like soldiers falling into line. Wyn twisted a tie around it, and Bessie grabbed the brown bakery bag they'd decided to use as their final packaging.

"Done." She held the bagged bread now, and she couldn't wait to show it to Oliver.

"I'm going to put it out on the counter behind the case," Wyn said as she fitted the cover over the blades. "Then we can offer sliced bread when people buy loaves."

"Can we do our rounds?"

"Yes," Wyn said. "I bought the one that could do every-thing we make here." She smiled again, and once again, Bessie saw the sunshine in her daughter's soul that had been missing before.

"When are you going out with Douglas?"

"Tonight," Wyn said. "He said there's a volleyball tour-nament on one of the beaches, and it's fun to just walk around, watch them play, get drinks, maybe something to eat." She wrapped the power cord up and around the slicer. "It sounded casual and fun for our first time out together."

"You do love a good food truck rally."

She giggled again. "I do. Get the door for me, would you?" She nodded to the swinging door that led out into the front of the shop, and Bessie moved to hold it for her though she could've kicked it open with her foot.

Wyn went by her, and a flash of gratitude for her good

daughter moved through Bessie. Her phone began to chime and chime and chime, and she knew that meant one thing: Wedding pictures from Bea.

She hurried over to her device, ready to see a grandbaby and beautiful people in beautiful clothes. But when she looked at her phone, she found Oliver's name on the screen.

Just found out the beach I was planning to take you to tonight is going to be hopping with a volleyball tournament.

Do you want to enter the touristy fray?

Or would you rather have a quieter night together?

Bessie warmed from head to toe, simply because of the last word of his last text. Together. She hadn't been *together* with someone for a long time, and it felt really, really significant.

Quieter, she tapped out. She wasn't looking for a loud, casual date while she tried to decide if she liked Oliver enough to go out with him again. Not only that, but she didn't want to be in the same space as Wyn tonight.

I was hoping you'd say that, he said. *Is five still okay? Too early? Too late?*

She smiled at his questions. He normally didn't second-guess their plans, and Bessie wondered what ran through his mind.

Five weeks had passed since she'd stressed in the driver's seat of her car and he'd knocked on the window. Five weeks since they'd partnered up for the Heritage Festival. Five weeks since he'd made her promise not to fall in love with him.

Bessie sure did like spending her late afternoons and

evenings with Oliver, and he seemed to be able to leave his smoothie shop whenever he wanted.

Five is fine, she said. *You can come earlier if you want to. I'll just be home.*

Oliver didn't answer, and Bessie sighed as she tucked her phone away. She got back to work on the quick breads, because they had a special order for them, and they needed to be baked, cooled, and wrapped for pick-up in only a few hours.

Once she finished them, Bessie would be done for today. She could head home, shower, and get herself together for her quiet evening with Oliver. That alone introduced more light into her life than she'd thought possible, and when Bea did send the pictures of her with the bride and groom, and her with her granddaughter, actual tears touched Bessie's eyes.

Maybe one day, she'd have everything Bea did. A happily married daughter, with grandbabies. A good, solid, handsome man at her side. Pure sunshine pouring from her eyes and smile in every picture.

Bea had always been several steps ahead of Bessie on the path of life, despite the two of them being very close to the same age. "It's not a race," she told herself, and then she started fantasizing about what the wedding pictures would look like at Wyn's wedding, Bessie standing next to her daughter, and Oliver standing next to the groom.

The doorbell rang, jolting Bessie out of the slumber she'd fallen into. It took her a moment to remember she'd laid down on top of her comforter for just a minute. She'd been playing word games on her phone, and her eyelids had grown heavy. She'd set her phone aside to simply rest, something she'd done plenty of times in the past.

She didn't always fall asleep. Today, she had.

"What time is it?" She fumbled along her side for her phone, found it, and then got to her feet. A frown tugged at her eyebrows. "It's only four."

As she looked at her phone, a text came in. *You said I could come early. Are you home?*

Her pulse picked up a beat, and then another. Instead of answering Oliver, she headed for the front door. She opened it, and he turned from the edge of the porch, as if he'd been about to leave.

"Sorry." She pushed her hair off her forehead. "I laid down for a minute to play games on my phone, and I fell asleep." She smiled at him, still fully waking up.

He smiled back. "That's okay. If you want to go back to sleep, I can come back." He wore a pair a navy blue shorts today, and his button-up shirt had short sleeves and came in a variety of lavender that few men could pull off.

"No," she said. "Come in." She stepped back out of the heat and humidity to allow him room to enter.

He pressed in close to her, his hand sliding up her arm and then dropping to her hip. "You look amazing."

"I just woke up."

"Yeah," he said. "Fresh from bed. Sexy." He pressed a kiss

to her forehead, which was about six inches too high. "Oh, your AC feels great." He'd eased past her by then, and Bessie hastened to close the door and seal the heat outside. AC wasn't free, after all.

"Did you go to work today?" she asked.

He turned to face her. "Nope." He tucked his hands in his pockets. "What gave it away?"

She nodded to his legs. "The shorts. I don't think I've ever seen you wear shorts."

Oliver's grin should be illegal, but he smiled at her anyway. No cops jumped through the windows to arrest him either. "I wore shorts to the fireworks," he said. "I'm almost sure of it."

"Maybe," she said, not really willing to concede the point. "Why didn't you go to work?"

"I'm allowed to take days off."

"I didn't say you couldn't." She also didn't want to fight with him. "Why can't you just answer a question? You never do, you know." She detoured away from him though every cell in her body pulled directly toward him.

"I don't?"

"No." She opened the fridge and got out the sweetened tea. "Do you want something to drink?'

"Yes," he said. "*And* I answered that question directly."

Bessie rolled her eyes as she set the pitcher on the counter. "You answer easy questions just fine. It's the hard ones you avoid." She looked straight at him. "Tell me I'm wrong."

He swallowed, and that was as good as a confession.

Bessie smiled at him, so he'd know he didn't have to tell her anything. She turned her back to get down glasses, which would also give Oliver a bit of breathing room. He seemed to need that from time to time.

"Do you talk to your parents?" he asked.

Bessie faced him again, surprise moving through her. "Yeah, sure," she said. "They're back in Texas, and my older sister lives three houses down from them." In short, Bessie hadn't had to consider the needs of her parents in her decision to move to South Carolina. "I text and call every now and then. Not like, every day or anything. I know some people are like that."

She poured sweet tea into a glass and nudged it toward him. "You?"

He shook his head, his neck moving slowly again as he swallowed.

Surprise blasted through Bessie. "You don't talk to your parents?"

"My momma died a few years back," he said. "And me and my dad never really got along." He picked up the glass of sweet tea and took a big swallow of it. That seemed to clear something in his throat, because he sat as he added, "Of course, that's my perception. My brothers say Daddy has no problem with me at all."

Bessie rounded the counter to sit beside him. She too had chosen shorts for tonight, because it was the beginning of August and about the temperature of the surface of the sun outside. They had little white daisies embroidered all over the denim, and she'd matched a flowery top to the bottoms.

"Why do you feel like that then?"

"Because I left," he said. "I'm the oldest in my family, and I didn't want what my dad had spent his whole life building." He took another drink while Bessie wondered if she should prompt him with more questions.

They'd talked about their immediate families—she knew he had two younger brothers, and he knew she was the middle of three girls. They'd talked about Wyn, and their businesses, the things they liked and didn't like, and of course—the Heritage Festival.

But this felt...deeper. This was Oliver admitting something to her, and Bessie needed to listen really closely to hear what it was.

"My great-granddaddy started the first furniture store in Birmingham," he said. "Blackhurst Furniture. There's been one of us at the helm for its entire existence."

Bessie nodded, catching the notes of bitterness in his tone. "I gotta say, you don't sound like you're from Birmingham." He spoke with a slight rolling lilt. If he left South Carolina, people might—*might*—be able to guess he was from the South. Other than that, he had a rather formal way of speaking.

Oliver sliced a look at her. "I took diction classes in college."

"You—" Of course he had. "You don't want to be from Alabama."

"The state itself is fine." He studied the depths of his

iced tea, like the swirling amber liquid might hold some secrets he needed to find. "I just never felt...at home there." He looked openly at her now. "Do you feel at home here, Bessie? On Hilton Head?"

"It's growing on me," she said with a smile. "I do love the beaches here. And the trees. It feels a bit like the Coastal Bend." She leaned against his bicep, glad the physical barrier between them wasn't too strong. "Why are you bringing this all up?" she asked. "And what does it have to do with you not working today?"

He'd flipped over several pieces, but she hadn't been able to put them all together yet.

"My daddy and oldest brother want to come to the island for the festival," Oliver whispered. "I took today off to meet with Grant and Ty about finding them a place to stay."

Bessie straightened, her pulse booming through her body. "Don't they know you're going to be really busy during the Heritage Festival?" She studied his body language —shoulders up near his ears, head turned away from her, holding very still.

He almost acted like a cat who thought he could go unnoticed if he didn't move.

Panic started to lash at Bessie's insides. "You're not backing out of the festival, are you?"

"No, of course not," he said quietly, his voice defying all the readings she was getting from his body. He sighed then, and everything inside him released. The shoulders went down. He swiveled his head to look at her. A smile even touched that mouth she hadn't yet.

"I want you to meet them," he said. "Which I know is a little crazy. We're still getting to know each other, and whatever."

"Whatever?" Bessie's eyebrows practically flew off her face.

"What?" he asked. "Yeah, whatever."

She laughed and shook her head. "You don't say things like whatever."

"I can use the word whatever whenever I want."

She sobered and looked right at him. Feeling brave, she even reached out and cradled his face in one palm. "Yeah, of course you *can*," she whispered. "But you, Oliver, don't."

"You think I'm stuffy."

"You are a little stuffy."

"You think I'm high maintenance for taking diction classes."

"You are a little high maintenance. I mean, you probably pressed those shorts before you put them on." She grinned at him. "They're amazing, by the way. You look great in them." Heat filled her face, because she wasn't used to vocalizing her inner thoughts, especially about how a man looked.

"I don't press my shorts," he said, turning away so she had to drop her hand. "They come back to me like that."

It took Bessie a couple of seconds to realize what he'd said, and then she let a string of laughter fly up to the sky. "Of course," she said through the giggles. "You send your clothes out to be laundered. Why didn't I know that?"

He gave her a blinding smile, and while this one wasn't

quite as sexy and illegal as others he had, it still sent a shot of happiness straight into her chest. He leaned closer, and then closer, his breath mingling with hers as she finished laughing.

"Bessie," he said. "I want a do-over."

"Yeah?" Her eyes drifted closed as he drew nearer. She couldn't wait another moment to kiss him, and every nerve ending stood at attention. "On what?"

"On that promise—" He cut off as an alarm wailed between them. She jumped back, adrenaline sending her pulse to her tongue and down to her toes all in one swift second. Oliver ducked his head, swore under his breath, and silenced his phone.

He looked at her, the moment between them broken and gone. "That was our cue to get going," he said. "I got us a special reservation."

Bessie slipped from her barstool, her chance at what she hoped would be a scalding hot kiss with Oliver lost. For now. "Okay," she said. "Let me get some shoes." She paused before she headed into her bedroom. "Are we walking far? Am I wearing sneakers or sandals?"

"You'll like the sand between your toes," he said. "So wear sandals."

She cocked her head at him. "I thought we weren't going to the beach."

"Why would you think that?"

Bessie rolled her eyes again and then fixed him with a glare. "There you go again," she said. "Refusing to answer my questions."

She turned and walked away while Oliver called, "You didn't actually ask me a question, sunshine."

Oh, but she had. A couple, actually, and she really wanted to know what promise he wanted a do-over on. As she slipped her feet into a pair of sandals that would weather the sandy beaches in Hilton Head, a gasp flew from her mouth.

He'd once told her, *You have to promise not to fall in love with me.*

Could he want a do-over on that?

Chapter Fourteen

Oliver couldn't believe he'd been interrupted for a second time. How many perfect circumstances could be created where he could kiss Bessie?

"Apparently you need one more," he muttered to himself as he rounded the SUV to open her door for her. They'd left her house with her enormous bag, and he'd driven through a soda shop before taking her to this tiny parking lot that could barely be counted as such.

She peered out her window, her Styrofoam cup clenched in her hand. "This looks like a stretch of beach where you'd bury a body." She looked up at him as he stood outside her door, a sprinkle of delight in her expression. "But it's not dark, and this can't be counted as a bayou, so..."

Bessie rose to her feet, and she looked like a million bucks in those daisy jeans and that sleeveless blouse. She wasn't as refined as Cass, and Oliver didn't want a woman like her anyway. She wasn't as high-maintenance as Lauren—

or even himself—and Oliver liked that she'd stopped asking about the dates he planned for them. The only thing she made sure of was footwear, after that "long hike" he'd made her take after getting the boiled peanuts.

"This is where some of the cannons were housed on the island," he said, taking her hand.

"Yes, I've heard of the history here," she said.

"We have a Civil War museum," he said. "Lots of historical stuff in the lighthouses too." He led her down the sidewalk and past the small park that no one used. The Port Royal Plantation wasn't exactly open to visitors, but Oliver had plenty of friends on the island. "This is also one of the quietest beaches on the island."

"It's in a neighborhood," Bessie said, moving to walk behind him as the trail narrowed. He took her past the remnants of the steam-powered cannon and down a fairly steep path to the beaches below. Always the gentleman, Oliver turned back to offer her a hand. His skin sizzled when she touched him, and Oliver didn't let go of her hand once they'd reached the beach together.

"There aren't going to be any food trucks out here," she commented.

His stomach growled, but he said, "Nope."

She paused, and he did too. They were the only two people as far as he could see. Of course they were. It was barely five o'clock on a Thursday afternoon at the beginning of August. Sane people stayed indoors in heat like this, and the only people he knew who ate dinner this early were well into their seventies.

And apparently, Bessie Clifton.

He grinned at her as she shaded her sunglasses and looked right and then past him to the left. "I gotta say," she started.

"There's nothing to eat?" he guessed.

She looked up at him, and he could just see the outline of her eyes through the darkened lenses. "Don't worry, sunshine." He leaned down and pressed his lips to her temple. "I've arranged for a private table for two."

"On this private beach," she said, her voice almost as dry as the sand.

"All the beaches on Hilton Head are public," he said. "So no."

"We had to go through a gate to get here."

"Yep."

"Do you have a second house here?"

He laughed. "You think I'm rich enough to have a second house on Hilton Head?"

Bessie didn't answer, and Oliver took his time enjoying the sound of the ocean as it roared ashore and the taste of the salt in the breeze as it brushed his face. "No, Bess. But I've got a good friend who works at the Country Club here, and we got in on his name."

He rounded a tall grouping of rocks and said, "And it's Gavin you can thank for this beautiful table." He indicated the dark wood table and two chairs that had been set up in the shady sand near the cliffs. "After you."

"Oliver." Bessie stared at the table, and then him. She released his hand and pranced through the sand. "I want this chair." She stood behind one that faced the ocean and looked to her right. "Or do I want this one?" She switched to the one that gave her a view of the water to her left.

"They're the same," he said with a chuckle as he arrived at the table. He pulled out the chair for her, and she reached up and ran those delicate fingers down the side of his face.

"Thank you," she murmured. She sat, and Oliver took the other chair. He'd activated his pin while Bessie had been putting on her shoes, and he'd texted Gavin that they'd be leaving soon.

"He said he'd leave a cooler," Oliver said, just now remembering. He wanted to share all of the hard things of his life with Bessie, and he'd started at her house. Just having his father and brother in town—on the island he called home—would be hard enough. And during the Heritage Festival? Which he worked the booth with his girlfriend?

It seriously couldn't be worse timing.

But he'd told them, *Sure, of course. Come. I'll see where I can find for you to stay.*

The island was usually booked to full capacity in June, July, and August. The Heritage Festival brought people from the mainland as far south as Beaufort, and all the way down from Charleston.

"I'm going to need a miracle to find somewhere for my daddy and brother to stay," he said as he located the cooler under the table, hidden by the soft white tablecloth. He pulled out two bottles of water and handed one to Bessie.

She took it but didn't twist open the lid. "Can they not stay with you?"

Oliver opened his water with a wrenching twist. "They could," he said slowly. "If one of us wanted to die." He gave her a wry look, and she blinked at him.

"That bad, huh?"

"It's just..." He sighed. "No. My house would be fine. I just don't like my daddy in my personal affairs."

Bessie gazed out to the water now, releasing him from the power of her eyes. "I haven't been to your house."

"It's three bedrooms," he said. "I should just have them stay there."

She took his hand in hers. "Not if you don't want them to." She offered him a small smile that started to set the mood. Oliver didn't dare lean in for a kiss right now, because Gavin should be appearing any moment. He did not want to be interrupted for a third time, and he'd already played a lot of cards to a friend he only talked to every few weeks.

"Do you kiss and tell?" he asked.

Bessie blinked, and then blinked faster. "I mean..."

"Grant and Blake have been asking me about you." He looked off into the distance too, finding where the water met the sky. The sun still had a handful of hours before it would be gone completely, but some gold had started to sink into the blue.

"I have told my friends about us," she said quietly. "They're interested, but I haven't said anything that would paint you in a bad light."

He lifted her hand to his lips. "I appreciate that."

Their eyes met, and the sky would surely crack open from the lightning passing between them. He wanted to tell her he wanted to kiss her. He wanted a do-over on the promise she'd made not to fall in love with him.

"You guys found it." Gavin clapped his hands as he came around the side of the rock behind Bessie. She twisted toward him, and Oliver put a big smile on his face.

"Yes, thank you." He half-stood and put one arm around Gavin. "It's great." He sank into his seat again, the sand, the sun, the surf, and the woman almost overwhelming him. "This is Bessie Clifton," he said at the last moment. She quickly shut her mouth, and he was glad he'd remembered his manners. "Bess, this is Gavin Fish. He's the head chef at the Country Club."

"So great to meet you," she said. "I requested quiet, and wow. You two know how to deliver." Her sunny smile landed on Oliver, and he practically preened in it.

"So we have our first course ready." Gavin's eyebrows went up. "Y'all ready for it?"

"Yes, sir," Oliver said.

"Did you want anything else to drink?" he asked. "I've got soft drinks, lemonades, tea, wine, beer…"

Bessie looked at Oliver, who looked at her. "I'd take a raspberry lemonade," he said. "But I'm driving, so I don't want anything harder."

"I'd love a London fog and a glass of rosé," Bessie said. She had never drunk either thing on any of their previous dates, and that only told Oliver how much more he had to learn about her.

"You got it," Gavin said. "Here's our fried green tomatoes and a roasted beet burrata salad." Two exquisite dishes got placed on the table by two more men.

"Thank you," slipped from Oliver's lips, but Bessie simply stared at the food.

"We have lamb or beef tonight," Gavin said, and Oliver looked away from the child-like wonder on his girlfriend's face. Just the fact that he could use the word *girlfriend* in his own head made him smile. He'd not used a qualifier with her while introducing her to Gavin, and he found he wanted to. Out loud.

"I'll have the beef," Oliver said, and they both looked at Bessie.

She startled and said, "Beef too, please."

"It'll be about fifteen minutes," he said. "I'll get the drinks out lickety split, Bessie."

She twisted and practically shouted, "Thank you," at his retreating form. When she faced Oliver again, he got hit full blast with her sunshine. "This is incredible. Do you see those beets?"

"I see them." He laughed lightly at the deep purple and bright golden root vegetables. "They look great."

"Did you ask Lauren about my beet obsession?" Her eyes narrowed. "Be honest now."

He nearly choked as he half-laughed and half-scoffed. "I did not," he said. "And Bessie, I will always be honest with you."

"Yeah?" She reached for the oversized serving spoon in the beet salad. "Then you better tell me what promise you want a do-over on."

Oliver simply watched as she put a healthy serving of beets, bitter greens, and burrata on her plate, then swiped her finger through the balsamic glaze. She stuck that in her mouth, and everything male in Oliver's body roared to life.

She looked at him, those eyes so open and unassuming, and he wished he was more like her. He'd been so jaded with women from his past experiences. Even aspects of his business sat behind stone walls, and he realized as he looked at her that Oliver needed to break out a hammer and start breaking down some of his assumptions.

"How many promises have you made to me?" He ducked his head when he realized he was staring. He speared a fried green tomato and put it on his plate. As he busied himself with getting some of the spicy sauce to go with it, he told himself he could not eat that. Not if he wanted to kiss Bessie, and he so wanted to do that.

Still, he dolloped the sauce onto his plate and looked at her.

"Just one," she said.

"That one," he said. "I want a do-over on that."

"You want me to break my promise?" she teased.

"Yes." He folded his arms. "We could just amend it if you'd like."

"To what?" she forked up a bite of beets and cheese and took it, her eyes hardly leaving his.

"You could promise not to fall in love with me within the first month." He nearly choked on the words.

Bessie nodded. "I could."

"Or, you could take a do-over on making the promise."

Hope filled his chest, but he contained it before it could leak out anywhere else.

"I could," she said again.

Oliver was suddenly tired of the game. He couldn't take in her beauty anymore. He didn't want to sit here and pretend he wasn't feeling the things he was. At the same time, he wasn't sure someone like her could even fall for someone like him.

"Do you think I'm lovable?" He watched a big wave crest and crash over itself as it continued toward land. It was a bully, running over anything that got in its way, and Oliver knew exactly how that felt. He'd bull-dozed his way through more than one meeting and situation in his life, and regret lanced through him.

"Oliver." Bessie spoke in a hushed, barely-there voice. "Of course you're lovable."

He flicked a look over to her, unable to do much more. "I keep everyone out."

"That's a choice." She let a pause go by. "Perhaps if you told me why you do that, I could help you figure out how to stop doing it."

He was exhausted from holding everything so perfectly. He felt tight from head to toe and even along the ends of his hair. He didn't need her reassurances, but at the same time, he'd really like to hear them.

Of course you're lovable.

"My daddy said I broke my momma's heart when I left. I was only seventeen. I never went back, at least not for longer than a weekend. He said she never recovered, basically insinuating that I'm the reason she died."

"Well, if that's true, it's because she loved you so much," Bessie said without missing a beat.

Oliver's eyes flew to hers, and she lit the world with her kind smile. "I'm sorry I'm such a downer."

"You're not."

"I'm sorry I do everything I can to push all your buttons."

"I don't mind it, to be honest."

"I'm sorry I can't answer hard questions."

"You've been doing fine tonight."

He cocked his head slightly. "You're annoying me with how fast you're firing everything back at me."

"Oh, am I?" Her eyes sparkled like diamonds, and Oliver let a fantasy play through his head—one where he lunged at her and kissed her with everything he had.

Instead of doing that, he moved slowly, inching toward her. Bessie only encouraged him with that smile and the way it started to straighten, with the way her eyes dropped to his mouth as if judging where it sat on his face, with the way she reached up and slid her hand along the side of his face and around to the back of his neck.

"Are you committing this time, Oliver?" she asked in a whisper, and she very rarely said his name. So rarely that his eyes drifted closed in bliss at having those three syllables spoken in her angelic voice.

"No matter what," he whispered back, and he managed to touch his mouth to hers. The sky, the sand, the rocks themselves exploded with heat, though Oliver knew that was all inside him.

He held there, tasting the tangy balsamic on her lips for a beat of time. Long enough to know he had to kiss her madly, deeply, to be truly satisfied. Then he pulled back, pulled in a breath, and did just that.

Chapter Fifteen

Bessie could not have imagined or planned a better dinner date than this one on the beach. A very private beach, no matter what Oliver said about Hilton Head.

He kissed her with the tenderness of a man in love. Bessie knew, because she'd been kissed like that before.

At the same time, she had absolutely never been kissed the way Oliver kissed her. He seemed to need his mouth on hers to keep breathing, and he kissed her and kissed her and kissed her with the same level of intensity and passion with which he lived his life. With which he ran his smoothie shop. And with which she assumed, he loved his family and friends —and hopefully a woman.

Her?

At the moment, yes, Bessie hoped this relationship would survive whatever storms came their way, because Oliver had been nothing but sweet and attentive that day.

He was most of the time, in fact, once Bessie got past his outer walls.

She cradled his face in both hands and whispered against his lips, "You're very lovable, Oliver, no matter what anyone says." She touched her mouth to his again. "Okay? Do you hear me?"

"Yes," he whispered back as he ducked his head to touch a kiss to her neck. "I'm sorry I'm so walled off. There's just something about you that makes me..." He lifted his head, the energy in his eyes burning like liquid mercury. "Want to put up more walls and then kick every one of them down. It's very confusing."

"Just what I want to hear," Bessie said into the intimate space between them. A few inches at most.

"I'm...not confused about you, Bess."

"Did you know that literally no one ever calls me Bess?"

His eyes softened. "Do you hate it? I'll stop."

She wanted to feel the fullness of his mouth against hers again, so she kissed him. "I don't hate it," she said after the moment of pressure. "If you're not confused about me, what are you confused about?"

"The fact that I want you," he said as he pulled back. There were no shy smiles, no sideways glances, no embarrassment at all. Bessie sure did like the maturity they both brought to the table. The sky had turned inkier during their kiss, and Bessie found it harder to see through the flat light.

"I haven't wanted anyone in a while," he admitted. "Every relationship I've had in the past few years has been a disaster. I put up another wall, and then another, and then another, until I'd built this, this...swamp in the middle, where I live and I keep everyone else out."

"You have friends," she said, catching a bit of his ire as he gave her a quick glare. She told herself not to fire back so quickly. This wasn't a showdown of wits, the way it had been when they'd first met.

"I just mean, you have Grant, and Blake. Harry and Scott. Ty. This guy Gavin—willing to set up a table out on the beach and then trek out here with food and drinks."

"Speak of the devil." Oliver nodded to something behind her, and Bessie turned as a waiter approached with her tea and her wine.

"Thank you," she said as he placed them on the table. Both were beautiful, and they made the ragged edges inside Bessie's soul smooth out. Or maybe that had been the kiss with Oliver. He certainly smoothed out rough places inside her too, and Bessie hadn't even known they'd been there until they were gone.

She lifted her earl gray tea latte to her lips and took a sip. "Oh, that's good." She offered the quaint gray stone mug to him, but Oliver shook his head, those eyes lit on fire again. She set down the cup. "What?"

"I've never seen you drink a London fog."

"We've been dating for five weeks." She could fire back on this. "The enormity of my life, my every like and dislike, has not been laid bare for you in five weeks."

He held up one hand in surrender, a chuckle accompanying it. "Fair enough."

"So tell me something you'd order at a restaurant that

you haven't yet." She trained her eyes on him, satisfied when he didn't look away. She'd learned that he only did that when he felt out of control. When he felt like he might reveal too much if he maintained eye contact.

"I'm confused, because I don't want to keep you out."

"So we're not going to answer the question at hand. Okay." She took a breath, though it was nice to hear that Oliver didn't want to keep her out. "I get confused when Wyn starts going over our budget at the bakery. It's so many numbers and decimals, and I get lost pretty fast."

Oliver grinned at her. "I don't understand why anyone likes riding a bicycle. The seats are so small."

Bessie almost burst out laughing, but she caught herself at the last moment. "How anyone can like marshmallows. It boggles the mind."

Oliver broke first, sending his booming laughter into the sky. Bessie grinned and grinned, because that was the best sound in the world—and she'd pulled it from him. His shoulders went down, and he unfolded his arms. Essentially, she watched him break down his walls right in front of her, and it was a glorious sight.

"Who doesn't like marshmallows?" he asked, grabbing onto her and pulling her closer. "It's un-American."

She couldn't really get closer unless she got up and sat in his lap, so she did that. He wrapped both arms around her, and she titled her head down to kiss him. He growled somewhere in the back of his throat, and oh, Bessie liked that noise too.

"They're going to be here any minute with the food," he murmured.

"Then you better behave yourself and stop kissing me." She grinned at him, and he grinned back. The moment lengthened and sobered, and Bessie closed her eyes and just breathed in with him. That alone was sensual and sexy, and she whispered, "I'd like a do-over."

"On what?" he asked in his low, husky voice.

"On that promise I made not to fall in love with you." She searched his face, finding little blooms of hope and joy— and dare she categorize some of them as love?—in his eyes.

"Done," he whispered just before he kissed her again.

HE DOESN'T WANT ME TO KISS AND TELL. BESSIE sent the text the following afternoon, after she'd finished her baking for the day. She sat in her air conditioned office, the plans for the Heritage Festival spread before her.

The problem was, they also bored her, and she needed something to pass the last hour she had here at the bread bakery before she could go home and take a nap.

Bessie... Bea sent.

What does that mean? Cass asked.

Bessie smiled to herself, her heartbeat pounding. Her fingers flew over her phone as she typed. *He kept me out too late last night too. He's a real beast.*

Her phone rang, and Lauren's name sat there. Bessie

hesitated, because she really didn't want to disrespect Oliver. In the end, she flicked on the call and said, "Hey."

Lauren said nothing, though Bessie knew the call had been connected. "Is he your boyfriend?" she finally asked.

"Yes," Bessie said, because that essentially told Lauren that she'd kissed Oliver. She didn't need to get into specifics.

Lauren squealed and said, "I knew it! I could just tell he liked you from the very beginning. Remember?"

"Yeah, remember how you told him he better plan lunch dates?"

"I—" Lauren cleared her throat. "I apologized for that. He caught me in surprise."

Bessie smiled, because she wasn't really mad at Lauren about anything. "Remember how Blake took you on that sunset dinner cruise?"

"Yeah," her friend said. "Why?"

"And you thought it was just so perfect. Remember that?"

"Yeah."

"I remember being so jealous," Bessie admitted. "No one has ever planned the perfect date for me. One that says he's been listening to me, and he knows what I like, and it's okay if it's not exactly what *he* wants. It's what *I* want, so he makes it happen."

"Sweetie, I didn't know. I'm sorry if I rubbed your face in it."

"You didn't." Bessie got up and looked out the open door of her office. Hillie still worked in the kitchen, and everyone else's job kept them in the front of the shop. "Lauren, I got my perfect date last night."

A smile sat in Lauren's voice as she said, "I'm so glad." She took a sharp breath. "So. Do we think he's The One?"

Bessie thought about some of the things he'd said last night. His questions about being lovable. The walls he had surrounding himself. "I think it might take us a little longer than you or Bea or even Cass, but...maybe."

"You just don't want to say and jinx it."

"I think it's probably wise if I just take things one day at a time," Bessie said. She'd lived her whole life like that, and she saw no reason to stop now. "And yesterday was a great day for me and Oliver. Today, he's working the afternoon and evening shift to train a few new employees. So I won't see him."

"You could," Lauren said. "If you get a hankering for some mango and strawberry all blended up deliciously."

Bessie laughed with her. "Yeah," she said. "In fact, I think I'll see if anyone else wants to get smoothies tonight too."

"I'm in," Lauren said with another laugh. "Oh, my twelve-thirty is here. Gotta run." The call ended before Bessie could even understand what had happened.

"Bye," she said to empty air. Then she re-focused on the texting thread, which had been going unchecked while she'd been on the phone with Lauren. Sage had told Cass that obviously Bessie had kissed Oliver, and they'd gone back and forth a little bit.

Joy, who worked at the library for a few more weeks

before her second grade teaching job started, had sent, *Yeah! Go Bessie! I just need a yes or no. Was it a good kiss?*

"Do you think I'd be telling you if it wasn't?" Bessie shook her head and didn't answer.

She's not answering, Bea said. *You guys, we need to leave her alone.*

Bessie's always been a little more private, Cass said. That was a kind way of saying that Bessie was more introverted and definitely didn't feel the need to voice her opinion or thoughts on everything. Bea and Cass often did, and they sometimes butted heads over their differences in opinion.

Oh! And Wyn got a second date with Douglas. She's pretty happy about that. Bessie sent that text, and that was her way of saying she wasn't going to say any more about Oliver. The last thing she needed to do was toss over more bricks and building materials for him to use to construct his walls.

"It's not your job to fix him," she told herself and the cool office.

Oliver would have to figure out how to deconstruct his walls...if he wanted her in his life. He sure did kiss her like he did, and while her phone continued to buzz and vibrate as her Supper Club friends congratulated Wyn on a successful first date, a message from Oliver came in too.

Missing you today.

Then he sent a laughing emoji. *I'm deleting these texts. I'm not usually so sappy.*

Bessie smiled. *Here's a hint*, she typed out. *Women like it when a man tells them he's missing them.*

Not always, he said. *Only if she wants him to miss her.*

Bessie would've scoffed and swatted at his chest if they'd been together. Or she'd have rolled her eyes. As she sat in her office, however, she realized something. Oliver liked arguing. He *liked* it.

And it wasn't exactly arguing; it was just continuing the conversation. "That's what he'd say anyway."

Bessie held her thumbs over her phone, ready to type something. What, she didn't know. She was a non-confrontational person. She didn't want every interaction to be him arguing with her. Or even presenting the other side.

You can trust me on this, he said. *I've told a woman I miss her and she didn't like it.*

Bessie's heart bled for him, and her thumbs flew into action. *Is she why you build walls around your heart?*

Partly.

She didn't know what to say. Bessie operated a lot on feel and with her gut, and both fired blanks at her right now. Again, she didn't want it to be her job to build up Oliver every time he had a moment of self-doubt. At the same time, wasn't that what partners did for one another? Offer reassurances of love and kindness? Hold them when they had a bad day and just needed a listening ear and a good friend?

That was what Bessie wanted, at least.

So she said, *I miss you too*, and left it at that.

Chapter Sixteen

S age Grady clipped the leash to Gypsy's collar and said, "All right, bud. You ready?" The dog looked up at her with layers of hair falling into his face. His tongue already hung out of his mouth, and he sure seemed to be smiling.

She'd loved the huge beast the moment she'd laid eyes on him. He'd wandered onto her hobby farm in Texas, and she'd been able to feel each individual rib. He hadn't been wearing a collar, and he had sores on his paws.

Sage had done her due diligence in trying to find his owner. She'd posted online in all the Sweet Water Falls groups, and she'd posted on her social media too. With the seven degrees of separation, she truly believed that if Gypsy was meant to return home, someone would've seen her posts.

No one had come forward, and Sage couldn't stand to see an animal in pain. She'd fattened him up, taught him how to walk on a leash, and let him sleep at the foot of her bed. She liked to tuck her feet under him when they got cold, though that didn't happen too often here in Hilton Head. Well, it did, because Thelma couldn't handle the heat, and she blew the AC twenty-four-seven.

"Let's go, bud." She led Gypsy—she'd named him as he'd wandered onto her property—outside. The morning air hadn't been super-heated and weighed down with too much water yet. Of course, it was only five-thirty in the morning, and only those who'd lost their minds got up this early to walk their dog.

Sage loved getting up early. She'd always been an early-bird, and this way, she could walk Gypsy before it got too hot. She also worked in a very busy salon, and she had to be there by nine.

Gypsy walked right at her side, the way she'd taught him, but he usually started out with a little too much oomph. "Don't pull me," she said to him. "Stay right by me." She increased her pace to keep up with him and give him a chance to exert his energy.

He panted like he'd run a marathon by the time she made it to the end of her apartment building, where she tugged on his leash to get him to stop. "We're meeting Edwin here." She looked across the beach that separated her building from the next one in this complex. Ed lived over there, but she didn't see him.

She'd met him a week or two ago as she'd been returning from her morning jaunt. He'd just been setting out with a tall boxer who definitely had a more aggressive personality than Gypsy. In fact, her dog sat and looked up at her expectantly, and she reached down and gave him a love pat. "You're the best dog ever," she said, practically cooing the words at him. "Yes, you are. Aren't you?"

Sage looked for Ed again, and this time, she saw him coming toward her. She wasn't sure if she had any romantic feelings for him. He stood taller than her, and he had plenty of muscles to wrangle his boxer away from Gypsy and anyone else they'd encounter on the beach. He had a quick smile, almost no hair, and a nice voice.

But she just wasn't sure if anything got tickled inside the way it needed to. She'd spent a lifetime with a husband who'd felt more like a roommate than a partner, a lover, and she wanted more. Of course, she'd just turned fifty-one this year, and she wasn't sure anyone her age was looking for the same types of things as her.

The men she'd met here in Hilton Head were either married, recently divorced and not ready for another relationship, or with a younger woman. Sage herself wasn't sure she was ready for another relationship, but then she reminded herself she was ready for one relationship, period. She couldn't have another when she'd never had one.

"Mornin'," Ed drawled as he approached. His dog barked once, but Gypsy just looked at him. "Hush, Pop." The boxer pulled at the thick lead, but Ed kept him in check with sheer strength.

"Morning," Sage said. "The water looks calm today." They started down toward it, and this part of the walk always made her calves burn. She didn't enjoy the way the sand shifted under her feet, giving her nothing to push against to take the next step.

Down closer to the water, it became harder, more solid, and she relaxed into their stride then. Ed wasn't much of a talker, and Sage normally initiated and carried all of their conversations. He walked next to her, his dog on his right, closest to the water. Gypsy trotted along on Sage's left, and she took in a long, cleansing breath.

"Did you try that oil I gave you?" she asked.

"Sure did," Ed said. "You were right. The itching went right away." He smiled at her, and Sage returned the gesture. There definitely was no fizz in their glances, and she sighed. She wasn't even sure why she was disappointed. She could still enjoy his friendship, as Thelma would never get up this early to go walking with Sage.

They walked along for several more steps. "What are you looking forward to this week?" Sage asked. Bea had just returned to town from her son's wedding, and that had kept the text string hot following Bessie's admissions that she'd kissed Oliver and Wyn had a new boyfriend.

Sage's heart shrank into a lump, which she then tried to stuff into a box. She was happy for all of her friends; she truly was. She'd been at Bea's side during her terrible divorce, so seeing her heal so quickly and find someone so wonderful so soon had shown Sage that life marched on.

In fact, Bea and Grant's love story had been the catalyst Sage had needed to confront Jerry about their loveless marriage. She'd finally been able to *see* what true, golden love looked like and felt like. She hadn't had it, and she wanted it.

Jerry had not wanted to give it to her, and they'd parted ways amicably. Their sons were grown, if unmarried, and their daughter had a baby and a husband in Santa Fe. There'd been no child support to work out, but Sage did get an alimony settlement for the next fourteen years. That money allowed her to make the move to Hilton Head and not have to work her fingers to the bone as she cut and colored hair.

She breathed in the sea air, once again grateful for the things she had in her life. She'd never dwelt on the things she didn't, choosing instead to be a glass half-full type of woman.

"What about you?" Ed asked, and she realized she'd missed everything he'd said. Her mind scrambled as she tried to find a memory of what he'd been looking forward to this week.

"Oh, I don't know," she said. "I have a ton of ladies coming to get their back-to-school hair done." She smiled over to him, noting that the sun had started to peek its head up over the water's surface. "So I'll be really busy."

"Better busy than idle," he said. "That's what my pappy always said."

"Mm." Sage dropped Gypsy's leash, wondering if the dog knew it. If he could somehow tell that he wasn't quite as constrained as he'd been a moment ago, though Sage hadn't been holding the leash very tightly.

He trotted along, getting a few paces ahead of her as he got to go his own speed. She loved providing him the extra freedom, and the beach sat empty this morning. Even if it hadn't been, she'd have let him go. She wanted him to learn to stay by her whether on a leash or not, and she yipped at him. "Too far," she said, and he slowed to wait for her. "Thank you. Good boy, bud." She gave him a pat as she and Ed swept into his space.

"Do you think I could let Pop off the leash?"

Sage swung her head toward Ed. "I don't—" She hadn't even finished speaking before he'd dropped the leash the way Sage had. "Think so," she finished as the boxer took off into a full sprint.

"Pop!" Ed yelled. He broke into a jog to go after the dog, and Sage yipped and snapped at Gypsy too. He begrudgingly came back to her side while Ed tried to catch his errant canine. Sage didn't think yelling was going to work, but Ed didn't even bring treats on their walks.

"I've got some liver," she called up to him. He faced her as his dog got further and further from them.

"I'll try that," he said. Sage quickly passed a few bits of dried beef liver to Ed, who turned and started running down the beach again. She could only keep walking and let them both go.

"I don't know, Gypsy," she said to the dog. "Maybe I should adjust your walking schedule by an hour. Then the beach will be full of people getting in their morning exercise." Then she could see if there were other single middle-aged men she could meet. Someone who could light a fire inside her with a single look.

Several minutes later, she caught up to Ed and Pop, both

of them panting as they stood on the beach. "You got him," she said cheerfully.

"He's going to be the death of me." Ed gave the dog a withering look, and added, "Can we turn around early? I don't normally run."

"Sure thing." Sage took one more step, paused, and then rocked back the way she'd been coming. She did an about-face and it took Gypsy a moment to swing around too.

"Thanks." Ed walked further up on the sand, and he had to keep tugging Pop away from Gypsy. In the distance, someone else had brought their dog out onto the beach, and Sage glanced over to Ed and Pop.

It looked like a wrestling match between the two of them for who got to decide when to step and how far. Sage switched Gypsy to her other side, and while he didn't normally walk over there, he could do it.

"Pop, stop it," Ed growled, and Sage looked over to him. Before she could catalog what was happening, Pop came to a complete stop, ducking his head. The collar and leash went *whoosh!*—right off his neck and over his head.

He darted toward her, toward Gypsy, toward the ocean, and he caught Sage mid-stride. She stumbled forward, fear flashing through her at the idea of falling.

Because she was so falling. She threw her hands out in front of her as if there'd be something to grab onto, and as she went down, all she could do was pray that she wouldn't break a finger, hand, or wrist.

After all, she used her hands to work.

She grunted as she hit the hard sand, remnants of sea creatures cutting against her palms. Shockwaves moved up her arms, but she didn't feel anything crack or pop. Pain smarted through her shoulders and knees, and she fell to her side.

Embarrassment as much as anything filled her instantly, and time rushed at her now. She hadn't even realized it had slowed before.

Two male voices talked at her, and Sage looked up, trying to make sense of it all. Besides Ed, who currently looked out toward the ocean and whistled loudly, another man had arrived on the scene.

He knelt in the wet sand, his face bearing concern. "Sage," Tyler Parker breathed. "Are you okay? That dog just clotheslined you." He threw Ed a dirty look the other man did not see and looked back at Sage.

With the brand new daylight haloing him from behind, Sage felt like choirs of angels should be singing. She'd worked with Ty to help her find somewhere to live here on Hilton Head. She'd met him several times now, and she'd never once felt any inkling of attraction.

Until this moment.

Their eyes met, and he reached out and brushed her hair back. "Talk to me, Sage. You're scaring me."

"Ty," she blurted out.

He smiled, and wow, that gesture on his rugged features had probably made a lot of women weep. It only made Sage grin back at him.

"Do you want to try getting up?" he asked. "Do you feel like you can?"

Sage hated that she was sprawled on the sand while he looked so clean and so vibrant above her. She took a moment to catalog her body, and then she said, "Yeah, I think I can." She put her hand in his, noting the foaming, fizzing, spitting energy moving from him to her.

She looked at him again, and his eyes had widened. Then a horrible groan came out of her mouth, and a whole new round of humiliation filled her.

Back on her feet—finally—she dusted the wet sand off her hands, hating the feeling of it, and looked around for her dog.

But Gypsy was gone.

Chapter Seventeen

❧

Tyler Parker kept one hand on Sage's arm, not sure if she was really okay. Her head swiveled left and right as she looked for her dog.

"What's his name?" he asked.

"Gypsy."

Behind him, someone said, "I've got him, Sage," and another man joined them. He held Gypsy's leash, and Ty took it from him.

Relief washed over Sage's face, and Ty's heartbeat thumped and thumped against his breastbone.

He'd met Sage before, and he wasn't sure what ray of sunlight she'd been bathed in, but he felt like he was seeing her for the first time.

Maybe that was because he'd finally ended things with Gloria a few weeks ago, and he felt freer than ever. *Not free enough to dive right into another relationship,* he told himself sternly.

He'd been with Gloria for over a year, and he'd been in love with her. He'd asked her to marry him twice—and he'd been turned down twice.

The last time had been in May, and things had shifted violently between them then. She wouldn't break-up with him, and Ty had finally gotten the job done just before the Fourth. Then he didn't have to spend another holiday with her family, pretending like he had everything he wanted.

"Are you sure you're okay?" he asked Sage. He'd been running toward her and...her friend, and he'd seen the boxer cut her off. She'd toppled, and she'd hit her chin right into the wet sand. A smudge of it still stained her face, and Ty wanted to reach over and brush it away.

He held fast to the leash in his hand instead. He wore the two leashes he used for his dogs around his waist, and both of his canines stood at his side, panting.

His breathing quickened a little too, but it had nothing to do with the running he'd been doing. But Sage's dark hair, her bright brown eyes, and the way she reached for her dog's leash.

"I'm okay," she said.

"You hit your head," he said.

She finally looked at him. "I did?"

"Yeah." He lifted his hand now that it didn't have anything to do. He didn't actually touch her, but he indicated the smudge of sand on her face.

She touched it, surprised as the sand that came away on her fingers. "Oh."

Ty glanced over to the other man, a strange surge of jealousy rising through him. He swallowed against it. "I'm Ty," he said.

"Ed." The man held his dog's leash tightly, and Ty turned his body so his dogs would be on his other side. That boxer put off some seriously high energy.

"Are you headed home?" he asked Sage and Ed.

"Yeah." She nodded, and while she didn't seem dazed, Ty wanted to make sure she got back to her apartment safely.

"I'll go with you," he said, and he guided Sage back into a walk. "Do you go walking every morning?"

A smile touched her mouth, and Ty liked the appearance of it. "Yeah," she said. "Almost every day, unless..." Her head gave a little shake. "Pretty much every day, yes." She looked over to him, and Ty felt like a strange part of a sandwich.

He walked on her right, her dog between them. His walked on his side, and Ed hovered close to Sage on her left, his boxer practically in the water.

"What about you?" Sage asked, her eyes falling down his body.

In that moment, Ty realized how little clothing he wore when he ran. A pair of black shorts that barely covered him and an arm-band that held his phone. His earbuds hung around his neck, as he'd taken them out when he'd rushed to help Sage after she'd fallen.

In the winter, he started out with a shirt, but he didn't bother in the summer.

"Ty?" she prompted, and he told himself to stay present.

"Yeah," he said. "Yep, I run most mornings. The dogs like it, and I used to train for marathons."

"You don't anymore?"

He shook his head. "Nah, my knees aren't the greatest."

"You must live close then." Sage gifted him with a smile, and she definitely seemed better now that they'd started walking.

Ty nodded down the beach. "Just down there. I usually run down to lifeguard station three, then turn back. It's about five miles."

"Wow," she said, and she sounded impressed. "We go one mile down and one back. We turned around early this morning, because Pops is really on one today."

"Yeah, seems like it," Ty said, though he didn't know Ed or his dog at all. He searched his memory, trying to come up with something more to say. Something to make this interaction more meaningful that watching her fall down.

"Are you working today?" he asked.

"Every day except Sunday and Monday," she said. "You should come in." Her eyes moved up to his hair. "Your hair is getting long."

He ran a hand through it. "Yeah."

"Are you still running from dawn till dusk?" A quick glance at his feet. "Quite literally, I suppose."

"Yeah, summertime is the best time to buy and sell a house." He grinned at her, as he really did love his job. He ran his own real estate firm here on the island, and he'd done really well for himself over the years.

"Seems like you said springtime was the best time to find a house." She looked up at him, not quite moving her head all the way. Was that flirting?

He cast a look to Ed, who watched the pair of them too. Were they dating? Ty couldn't quite get the vibe between them, and then his feet touched sidewalk.

They both stopped walking, so he did too. Ty looked from Sage to Ed and back.

"Well, I'm this way."

Sage blinked and spun toward him, almost like she'd forgotten he'd walked in with them. "Thanks, Ed. See you later."

"Yeah." He nodded to Ty, turned, and left.

Things settled in Ty's stomach, and since he'd rather be forthright and know what ground he stood on than tiptoe around, wondering if he could text her about getting dinner together.

"Are you and he...?" He cleared his throat as Sage's attention returned to him. "Are you and Ed together?"

"Together?"

"Dating?"

Sage's face blanked for a moment, and then she shook her head quite emphatically. "No," she said. "We walk together in the morning is all. There's nothing between us."

Relief cascaded through Ty, and every muscle in his upper half relaxed. He hadn't even realized how tight he'd been.

"Great," he said as he tugged his dogs closer as his retriever started to stray. That drew Sage's attention to his canines, and she grinned at them.

"What are their names?" She ran her hand over his black lab's head.

"That's Brother," he said. Nodding over to the golden, he said, "That's Sherman."

"Interesting names," she said as Sherman came over to sniff Sage.

"They're rescues," he said. "I've had them for five or six years, and I got them together."

She beamed up at him. "That's great."

"Where did you get Gypsy?"

Sage straightened and started down the sidewalk toward her apartment. Ty probably needed to get going back to his place, because he still needed to go another mile down the beach, shower, and meet a client for a showing by eight-thirty.

Still, he went with her, because he didn't want to leave yet. He could send a text and say he was running late. It certainly wouldn't be the first time.

"He wandered onto my hobby farm in Texas." She glanced over to him. "I rescued him, and when I couldn't locate his owners, I kept him."

"He's really good," Ty said.

"I've worked with him a lot," Sage said. "He's big, and Thelma and I have already started talking about finding somewhere with a yard for him."

"I know a guy if you need a recommendation."

She laughed and that only made Ty happier than he'd been in a while. Even when he'd been with Gloria, he hadn't been this happy.

Free and happy.

"If you have time, come in and get a haircut," she said.

"Just not this morning. I'm double-booked this morning, and you'll have to go to someone else."

"I don't want someone else," he said, and what he meant by it, he wasn't sure.

But thankfully, Sage kept her pretty smile on her face, nodded, and said, "Have a good day, Ty."

She went inside her apartment, her big, furry, black dog trotting in behind her.

Ty gazed at the closed door for a moment or two before he realized it, and then he looked down at his dogs. "Come on, guys," he said. "Don't look at me like that."

Both of their tongues hung out, and Ty hit the beach running again. He'd worked out a lot of his troubles by pounding his feet into sand and pavement.

But the run home was one of the easier ones he'd ever done, because he couldn't stop smiling about his run-in with the beautiful Sage Grady.

Chapter Eighteen

Oliver turned at the sound of a female voice he knew. Not Bessie, but one of her good friends, Joy.

One of his friends, Scott, stood at her side, his eyes still up on the menu board at The Mad Mango. The man probably had the thing memorized, because he'd come in countless times.

"Take this down to the register, please," he said to one of his employees, and the young woman nodded as she picked up the smoothie he'd just finished making.

Oliver moved over to the ordering station, his smile sliding onto his face easily. "Hey, guys."

"Hey, brother." Scott reached up and held out his fist. Oliver bumped it and looked at Joy. She looked perfect at Scott's side, and she smiled at him too.

"Hey, Oliver."

"What are you guys doing today?" On a Monday, he'd expect them both to be at work. But they wore tees and shorts, with sunglasses perched on Scott's head. He sported a healthy tan, as he owned and operated a landscaping company and he worked outside most of the time.

"We're playing hooky today," Joy said with a grin. "Starting with smoothies before lunch, and then...I don't really know what else Scott has planned."

He grinned at her and said, "If you have a plan for your Day of Nothing, that defeats the purpose."

"He has a point," Oliver said. "I only tell Bess enough so she can dress appropriately and be prepared with the right shoes."

Joy's eyebrows went up, and Oliver's chest fell into itself. "Bess?" she asked.

Oliver's gaze flitted over to Scott, and he practically yelled, "I'll have the Rainbow Sunshine."

Oliver tapped on the tablet in front of him, embarrassment heating his face. He looked up at Joy, who'd engaged in a silent conversation with Scott. Oliver didn't like that, but he wasn't going to grump his way between them.

"What do you want, sweetheart?" he asked, glancing back to Oliver.

"I think I'll go with the Surfer Boy," she said. "Bessie's always telling me that's her favorite." Her eyes landed on Oliver, and he nodded.

"You two should double with us," she said next, and Oliver froze. He'd been hoarding Bessie to himself, he knew that.

"Yeah," he said. "That would be great."

Joy's face bloomed into a smile. "Great," she echoed. "I'm texting Bessie right now."

"We're pretty busy right now," Oliver said as he tapped in Joy's order. "The Heritage Festival is only a few weeks away, and my dad and brother are coming into town." Oliver swallowed, hoping his worries about his family showing up in Hilton Head weren't immediately obvious.

"Don't give me the busy excuse," Joy said as another couple joined the line. "We have a wedding the week before your Heritage thing, and I know you see her every day already."

"Yeah." Oliver glared at Joy now. *He* didn't have to be besties with her. "But sometimes that's just me stopping by the bread bakery and sneaking into the back."

"Oh." The hardness on Joy's face softened. "That's so sweet." She smiled at Oliver, who couldn't keep up with the hot-cold of the woman. "What are you guys doing tonight?"

"We have a meeting for the Festival," he said. "We have to show our booth layouts for approval, and we have to turn in our tax permits."

Joy blinked, and Scott tugged on her hand. "Come on, my Joy. Let's get our drinks, and we can catch up with Ollie later. We have his number." He gave Oliver a smile, and thankfully, Joy went with him.

Unfortunately, he still stood at the ordering station, and a small line had accumulated during his personal conversation. He put on his bright business smile and asked, "What can I get for you?"

"Can I get the Birthday Beach Surprise without banana?"

Oliver bristled, but he'd learned how to do it without showing it. He gave a single nod and typed in the order. The next customer gave their order, and Oliver keyed it in. He took care of the line, then swapped back to the behind-the-scenes work.

He liked to be out on the line every now and then, just to make sure his employees knew he could do the work they did. He also gave tips for things, ensured the smoothies got made and the equipment cleaned the way he wanted, and he couldn't stand being trapped behind a desk all day.

He normally worked more evenings, but since his relationship with Bessie had started, he'd been leaving the nighttime work to his assistant manager.

Leo did a great job, and Oliver never saw anything amiss in the mornings when he came in.

When he stepped into his office and checked his phone, he saw Bessie had texted. *You agreed to a double-date with Joy and Scott?*

A growl came unbidden, and Oliver started angry-tapping out a response. *Why is that so surprising?*

Before he could send it, he paused. That was the exact response Bessie said she hated. A non-answer. A question answered with a question.

Letting her know his thoughts wasn't bad. It didn't make him weak, and Oliver erased his reply.

Yeah, he said instead, his mind working really hard to

find the rest of the answer. *She invited us, and I figured it wouldn't hurt. They're your friends, and they invite their*

He stopped there, because he could not send the word *husbands* to her. Could he?

"Significant others?" he wondered as she toed his office door closed and went to sit at the desk. He sighed as he sat down, rolling his neck as he did. When he focused on his phone again, he saw that the text had been sent.

"No," he said, his pulse jumping up and down and flapping around. "No, no, no."

Bessie wasn't a very confrontational woman, but she didn't seem to have a problem calling him out. He fully expected her to force him to complete the thought, and his thumbs hovered above his phone, still trying to figure out what to say.

She texted, *Can I call you?*

Instead of answering, he tapped to dial her. The line only rang once before she picked up, and Oliver looked up to his framed business license hanging on the wall as he listened to Bessie's pretty little voice say, "I really want to know what word goes in that blank you left in your text."

He grinned. "I'm sure you do."

"Well?"

"I couldn't think of what to put there," he said. "And I somehow sent the text while crossing my office and sitting down."

"So you're not working out on the line?"

"Not at the moment. Scott and Joy came in, and I finished up the orders, and then I retreated."

"Mm, I can just picture it." She was teasing him, but Oliver knew one of his special talents was retreating. Sticking around took so much more work, and his patience for things he deemed over was literally zero.

He'd been learning that sometimes there was more to see, more to be had, if he'd stick around and dig deeper. For Bessie, he was really trying not to run at his first inclination to do something.

"I was going to put 'husbands' there," he said honestly. "I mean, Scott will be Joy's husband soon, and the others are married."

"Sage isn't."

"Right," he said. "You and Sage aren't. And then I wasn't sure if I should hit you with that word. I was contemplating 'significant others' when I realized the text had sent."

He leaned back in his chair and closed his eyes as he faced the ceiling. "What would you put there?"

Bessie remained quiet for a moment. He could hear low background noise over the line, so he knew she was still on the call. "Maybe husbands," she said. "Boyfriends. Significant others."

Oliver's throat constricted, but he pushed past the discomfort. "You're the first woman I've dated seriously in years."

"Oliver."

He sat up, then got to his feet, unable to stay seated for yet another confession. He felt like he gave one every other day to Bessie.

"It's true," he said. "Either I knew I was dating a tourist and it wouldn't last—not everyone is Grant and Bea. Or after a month or two, I found I didn't like the woman that much."

He cleared his throat, and that meant he couldn't speak again before she said, "We've only been dating a couple of months."

"Yeah, I want to keep at it," he said quietly. "That's what I mean, Bess." He paused on the nickname he used for her. "You're the first person I've wanted to *keep* dating in the past several years."

"You went from 'years' to 'several years'."

"Feels like forever," he whispered.

"Okay." She exhaled, and he heard it loudly over the speaker. "You're right. We get together as Supper Club friends, but we sometimes all gather together for things."

"Like Beach Day," he said.

"Right," she said. "Barbecues. Summer parties. Whatever."

"Women like too many parties and 'whatevers'."

She laughed and Oliver joined her. "Are we ready for tonight?" she asked.

It was his turn to exhale like he held the weight of the world. "If you can handle standing out in the sun while the committee comes around, then yes."

"I have my overlays ready."

"Me too."

She paused, and Oliver should say good-bye and get back to work. Surely something needed to be done. He'd let her scatter his thoughts, and he couldn't remember what he'd come in here to do.

"Oliver, I want you to know I appreciate all you've taught me this summer about the Heritage Festival."

He usually knew how to accept praise. He could shake someone's hand, smile and laugh, and throw a compliment their way too. It was his classic avoidance behavior, and he didn't have an alternative.

"You're welcome," he said, his tongue tripping over the words. "I've enjoyed it, believe it or not."

"Yeah, because you like being in charge," she teased.

He chuckled. "Yeah," he said. "I do."

"You like bossing me around."

His breath froze in his lungs. "Is that what I've been doing?"

"No," she said quickly. "I was joking. I *need* to be bossed around for this. I've learned a lot, and I wanted to say thank you."

"Okay," he said gruffly. "You've said it."

"Okay," she said too, and now a line of tension connected them through the phone.

"I'm going to be here until almost the meeting," he said. "Do you want to come pick me up?"

"Yes," she said. "I'll see you then."

"Can't wait," he said, and the call ended. He slid his phone onto his desk, his thoughts tangling and untangling. He paced to the door and then back to his desk.

"Do I boss her around?" he asked himself. She'd told him a week or two ago that everything he said sounded so authoritative. He didn't know how to change the way he spoke, and he *did* know a lot about the Heritage Festival. About running a small business in Hilton Head.

"But not about women," he muttered to himself. He didn't have brothers or a father to talk to about this kind of stuff.

But he did have friends, and the August Supper Club was coming up. Perhaps he could have a Boys' Night on the same evening and get some male perspective on his relationship with Bessie.

When he reached his desk again, he snatched up his phone and sent a text to Grant, Harrison, Blake, Scott, and Ty.

Who's doing Supper Club this month? he asked. *Who wants to come to my place for hamburgers and fries that same night?*

He sent the text, his fingers already flying over another message. *Wait, it's Cass. So Harry's outdoor kitchen is out. My house. Next Thursday. Bring your appetite and your advice. I want to talk about Bessie.*

Before he could chicken out, he sent that text too, and then he collapsed into his chair.

"The schedule," he muttered to himself. That was his afternoon task, and he shook the mouse on his desktop to get it to wake.

His phone buzzed and buzzed and kept buzzing so much it started jiggling and dancing across the surface of his desk. He picked it up, expecting an onslaught of messages.

He wasn't disappointed, and his stomach clenched at Grant's text. *Wow, you want to talk about Bessie. This is huge.*

I'll be there, Blake had said.

I'm in, Harry said. *I'll bring dessert from Gourmet Goods.*

He silenced his phone completely so it wouldn't even vibrate, because he'd just spilled more—to Bessie and his friends—than he ever had before.

And it felt good.

Chapter Nineteen

B essie wiped her forehead, but the sweat she cleared would only return. She didn't want to complain like a petulant child, but it was *hot*.

For the days of the Heritage Festival, they'd have a tent over their six-sided booth. Oliver had already pinned the papers to the grass where they'd set up two six-foot tables. That separated their two booths and gave them space to store their change, extra products and ingredients, and power cords.

"I got my mobile credit card device," she said to Oliver, and he turned from where he worked to tape down where he'd have a blender. He took the Heritage Festival very seriously, and he'd said he'd done things another way previously, and his Festival had been "a disaster."

Bessie would kind of like to see what a disaster for Oliver Blackhurst looked like. He was always so polished and perfect, even on a hot evening in the sun. He *glistened* with sweat while it poured from her by the bucket-full.

"That's great," he said. "We can test it tonight if you want."

"Sure," she said. "It'll go here. I only have the one. Will that be okay?"

"A lot of people bring cash," he said. "And you have two other mobile ways to pay. If they want to use a card, they can wait for it if it's busy."

"How many do you have?"

"Two," he said. "One will be fine, Bess."

Reassured, she nodded. "Okay." She took a deep breath, but that only reminded her that doing so might drown her. "I'm going to have to underbake my bread, so it can sit out here in the sun and finish baking."

"It's hot." He moved to stand next to her. "What does *stand of extras* mean?" He looked from the paper she'd placed there to her face. Without waiting for her to answer, he grinned and then touched his lips to hers.

"It's too hot for kissing," she murmured against his lips.

He laughed as he put a touch of space between them. He hadn't been awkward when she'd showed up at The Mad Mango an hour early. He'd simply welcomed her to his office and kept working.

They'd arrived precisely on time for the approval process, but Amy and her team hadn't been by their booth yet.

Bessie wasn't ready, but it wasn't hard to put sticky notes to the top of the table that labeled her bread. They'd bring it over in baskets and keep it in those, so the booth looked homey and inviting.

"I'm going to put other things here," she said. "I have a tiered rack of jams, and Wyn is working out if we can have enough power for refrigeration."

"Bess, I'm running nine blenders. I'll have a chest freezer here. You can put anything you want in it."

"My compound butters?" she asked.

"Sure, sunshine." He smiled down at her, and it so wasn't fair that he wasn't dripping wet for how hot it was. And with him standing so close, and looking at her with so much joy and emotion in his eyes? He only made the air immediately surrounding her that much warmer.

He moved back to his side of the booth, and it took four or five long strides for him to reach his side. The booth had been built out of a wooden frame, and Oliver had plastic tablecloths to cover it. He said it made the surface more even, and it was easy to keep clean.

Bessie moved down to the corner of her side of the booth, where the side met the front. She and Wyn had brainstormed the layout of their booth extensively, and they'd decided this corner would be their sample station.

Wyn had found three people to work this area, all of them outside the booth. They'd have bread samples on trays, and then this corner would house their butter and jam samples. The amount of tasting spoons her daughter had ordered...

Bessie was sure they'd have enough for ten Heritage Festivals, but Wyn said she'd done some research and had talked to several other bakery owners who'd participated in festivals in the past. In fact, Wyn thought they might need to make an emergency run to the restaurant supply warehouse just across the bridge—where her boyfriend worked.

A smile touched her face. She'd enjoyed seeing Wyn come to life right in front of her. Bessie hadn't even realized how...tired and run-down her daughter had become. She'd known the job in Oklahoma had been bad there at the end. She'd known Wyn had been in love with her boyfriend there, and that the break-up hadn't been easy.

She maybe hadn't had enough brain cells to have the vision she'd needed. Guilt touched her, but it only pricked her heart for a moment before he spiraled away. She'd had her own set of challenges, and Bessie couldn't be expected to know everything, about everyone. Now that she lived with Wyn, she had a much more close-up view of her daughter, and moving here and taking on Flour Power had definitely breathed life into Wyn.

Into Bessie too, if she were being honest. Since Oliver had been so honest with her, revealing many things about himself, his mentality surrounding dating and women, and his family situation, Bessie had been trying to be completely honest with him too. That had extended to herself as well, and she could admit she was far happier here, running her own bakery, than she'd been in Sweet Water Falls working for someone else's.

"Oh." She spun toward Oliver as her mind continued to wander wherever it wanted. "My banner is going to be ready tomorrow."

"Yeah?" He smiled at her over his shoulder. "That's great."

She'd hang that in front of the middle tables, further concealing them, and delineating her booth from Oliver's. They'd be able to walk back and forth into each other's space just fine, but they'd wanted it to be clear that there were two businesses in their booth.

Based on the emails Bessie had gotten from other small business owners, they were all doing the same. She wasn't sure what the committee wanted to accomplish by making them pair up, because she and Oliver were definitely making two smaller booths out of one bigger one.

"I think I've got mine," she said. She was bringing nine types of bread to the Festival, and that meant three big baskets for each of her tables. They didn't serve drinks at Flour Power, but for an ultra-hot summer festival in the park, Wyn had suggested they do bottles of water, lemonade, and sweet tea. She'd spent half a day last week seeking out the best places to buy such things in bulk, and Bessie's business credit card had been groaning for weeks.

"Yeah?" Oliver took her hand in his and surveyed her table that butted up to his. "A cooler of drinks?" He looked away from her note on the table to her, and his eyebrows drew down into a sexy V. "Bess, I'm serving smoothies literally right next to you."

He indicated the sign three feet down that said *Blender 1.*

Pure foolishness strung through her. "I can't believe I didn't..." She shook her head, pulling her hand away. "Let me text Wyn." If they couldn't cancel, and they couldn't sell the drinks here, Bessie would put them in the shop.

It's not a total loss, she thought as her daughter's phone rang. She drifted away from Oliver, wishing her mind worked on a business level the way Oliver's did. She felt so scattered, like every thought and whim, every little whisper of an idea, was the right one. She seized onto all of them, because she had so few.

"Hey, Mom," her daughter answered. "How are things going over there?"

"Good." Bessie left the booth, hoping not to have this conversation in front of Oliver. "Are you on your way here?"

"Yep."

"Uh, Oliver just reminded me that he's selling *drinks* right next to our booth."

Her daughter let the silence say it all, and she said, "I'll cancel our order."

"Can you do that?"

"I'm sure I can," Wyn said. "We'll just make sure we have enough to drink for our employees. The forecast still isn't to the days of the festival, but it'll probably be really hot."

"Probably." Bessie sighed. "Why didn't we think of Oliver's smoothies, literally in the booth a foot from us?"

When Wyn didn't answer, Bessie could picture her daughter's set jaw. The blazing look in her blue eyes. "I don't know," she said. "I'm starting that business class in only a couple of weeks, Mom. I'm still learning." She sounded embarrassed and apologetic, and that was the last thing Bessie wanted.

"It's okay," she said. "I didn't think of it either."

Clicking came through the line. "I found the order for the drinks," Wyn said quietly. "I'm going to call right now."

"It's almost seven."

"I can leave a message, and Douglas will be here in a minute, so I have to go."

"Okay," Bessie said brightly. "I'll see you both soon." She wasn't sure if Wyn heard the last part, because the call had already ended by the time Bessie lowered her phone a moment later. She sighed, because the last thing she wanted was to upset Wyn, to point out the obvious inexperience they both had.

Not only that, but she was meeting Douglas Polletson for the first time that evening. Wyn wanted to see the booth physically after Bessie had mapped it all out, and Douglas wanted to see Wyn. They were planning to stop by for only a few minutes, and then they had dinner planned.

Bessie had planned to head home after she got her layout approved, where she'd eat leftovers from last night's dinner out with Oliver, take a bath, and go to bed. Even with that timeline, she'd be an hour behind on her bedtime.

She turned and faced the booth, and she'd walked about thirty feet away. From this distance, she could easily see how amazing this booth placement was, and she closed her eyes behind her sunglasses. In her imagination, the Heritage Festival had started, and the park teemed with people.

They loitered around her booth, taking her card so they'd know where to come next time they wanted bread, and they wandered down to Oliver's booth to get a smoothie to sip on while they wandered through the rest of the booths.

She opened her eyes and found Oliver looking in her direction. He raised his hand, and Bessie smiled. She made her way back to him, and as she stepped into the booth, he said, "I didn't mean to chastise you."

He wore sunglasses too, but she still felt him scrutinizing her. No, searching her face to make sure he hadn't offended her. For someone who didn't know Oliver—a camp she'd been in before—she could easily see how intimidating and grumpy he could be.

But right now, as she slipped both of her hands into both of his, all she saw was a really hot man looking at her to make sure she wasn't upset. When she'd made the mistake, he wanted to make sure she wasn't mad at him.

"I called Wyn," she said. "She's going to cancel the order." She swallowed and looked down at their joined hands. "Oliver, I'm so out of my league with the bread bakery. Neither Wyn nor I are very business-minded, and I just feel so...stupid."

"Sunshine." He folded her into his arms, a place Bessie wanted to always be. He didn't say she wasn't out of her league. He didn't tell her she knew more than she thought she did. He simply held her, and Bessie let her emotions storm through her chest, because she didn't have to hide who she was and what she'd done.

"I'm sorry," she whispered against his chest.

"We all start at nothing and learn as we go," he said.

"Did you?" She pulled back and looked up into his face.

"I've had The Mad Mango for about twelve years," he said. "I'm forty-six. So what did I do for the first thirty-four years of my life?"

Bessie smiled up at him. "I have no idea."

"I learned what I needed to know in order to open the Mango and keep it open."

"Have you had failed businesses in the past?"

"Three of them," he said as he leaned down and touched his lips to her forehead. "You're doing great."

She closed her eyes and let his words sink into her brain. She needed to hear them more than she even knew. Bessie became aware of just how juicy their points of contact were, and she stepped back before Oliver noticed how...moist her hands were.

"You're still okay to meet Wyn and Douglas tonight?"

"Yes," he said, no swallow in sight. "I have met your daughter before, sunshine."

"I know." She looked out toward the parking lot anyway, but she didn't see Wyn yet. She told herself to relax. Wyn liked Douglas a lot, and therefore, Bessie wanted to as well. "Is your family still planning to be here for the festival?"

"Yes," Oliver clipped out, and Bessie dropped the subject as quickly as she'd brought it up. He'd told her he was going to try to get them to come the week after, so they wouldn't be so busy, but apparently he'd failed.

Well, she thought. *There's a first time for everything.*

She tucked her hand-drawn maps for the booth away just as Amy Flannigan chirped, "All right. This is one of our platinum sponsors. Let's see what they've got for us."

Chapter Twenty

B essie's nerves screeched at her, but she listened to Oliver do his presentation flawlessly. He indicated the signs he'd printed and talked about what he'd have and where. He smiled through it all, and he even laughed a few times.

Amy ate right out of his hand, and the rest of her committee seemed equally as impressed. Bessie hardly knew him when he was in business-mode, but she liked watching him in action. She liked that he had different sides to him, and that he pulled back on his business life to let a more personal side of himself emerge while they were together.

"Perfect, as always, Oliver," Amy said, and Bessie had been on earth long enough to know flirting when she saw and heard it. The committee chairwoman turned her attention to Bessie. Her smile didn't slip a single centimeter as she said, "All right, Miss..." She checked her clipboard. "Clifton. Flour Power. Let's see what you have planned."

Bessie took a deep breath, nearly drowned, and she tried to adopt the most Oliver of skins she could as she said, "Hello, everyone. I'm Bessie Clifton, and I own Flour Power —a specialty bread bakery—with my daughter Wynona."

She proceeded to go around the booth from the far corner back to the middle table which touched Oliver's. During her presentation, Wyn arrived, and she stepped into the booth with her mother.

"Sounds great," Amy said. "You guys are going to draw a lot of power in this booth." She looked around her feet. "I'll make a note that you need a couple of extra extension cords."

"That's great," Bessie said. She turned to Wyn. "This is my daughter, Wynona. She'll be here with me during the whole three-day festival."

Pleasantries got exchanged, and Amy turned to her people. "That's it, guys. What did you think?"

Bessie couldn't hear any of their replies as they walked away, and her muscles seemed to melt into marshmallows.

"Has anyone ever not passed this booth inspection?" Wyn asked.

"Oh, yeah," Oliver said. "Amy's hardcore." He chuckled, and that alone drew Bessie's attention. Wyn moved to hold Douglas's hand, and Bessie jolted out of business mode and back into mom mode.

"Mom," Wyn said with a smile in her direction. She then turned it on Douglas. "This is my boyfriend, Douglas Polletson."

"It's so great to meet you," he gushed, and he stepped

forward to shake Bessie's hand. "Wyn says you're not from here, so I won't kiss you." He laughed lightly, and he didn't wear a stitch of concern or anxiety on his face.

He did wear a full beard, and how he could handle that with all the heat was a mystery to Bessie. He stood several inches taller than Wyn, who wasn't terribly short for a woman. He had a hint of auburn in his brown hair, and he basically glowed as he moved back to Wyn's side.

"Douglas, my mom, Bessie."

"I'm so happy to meet you." Her chest stormed with emotions, because she just had the strongest feeling that Wyn and Douglas would end up married. She moved right into him. "I may only be Texan, but we're hugging."

She giggled as he hugged her, and as they parted, Oliver eased into her side. "And this is my boyfriend, Oliver."

"Hey, Douglas," Oliver said. "I know Douglas. He runs the restaurant supply warehouse." He swallowed, which meant something.

"Howdy, Oliver." Douglas didn't seem to think there was anything weird or awkward between the two of them, but oh, Bessie saw him swallow again.

"The booth is going to be great, Mom," Wyn said.

"I hope so," Bessie said. She could lay out the booth. She had the credit card reader now. All the pieces had been put down. But it didn't matter if she had a basket for nine-grain bread if she couldn't bake all the loaves she needed for the event.

You can, she told herself. She'd put in a few long days for this, and then she'd rest.

ELANA JOHNSON

"We're gonna go to dinner," Wyn said, and as Douglas shook Oliver's hand, she stepped into Bessie for a hug. "So, what do you think?"

"I think he's amazing," Bessie whispered to her daughter. "We can talk more tomorrow." She pulled back and smiled at Wyn. "Have fun," she said in a more normal volume.

"*So* great to meet you," Douglas said again. He possessed so much energy, and she watched as he and Wyn left the booth, reconnected their hands, and headed out.

"We're free too," Oliver said. "Do you want to drive-through somewhere? Or just go home?"

Bessie would like to say she had the time and energy to go out to dinner. But the fact was, she didn't. So she said, "Can you just take me home, baby? I'm tired."

"Absolutely." Oliver took her folder from her, then led her to his SUV.

Once settled, she asked, "What's with you and Douglas?"

Oliver's head whipped toward her. "Uh."

Bessie simply waited for him to answer. When he didn't, she said. "Come on. I literally admitted to you an hour ago that I have no business training. I was going to serve drinks out of my booth."

Oliver's eyes grew stormy, and he flipped the SUV in reverse. "I dated his sister a while back. I don't even think he knew, but *I* know, and I was a little awkward there for a second."

"His sister?" Bessie's eyebrows rose to her hairline. "How old was she?"

"A lot younger than me," he grumbled.

"Do you want a younger woman?" she asked.

"Absolutely not." He tossed her a dark look. "Her age was a huge reason I couldn't stand to see her after only three dates."

Satisfaction drove right through Bessie's chest. "Good to know," she said airily.

He captured her hand in his. "Is someone jealous?"

She looked over to him, catching the grin on his face that had chased away the storm clouds. "You've dated a lot more than me," she said. "Yeah, it makes me a little nervous that you have so much more experience. I wouldn't call it jealousy."

"What would you call it?"

"I just want to know what interests you. Who you're interested in."

"You," he said bluntly. "I'm interested in you."

"Why?"

"Are we going to play this game?" He steadfastly refused to look at her, though he'd turned out of the parking lot and the road in front of them was straight.

"Is it a game?"

"If I tell you why, you have to tell me too."

"Fine."

"Fine." He blew out his breath. "Initially, it was your eyes. I love your eyes. They're this color I can't even describe. Not too bright. Not washed out. They're...perfect."

Bessie adored the tenderness in his tone. She could listen to him say, "I love your eyes," every day of the week, every hour.

Her smile formed on her face, and it would not leave. "It was a physical attraction up front for me too," she said. "I'm a real sucker for a man with dark hair and dark eyes. It's so... mysterious. And you were *so* stormy, so gloomy... I thought you were good-looking, and I wanted to know why you were so prickly."

He lifted her hand to his lips, pressed a kiss to the back of it, and said nothing more. Bessie didn't want to play this game either, because it might make her delve into places she hadn't gone yet.

At her house, he stood on her porch and kissed her good-night, and as Bessie faded to sleep, she had the very real feeling that she'd started the journey toward a better life by moving here and opening the bread bakery.

But she couldn't get all the way to perfection and bliss on her own. That was when Oliver had shown up, a knight on a shining, white horse, to take her the rest of the way.

"YOU REALLY LIKED HIM?" WYN ASKED AS BESSIE shaped pitas the following day. "You met him for two minutes."

"He has a good spirit about him," Bessie said, glancing over to her daughter. "Why are you so nervous? It doesn't really matter if I like him."

"Mom." She rolled her eyes, and while she was twenty-three years old, the gesture and tone reminded Bessie of someone a decade younger, upset with their mother for not letting them go to the mall with their friends.

"Of course it matters if you like him," Wyn said. "It's only me and you. You and me. And if it's me and you and him, of course you have to like him."

"I did like him," Bessie said again. "I'd love to get to know him better." She placed the pita on the sheet tray and reached for another ball of dough. "Wyn, it's been a few weeks. You have plenty of time to fall madly in love with him—and I have plenty of time to get to know him."

She nodded, but her eyes still carried a hint of worry. "I'm falling too fast for him, just like I did for Sawyer in Oklahoma."

Bessie could shape pitas without looking at them, and she took the opportunity to study her daughter. "Wyn," she said, but her daughter had gone inside her own head. "Wynona."

That got her to look up. "You should talk to him about it."

"About what?"

"Oklahoma," she said. "Sawyer. How fast you fall. Then he'll know where you are, and why you're scared."

Wyn blinked at her. "How did you know he asked me what I was afraid of?"

Bessie smiled and focused on her dough. "I didn't," she murmured. "I just know you, and I can feel your nervous energy. He seems like maybe he can too, that's all."

"I wish I could feel things like that," Wyn said with a sigh. "Momma, am I even ready for a serious relationship right now?"

Bessie looked up at her. "You don't think you are?"

"I don't know."

"Tell me why you wouldn't be."

"Sawyer and I only broke up nine months ago."

"Okay, but you weren't engaged."

"I loved him," Wyn whispered. "Can someone just get over loving someone in nine months?"

Bessie put the last pita on the tray and dusted her hands off. "Wyn, my baby. There's no timeline for love. Some people fall in love at first sight. Some date for years. Some can move past someone else quickly, while other hearts are slow to heal. You can't put a specific number of months on it."

She nodded, but her teeth worried her bottom lip. "You liked him, right?"

Bessie grinned and nodded. "I liked him, honey. Tell you what. Why don't you invite him to, I don't know. Get smoothies with us. Then I can see Oliver, and I can spend time with both of you."

Since Wyn worked until four or five, and Bessie went to bed so early, they didn't see one another a whole lot in the evenings. If she went out with Douglas, Bessie was asleep by the time Wyn got home.

"Yeah," she said, pulling out her phone. "Smoothies." She started texting. "Are you seeing Oliver tonight?"

"I see him almost every day, so probably," she said. "We don't have specific plans."

"Would it be weird to go on a double date?" She looked up, her eyes wide. She blinked, and the answer sat there. "Never mind. I think it would be weird for me."

Me too, Bessie thought. The last thing she wanted was to put her affection for Oliver on display for her daughter. Thankfully, she didn't have to say so out loud. She didn't talk about her dating life much, to anyone. She wanted to respect Oliver's wishes in that regard, and besides, Bessie didn't like the spotlight to shine too brightly on her.

"Are you going to come to Supper Club next week?" she asked.

"Yes," Wyn said almost absently. She finished her text and met Bessie's eyes again. "Maybe the ladies there will have some advice for me."

"Advice about what, Wyn?" Bessie didn't mean for her voice to come out so pointed, but she'd literally been reassuring her daughter for a half-hour. She moved the pitas to rest and checked her list for what she needed to make next.

Pretzels. She'd started a social media page, and she'd told people the pretzels would be fresh on Fridays, Saturdays, and Sundays starting at noon. So she better get cracking. It was first-come, first-served with these specialty items, and Bessie started prepping to make thirty-five pretzels.

"I don't know," Wyn said. "They have good advice about dating and stuff."

"So do I," Bessie said, starting to get annoyed.

"It's different when I hear it from them."

She worked hard not to roll her eyes, because she didn't see how Lauren telling Wyn it was okay to fall in love fast meant something more than when Bessie said it. Not only that, but none of those women knew what had really gone on in Oklahoma. Wyn should trust Bessie more, not less.

"Okay, well, let Cass know you're coming. She asked me, but you have her number the same as me."

"Okay." Wyn went back to her phone, and Bessie let her frustration at being overlooked in favor of someone else's opinion bleed out into the pretzel dough. As she shaped them to drop into the pot of boiling water, she decided she was going to keep one for herself today.

For her and Oliver, who'd commented on her social media post about the pretzels that he'd never really had a good one.

"This afternoon," she muttered to herself. "He will."

"So," she said a few hours later. Oliver chewed his first bite of pretzel, his face giving nothing away. "What do you think?"

He swallowed, but this was a normal gesture, not one that signaled his distress. "I think." He reached for the pretzel and pinched off another piece. "I need another bite of this, because it's the best thing I've ever put in my mouth."

Delight filled her from head to toe. "Are you being serious?"

"Maybe it's this cheese sauce." He dunked his pretzel in it and popped the whole thing in his mouth. "These are incredible," he said with a full mouth.

She giggled and said, "I made the cheese sauce too, so I'm taking credit all the way around."

He finished eating and said, "You should. And you know what else you should do? Sell these at the Heritage Festival. People will go nuts for these."

Trepidation threaded through Bessie. "I can't mass-make them," she said. "Not the way I can bread dough. And the two-step boiling-baking process takes too much time."

"Do they freeze?"

"Yes," Bessie said, falling almost into robot mode. "For up to three weeks." By the time she finished speaking, Oliver's eyebrows had lifted. His gauntlet had been laid.

Bessie sighed. "I was thinking I wouldn't sleep for five or six days. Now you want me to start giving it up now?" She groaned as she leaned into him.

He chuckled and held her in his arms as they sat at her kitchen counter—their meeting place this afternoon. "I don't know about the sleep," he said. "But I have to have this pretzel in my life every day."

He might as well have proposed, because complimenting Bessie's baking was her love language. He sure did seem like he'd been dipped in gold, and Bessie wondered for the first time if perhaps *she* was the one falling too fast.

Then she decided that even if she was, she could do what Wyn couldn't seem to: She could take her own advice.

It was okay to fall in love quickly.

She threaded her fingers through Oliver's. "You've never been married."

He made a noise of assent, and she already knew he'd never been married.

"Do you want to get married?"

His eyes came to hers. "Yes," he said simply. "I'd get married to the right person."

"Have you been worried about finding her? Is that why you never got married?"

"No, sunshine." He picked up the last bite of pretzel, coated it in cheese sauce, and ate it. Gladness spread through her that he'd liked it. "I never got married, because I wasn't dating for that purpose. I was so focused on my businesses, that dating was this...afterthought."

"And now?"

"Now, I have Mango, and it does well, and I've been...looking."

"Until your no-dating pact with yourself."

"I wasn't having any luck." He didn't smile, and he didn't defend himself further. "I had to learn some things, just like I did with starting and running a business." He looked away, and Bessie didn't like that. "I still have a lot to learn, but I'm trying."

"Hey." She guided his face back to hers. "You're doing great." Her eyes flitted between the two of his. "Oliver, I—"

"Don't," he said, and then he pressed his lips to hers. She wasn't sure what he thought she might say, but it didn't matter. She could say a lot with a kiss, and she focused on doing that. She was definitely falling for him, and she had fantasies of what a life with him would really look like.

She'd never been kissed the way he kissed her. She'd never been courted the way he courted her. She'd never been taken care of the way he took care of her, and she wanted all of the above and more.

It was something she'd thought she'd never have, not after her marriage had ended. She'd thought maybe she'd had her chance, and she hadn't chosen well. After all, she was almost fifty years old, and who found the love of their life at that age?

Maybe you and Oliver, she thought, and oh, it was a beautiful thought.

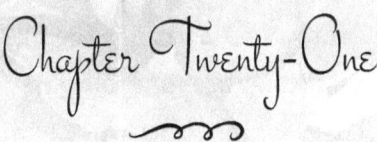

Chapter Twenty-One

C assandra Tate leaned into her husband, Harry, and kissed him. "Have fun at Oliver's." She stepped back. "I want all the details."

He smiled at her. "I know you do." He picked up the boxes of pastries he'd bought at Gourmet Goods on his way home from work. He'd brought the peach-mango tarts that she loved, but the rest he was taking to Oliver's planned boys' night.

"But you won't give them to me." She sighed and went back to the only thing Cass was making for Supper Club that night—Mexican hot chocolate. She'd also serve raspberry frappé, but she'd bought that. And no dinner in South Carolina seemed complete without lemonade and sweet tea, and Cass and Harry had those staples in their fridges all the time.

She'd also cut up watermelon just before they started, after the picnic feast she'd ordered had been delivered. She'd done tacos in the past. They'd had a grill night. If supper was being served at Bea's or Bessie's, they enjoyed a home-cooked meal. Even Joy did a lot of homemade items with family recipes.

But Cass liked to order catering. She liked being able to fold everything up into aluminum foil trays and stash it in a trash bag. She liked being able to work with her clients on the days she hosted Supper Club, and she liked being able to enjoy her friends instead of being too tired to chat and anxious about what time everyone would finally leave.

"I'll save you a barbecue meal, okay?" She gave him a smile as he picked up his ball cap and put it on his head.

"I'll tell you what I can," he said. "Oliver isn't very open about, well, anything. Just the fact that he said he wants to talk about Bessie is huge."

Cass nodded and went back to stirring the hot chocolate.

"Save me some of that too, hon." Harry slid a kiss down her cheek to her neck, where he got serious. She pressed into the touch, because it sent a thrill through her. After her husband had died, Cass had never dreamed she'd find someone to love her the way Harry did. She knew she had certain...eccentricities, and she loved shopping, buying nice things, and a certain lifestyle.

Harry had taken all of it—he'd taken her just as she was —and he loved her unconditionally. He hadn't gotten the library bid, and when he'd found out, he'd been an odd mix of upset and happiness. He worked dang hard, and Cass had been secretly glad he hadn't gotten yet another huge project.

He managed to stay busy with his construction firm, and they had everything they wanted or needed.

"See you soon, baby." He left, and only moments later, her son walked in the same door her husband had used to exit.

"Mom," Conrad said. "Harry said I could go to Oliver's with him. Is that really true?" He wore hope in his eyes as he hooked his thumb over his shoulder.

"If he says you can, then you can," Cass said. She stirred the hot chocolate without looking at it. "Did you forget I had Supper Club tonight?"

He wore the khaki shorts and dark green shirt of the tour company he worked for every summer. He lived with her, and he saved money for college. He'd be a senior this year, and then Cass suspected he'd apply for law school though he hadn't said as much.

He'd dated a lot the first couple of years at Baylor, but this past year, he hadn't had a girlfriend or even gone out with anyone all that much.

Her happy-go-lucky son grinned. "Yeah, I forgot."

She smiled back at him. "Go with Harry then. Oliver's having burgers and fries."

He surveyed the counter, but the food hadn't arrived yet. "What are you guys having?"

"Barbecue," she said. "Ribs, chicken, and brisket. Baked beans and cole slaw. Cornbread." She indicated the hot chocolate. "Hot chocolate, and watermelon."

He looked torn for a moment, and it was just like him to let his stomach decide.

"Go with Harry," she said firmly. "I'll save you both a plate, and you won't have to be sequestered in your bedroom."

"Good idea." He ducked back into the garage, and then he dashed back into the house thirty seconds later. "He says I have time to shower and change."

Cass would never be able to do that, but Conrad could shower and change in less than ten minutes. In that time, the food got delivered in the beautiful and recyclable aluminum foil trays that Cass couldn't stop smiling at.

She had the delivery men put the proteins first, then the sides, and she put her big pot of Mexican hot chocolate down on the end, near the refrigerator. She loved to fill a glass with ice, then pour the hot chocolate over it. It thinned it a little, dulled some of the spice, and brought the liquid to a tolerable drinking temperature.

Of course, she loved Mexican hot chocolate as-is too, and she poured a little from the ladle into a small cup and swirled it. The rich, deep flavor of chocolate rose to meet her nose, and Cass found herself smiling again.

The house sat silent as she tasted her chocolatey creation, and she sighed in bliss.

"Bye, Mom," Conrad said as he rushed through the kitchen again.

"Take notes on Bessie," she called after him, but her son didn't answer. He wouldn't take notes on a woman twice his age either. The garage door slammed, and Cass moved to her double-wide fridge and took out the watermelon.

She set to the task of cutting that into bite-sized cubes, and she'd just finished when the front door opened.

"...is what I'm saying," Bea said as she entered. Cass couldn't see who she'd arrived with, as the kitchen sat past the foyer, the staircase leading up, and around the corner from the family room.

"I know what you're saying," Joy said. "I'm saying we should let her talk about it. Bessie has been tight-lipped for a reason."

The two women arrived in the kitchen, and Bea put her purse on the built-in desk and took in the spread of food and then finally Cass as she stood at the kitchen sink and washed the watermelon from her hands.

"Look at all of this," she said.

"You sound shocked we have food for Supper Club." Cass gave her smile and grabbed a towel to dry her hands. She then moved to hug Bea, her closest friend in the whole world. The two of them had been the first to move to Hilton Head, and Bea held a very special place inside Cass's heart.

She'd been the one to finally take Cass to the Everglades National Park after West's death, as Cass had planned that trip for her and her husband, and then he'd died before they could take it. She'd met Harry on that trip, and their friendship had bloomed into love over time.

She couldn't imagine her life without Bea in it, nor Harry, and she could hardly remember her life with West in Texas. Of course, she still could, and she sometimes reflected on those times.

But Supper Club here on this barrier island of South

Carolina was exactly as it had been in the Coastal Bend of Texas. The same amazing women. The same friendships— only stronger. Better.

She stepped over to Joy and hugged her too. "Only another two weeks until school begins," she said. "Are you nervous?"

"Beyond," Joy admitted into Cass's shoulder.

She pulled back and smiled at Joy, whose natural beauty shone through her like a beacon these days. "But you're not nervous about the wedding, right?"

Joy totally was, but she shook her head. "Whatever it will be, it will be."

"It's only three days away," Lauren said, and Cass spun toward her as she hadn't heard her come in. She'd pinned her dark hair out of her face today, but plenty still hung over her shoulders from the back. She wore almost no makeup, but her blouse boasted bright blue stripes that went from large to small as they moved down her torso.

She wore white shorts—classic fashion that Cass appreciated—and she carried a box that made Cass's mouth water. "You brought the piña coladas."

"I couldn't help myself."

"I'm going to get full just on drinks," Joy said, and when Cass glanced over to her, she'd already made herself an iced hot chocolate.

That alone made Cass burst with joy. She wanted her friends to feel comfortable in her home. She wanted to feed them and have them enjoy it. She wanted to participate in their lives and have them solidly in hers.

Lauren put the box of piña colada mix on the counter and opened it. "I'll get it all out."

Cass had already set the table with a sunny burnt orange table cloth, and while some of the ladies used paper products to eat off of, Cass used real dishware. It was easy to load into the dishwasher, and everyone would help do that before they left.

Then she'd whip the tablecloth in the laundry, and she'd be able to go to bed happy.

"Your place settings are always so immaculate," Bea said as she ran the tip of her finger along a pristine white charger. It held a clear plate, which only added to the lightness of summer, something Cass loved.

It didn't get too wintery here, just as it hadn't in Sweet Water Falls, and Cass loved the off-season on Hilton Head. It went back to feeling like a small-town community, and it was a slow, quaint life Cass really craved.

"We're here," Sage sang, and she and Bessie came bustling into the kitchen. They both looked more vibrant and happier than Cass had seen them even a few days ago.

"What's going on?" she asked immediately, glancing from one to the other. Bessie carried a few loaves of bread, and she spilled them onto the desk beside Bea's purse.

"I brought bread for everyone," she said.

"Are you not selling through your inventory anymore?" Lauren asked. "I can't even get the sourdough if I don't go before nine a.m."

"I made these special for you guys." Bessie beamed at them. "Lauren, yours is the sourdough, so don't let Bea steal it from you. Cass, I brought you and Harry the cheddar asiago, because I know he loves that with a lot of butter for breakfast."

"He does," Cass murmured, not at all surprised by Bessie's thoughtfulness. She learned and remembered the minute details, because she cared about people.

"Joy, yours is straight-up cottage white." She smiled at her friend as she gave her a side-squeeze. "Because I know you're going to be hosting a few people this weekend, I made you two loaves."

"Bessie, you're the best." Her future sisters-in-law were staying with her starting tomorrow, as Scott's parents would be bunking with him.

"If it's not sourdough, mine better be the nine grain," Bea said.

"What else?" Bessie walked over and hugged her too. "My daughter will be here soon. She wants to talk about Douglas." She stepped back and looked at everyone. "I told her what I thought already, and well, she obviously thinks you all will know more than me."

Cass's breath caught in her throat. "I'm sure that's not true," she managed to say. She glanced over to Bea, needing someone to back her up.

But Bea said, "Sometimes kids just need their parents' words validated." She looked nervous, but she brushed her growing-longer hair out of her eyes. "What did you tell her? I'm sure we'll agree."

The doorbell rang, pausing the conversation. "I'm coming in," Wyn called, and Bessie went to greet her. Cass followed, because she did want Wyn to be here if she wanted to be.

"I'm so glad you came," she said to the younger woman. She gave her a quick squeeze and noticed she carried a brown paper bag. "You don't have to bring anything."

"I know." Wyn gave her a nervous smile, though she'd interacted with Cass and her mom's other friends plenty of times. "But these compound butters need to be eaten, and a little birdie told me that you like the roasted garlic one."

"I do." Cass took the bag, noting the weight of it. "Conrad adores it too. He uses it to make grilled cheese sandwiches, and I have to say, they're delicious." She grinned at Wyn and turned back to the kitchen.

"All right," she called over the smaller conversations. "The food is here. Let's load up, and then we can talk." Cass looked at Bessie, though she didn't intentionally mean to. Several others did too, and she wished she could take that burden from Bessie. She couldn't, but she could fill her full of good food and hope she'd open up.

She chatted with Lauren about her garden, her marketing consultations, and how things were going with Blake now that they'd been married for eight months. She was upbeat and positive, and Cass loved the changes in her since she'd moved here, opened her own firm, and fallen in love with a good man.

They settled at the table, and for some reason, the conversation stalled. Cass forked off a bite of her brisket and swept it through the tangy raspberry barbecue sauce. "Should we start with a bit of news?" She glanced to Joy, who sat next to her on the left. "Just one thing going on that you maybe haven't told anyone. Or if you have, maybe not the whole group."

No one said anything, and Cass, as the host, decided she better lead out. "Harry and I are leaving for Jerusalem in about a month, and I'm a little nervous, because I've never traveled outside of the country." She smiled around to everyone. "And Conrad is most likely going to go to law school."

She took her bite of food and looked up.

"Shelby is going to move here for her senior year," Bea said. Tears already tracked down her face by the time Cass looked at her. "I'm thrilled, but terrified. She's thrilled, but terrified. It's just a big change."

A beat of silence went by, and then Joy said, "Yeah, because you and Grant aren't used to having her full-time."

"Did something happen with her mom in Alabama?" Lauren asked.

Bea shook her head. "Her job is requiring more travel now," she said. "She's gone to Mexico or Montreal about half the time these days. It's just not conducive to having a seventeen-year-old."

"I thought she was eighteen," Cass said.

"She is," Bea said. "But that doesn't mean she's an adult. And she's still in high school."

"Well," Sage said slowly. "This will get her away from that boyfriend she wasn't sure she liked, right?"

Bea nodded again, her tears drying up. "I'm kind of a mess over it, and I don't know why."

"It's a big change," Cass said matter-of-factly.

"I have something," Lauren said. She wore a look of anxiety on her face. "It's kind of a weird situation, but Blake's ex-wife is going to move in with us for a few weeks." She cleared her throat. "A while. Until she can find a place of her own that's safe."

"Safe?" Cass asked, as did Bessie and Sage. "What does that mean?" Cass added.

"Jacinda had this boyfriend," Lauren said. "Out on Carter's Cove, and he...he's why Tommy came to live with Blake last year," she said. "He's been—" She brushed at her eyes. "He's been hitting her. She needs to get out of there, and in fact, Blake and Tommy are there tonight. Getting all of her stuff out. They took a couple of cops, because they don't really know what this guy will do."

A sense of solemnity settled over the group. Cass didn't normally like Supper Club to be tense, but she couldn't control the happenings of her friends' lives. Things weren't always rainbows and unicorns.

Husbands passed away. They cheated. They drifted out of love.

Work took priority in some lives, and sometimes, people didn't treat each other right. Moves had to be made, and children protected.

Businesses got started, and with every new day, there was a new opportunity to live. Really live.

"I hope it goes okay," Bea said. "You'll let us know when they're back?"

Lauren nodded, and she took a deep breath. It settled in her shoulders, boxing them up and making Lauren look stronger. She smiled around to everyone. "I didn't mean to kill the mood."

"I can lighten it," Sage said. "I met a man."

That simple statement sucked the air right out of the house. "What?" Cass managed to gasp.

"When?" Bea asked.

"Where?" Joy threw at her.

Sage sat there and scooped up another bite of baked beans. She ate it, a glow around her that Cass had noticed but hadn't known what to attribute it to. Now she knew.

"You all know him too," she said. "I've met him before. He helped me and Thelma find an apartment."

"Hey," Wyn said. "Where is Thelma?"

"Not now," Bessie hissed, half standing. She planted both palms on the table, her blue eyes practically firing electricity across the table to Sage. "Are you telling us you've met... Ty?"

"Yes," Sage said with a bright smile. Then a giggle.

Cass looked from left to right, from Bessie to Sage.

"Keep talking," Bessie said.

"Sit down, Mom," Wyn said almost under her breath, and Bessie settled back into her seat.

"It was just this thing during my morning walk," Sage said. "But I don't know. There was something new between us." She grinned even wider. "It was exciting. Is this how you've all felt?" She looked around at all of them. "Because wow, if so. You've been holding out on me."

That did cause a ripple of laughter to go around the

table. It didn't stop everyone from zeroing in on Bessie and Joy.

"Mine's easy," Joy said. "I'm scared out of my mind to do two huge things in literally the next two weeks. I'm quitting my job tomorrow. I'm getting married again on Sunday. And I start teaching second grade only a few days after returning from my honeymoon." She filled her mouth with an enormous bite of cornbread, and that was her signal to the group that she wouldn't be saying any more.

"All right," Bessie said with a sigh. "I know everyone wants to know what's going on with me and Oliver."

"I was actually going to ask how the Heritage Festival was coming," Lauren said.

Bessie laughed and shook her head. "You were not." She glanced at her daughter and startled. "Oh, Wyn. Would you like to go first?"

"Yeah," she said. She shifted in her seat, squirming as her nerves obviously coursed through her. "So I'm dating Douglas. I know my mom's told you about him."

Cass had heard of Douglas, yes. But just like Bessie hadn't shared many details of her own relationship, she hadn't given them much about Wyn.

"I sure do like him," she said. "I feel like I'm falling too fast, and well, my mom says people fall in love at all different rates, and I don't know." She brushed her hair off her face, which only revealed more worry in her eyes.

"What don't you know?" Joy asked gently.

"I have—I left Oklahoma after a break-up I didn't want." She brushed at her eyes. "I was in love, and he wasn't, and I don't know. It feels like I should take more time to really be ready to even be in a relationship with someone."

Wyn was such a sweet girl, and Cass could see her daughter easily in the young woman. She wanted to wrap her up and tell her she still had plenty of life to live. That she didn't have to rush from one man to another. At the same time, she wasn't Jane, Cass's daughter who flitted from state to state, even country to country, and person to person.

Wyn looked up, her eyes brimming with unshed tears. "I don't want to hurt Douglas. I don't want him to be my rebound."

Silence filled the kitchen and dining room again, and Cass felt like she needed to jump up and get out the tarts. Dessert always cheered everyone up, and as a few of them had finished eating, they had nothing to do but stare at Wyn.

Finally, Bea said, "I'm the wrong one to ask about falling fast. I met Grant, and ten days later, I knew I wanted to keep seeing him, and we were married within six months of meeting."

"People definitely fall at different rates," Joy said. "And in different ways. When I walked away from Scott for the last time, it nearly broke me. That's how I knew I couldn't do it again."

"Blake and I took a few tries," Lauren said. "But we're rock-solid now."

Cass realized that she'd experienced something similar. "I obviously loved West when he died," she said carefully. She'd boxed up a lot of her memories and emotions surrounding her husband. Harry was always so good to let her grieve in her own way, and whenever she needed to. Sometimes the situations at hand simply sparked something so strong that she wept. Or had to say something.

"I did have to take some time," she said. "There were things that had to be taken care of. We shared a house that I found I didn't want to live in alone." She glanced over to Bea. "My friend was here, and I needed something fresh."

Wyn nodded. "I've really liked being here, working with Mom." She leaned into her mother, who put her arm around her protectively.

"When I started to date Harry," Cass said slowly. "I just told him what was going on with me, and that I needed time to sort through it all."

Wyn looked at Bessie, and she raised her eyebrows at her. She'd clearly told Wyn something similar, and Cass was glad she'd been able to back up Bessie in some small way.

"All right." Wyn drew herself up again, a smile already on her face. "Thanks, everyone."

All eyes turned to Bessie, and she casually lifted her glass of golden sweet tea to her lips and took a long drink. "I suppose it's my turn."

Cass rested her chin in her hand and gave her friend a smile. "I suppose it is."

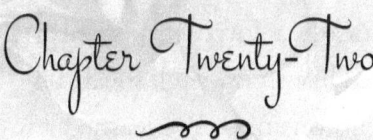

Chapter Twenty-Two

B essie didn't particularly want to put herself on display, and she certainly didn't want to drag Oliver into any mud. At the same time, he'd told her mere hours ago that he was hosting all of the men at his house that evening.

She'd been surprised on top of surprised, but they hadn't had much time to discuss it. "I know he's got everyone at his house tonight," she said slowly, trying to decide how to start. There simply was no good entry point.

At the same time, she could easily defer them all by saying, "We've been dating for almost two months. As far as two-month old relationships go, I think it's going pretty well."

"Two Supper Clubs ago, you wanted to claw off his face," Lauren said with a smile. And she wasn't wrong.

Bessie wanted to tell Lauren it wasn't Supper Club where she'd first shown up after punching dough with the thought of it being Oliver's face. That had been at their afternoon tea.

Instead, she giggled and shook her head. "He's..." She drew in a breath and felt like sighing it out. "He's a sweet man buried beneath a lot of experiences that have jaded him." She nodded like that was all she'd say.

"He's smart in business. I've learned a ton from him by doing the Heritage Festival. Wyn and I meet every week, and we have lots of notes." She leaned away from the table as if it had electrocuted her. "Oh, you didn't tell them you're starting business classes."

Wyn's face lit up. "Yes, I'm taking a couple of classes through the extension programs at the university." She gave Bessie a look that said she didn't want to talk more about it. "We'll see how it goes and what I can learn."

"That's amazing," Cass said with a smile. "I heard a rumor that Oliver's father and brother are coming to town." She looked down and picked up her last piece of cornbread and innocently put it in her mouth.

Bessie nodded, her eyes landing on Joy. "Yes, in a few weeks. I can admit I'm a little nervous. He doesn't even talk to them all that much, so it's not like when Joy met Scott's family."

"My kids didn't approve of me and Harry," Cass said. "I think sometimes Sariah still doesn't." She gave a sad smile, but Bessie heard the emotion behind it.

"You don't have to impress them," Joy said quietly. "That's what I learned. Oliver won't think any less of you."

"Probably not," Bessie said. "Anyway, most days, I'm not even sure which way I'm going. I bake and bake and bake, and then I relax with Oliver. He plans everything, picks me up, and I sip smoothies on the beach." She smiled, because that had literally been their afternoon yesterday. "He's... sweet. I like him."

"She likes him," Sage teased. "Seriously, that's great, Bessie."

"We should plan another big dinner for everyone," Bea said.

"Maybe something like 'you survived the first week of school and the Heritage Festival'," Cass said.

"Mid-September," Sage suggested.

"For Supper Club," Joy said. "It's my month, and I can invite all the men." She looked over to Sage. "Even Ty." She raised her eyebrows. "Maybe that'll spur things along for the two of you."

Sage shook her head, but her smile didn't diminish. Bessie let them plan a big meal in September, because she would like to see Oliver with the other men. She'd like to see him through the eyes she had for him now in a large group. He'd never really come to anything before, at least not for longer than a few minutes to deliver smoothies.

"Anyway," she said into a break in the conversation. She stood and picked up her empty plate, then Wyn's. "Sorry there's not a lot of details. It's still new, I think. I'm not Bea either, and I think we just need more time together."

"Fair enough." Bea started clearing the table too.

Everyone pitched in, and Cass brought out a blue pastry box full of peach-mango tarts, which she then took outside to the back patio. It faced east, so with the sun going down behind the house, the shadows had cooled the pavers and cast the beach in streaks of light.

"Beryl, move over, bud," Cass said to her golden retriever. He'd been sunning himself on the patio near the couch, and Bea took a tart and went to sit on the end of it. The dog looked up at her, and she grinned down to him.

"Can I give him a little bite?"

Cass nodded, though her mouth pinched a little at the corners. "Conrad feeds him a little bit of everything. The only reason he hasn't ballooned up is because Harry makes him run the beach with him a few times each week."

"That's how I met Ty," Sage said casually as she plucked a tart from the box. "He was running with his dogs. He has two."

"Ooh, a dog man," Bessie said. "I can't believe we didn't know he was perfect for you until now." She giggled as she took a tart too. She perched on one of the chairs surrounding the table on the patio, as the couch had filled up, and she didn't want one of the rocking chairs.

"We don't know that," Sage said. "But he came to get his haircut, and I don't know. There's a fizz there."

"You know what you have to do with a fizz, right?" Bea asked.

"No." Sage took a bite of her tart and looked to Bea. "What?"

"You have to throw in a firecracker. See if it explodes."

"This isn't a science experiment," Cass argued. "Why don't you just text him?'

"No," Bessie said quickly. "If he's interested, he should ask her." She glanced around at her friends and daughter. "I'm a traditionalist. What can I say?"

"I'm not going to rush anything with him," Sage said. "Maybe he didn't feel the fizz."

"What do you think the guys are talking about?" Lauren asked as she perched on the arm of the couch. She hadn't picked up a tart, but she nursed a mug of hot chocolate.

Bessie felt the weight of all the women's eyes again, and she shrugged. "I don't know," she said. "To be honest, I was shocked when Oliver told me he'd invited them all to his house." She glanced over to Bea and then Cass. "He hasn't done that before, has he?"

"I don't think so," Bea said, but Cass flat-out said, "No." They exchanged a glance that Bessie couldn't decipher. "Oliver's definitely their friend," Bea said. "But he hasn't been one to just come hang out. Not like Blake."

"Scott doesn't do much hanging out either," Lauren said, and Bessie suddenly didn't feel so left out.

"He is who he is," Bessie said. "I think he knows who that is, and I'm not worried about it." She couldn't be, even if she'd just fibbed a little. But now that they all lived here, it wasn't like they were getting together every day to have nail-painting parties, lunches, or to go shopping.

They all had individual lives, with jobs and families.

Bessie did too. She knew who she was, and what she wanted, and it was okay if she stood on the sidelines. She needed a man who wanted to do the same, and in that moment, she realized that Oliver was exactly that man.

He very well could be perfect for her—if she wouldn't compare him to her friends' husbands and what they did. After all, they all had different DNA, different lives, and different personalities.

The miracle was they meshed somehow, and an intense love for her friends—and their husbands—draped over her like a warm blanket.

"I think I'm falling in love with him," she whispered, but the conversation had moved on to something else, and no one heard Bessie. She'd effectively taken her time in the spotlight, and then faded to the background.

Which was fine. She didn't want her friends to be the first person who knew she was falling in love with Oliver anyway. She'd advised Wyn to talk to Douglas about her past and her feelings.

Now she just had to do the same thing with Oliver.

THE FOLLOWING DAY, BESSIE PULLED UP TO THE Mad Mango. She'd been here so many times in the past several months. Her eyes automatically went past the smoothie shop and along the sidewalk that went to the other half of the building. A Chinese restaurant had taken the space, and with the number of cars in the small parking lot, they seemed to be doing well enough.

The air conditioning cooled her inside the smoothie shop, and since it was almost two o'clock, the line extended down the counter. She expected to find Oliver working the line, either taking orders, making smoothies, or ringing people out. He had an immaculate system to get people through the line and out the door, and Bessie indeed found him working the tablet where people paid for their smoothies.

He had two stations open today, and out of everyone working behind the counter to make fresh fruit smoothies, only Oliver didn't wear a visor. He wore his authority like a hat, that was for sure, and Bessie loitered out of the way but not in line, watching him.

A couple of his employees asked him questions, which he answered quickly. He smiled at every customer, and he was the dark picture of male perfection. As the line dwindled, she pushed away from the wall and approached. She held up the round of cinnamon chip bread she'd brought for him. It had become a bestseller pretty quickly, and she'd snagged a loaf for him before stocking the case this morning.

His face brightened, and that illegal smile touched his mouth. He checked the line, then held up one finger to indicate he'd be another minute, and went back to work.

Several minutes later, he led the way into his office, and Bessie put the bread on the corner of his desk. Surprisingly, he didn't keep everything filed and straightened at ninety-degree angles. It was the one corner of his life that he seemed to allow for a little chaos.

"It's so good to see you," he murmured as he closed the door and approached her. She moved away from him, enjoying the dance between them. He sandwiched her between his body and the cupboards behind his desk, planting one hand against it as he leaned in.

He kissed her, and this one had a different energy to it. He was insistent and gentle at the same time. Seeking and taking simultaneously. Fire licked through her abdomen, and Bessie simply tried to keep up with him.

When he broke the kiss, he didn't put much distance between them. "You smell amazing."

"Things last night must've gone well."

He smiled slightly, and that was as sexy as his full grin. "We had a good time, yes."

"What did you talk about?" Bessie's curiosity couldn't be sated, not until he told her if he'd brought up their relationship. "I told my friends we'd only been dating for two months, but that I sure did like you."

He pulled back a couple of inches then, searching her face. "You did?"

"Yes. Not many details." She fiddled with the collar on his polo and pulled him back to her for another kiss. Against his lips, she said, "I may have used the word *sweet* to describe you."

He chuckled and moved his hand from the cupboard to the back of her neck. He held her there, his expression sobering. "I talked about you," he said. "Because I need their help to keep from losing you."

Confusion made her frown. "What do you mean?"

"Nothing I haven't already told you," he said. "I'm serious about you, sunshine, and I haven't been serious about anyone in a long time. I don't know what I'm doing. They're in serious relationships."

"What did they tell you?"

He looked down. "I like this shirt."

"Oliver."

He backed up then, and Bessie straightened her shirt, which was a plain purple blouse with bell sleeves. Yes, she'd gone home to change before she'd come over here. She didn't need to show up covered in flour and pumpkin seeds to see her boyfriend.

"They were actually pretty vague," he said. "They said I'd know what to do, because it's not really something I can plan or control."

Bessie saw the reason for the difference in him. "Ah, and you love to plan and control."

He didn't confirm that he did, but he shot her a dark look that used to irritate her. Now it only lit her blood on fire, because she knew there were so many complexities to this man.

"Oliver," she said, and he sighed and turned away from the window that looked out into the shop. She approached him the way she would a hurt puppy. "They're right, you know. *We'll* work through whatever comes our way as we keep seeing each other."

She arrived in front of him and ran her hands up his chest, feeling the hard muscles beneath the fabric. "Together. We're in this together."

"I'm falling for you," he whispered.

"Funny." She grinned and leaned into him, relying on him to keep her upright. "I'm falling for you too." She kissed him this time, and she kept it slow and sweet, because she wanted to explore this feeling for a moment too.

It sure was...nice.

Chapter Twenty-Three

J oy Bartlett hunched over the sewing machine, only one last panel to attach to her dress. Yes, she'd started with a Bride of Frankenstein dress from a Halloween costume. It had come with a pot of red paint to emulate blood, and the idea for her beachy wedding dress had spiraled from there.

She couldn't wait to show it to everyone, and she glanced at the clock she kept on the edge of her sewing table. "Soon," she said, the pressure mounting behind her eyes.

Scott's mother and sister would be there. His sister-in-law, who lived right here on Hilton Head. Joy had spent quite a bit of time with Rowena this summer, prepping for the wedding. She alone knew the wedding dress would not be all white.

Yes, Joy had started with white fabric. But that little pot of red paint... She hadn't gone to darker colors like red or blue. But if there was anything better than pastels and sunshine and a sandy beach, Joy didn't want to know about it.

She was going to be married in the dress of her choice, out in the open air, with her gorgeous husband at her side. Her sons had arrived yesterday, but they'd both gotten a hotel, as Joy's house was full of Scott's family.

Her daughters-in-law were already here, tending to the fondue bar that Joy was serving tonight for all the women closest to her. She'd wanted them here to show them her dress. She and Scott would be married at eleven o'clock tomorrow, a time she'd chosen so she wouldn't have to get up early and would have time to get her hair and makeup done.

Scott was with his father, his brothers, and her sons that evening. Joy loved the melding of two people and their families, and she smiled as she wrestled the fabric under the needle to make sure she wouldn't flash anyone at her wedding tomorrow.

The panel finally complied, and Joy sat back. She released the pressure foot, stood up, and lifted the dress from the table. It went back on the hanger, and Joy stood back in her tiny sewing studio and surveyed the dress.

It was absolutely everything she wanted, and she took the can of liquid starch and sprayed the dress one final time. It dried in no time flat, and Joy went out into the main part of the house, leaving open the door so she wouldn't pass out when she went in to get dressed.

She could dress herself, and she could walk easily in the

dress. She could sit, stand, and dance. She'd made sure of that.

She and Scott were getting married on the beach, which was a public space. The first people there to set up umbrellas, shades, tables, or chairs got to use the space. Nothing could be left overnight, but Joy wasn't worried about it.

Getting married in front of strangers wasn't her goal, and Cass had a stretch of sand that wasn't a popular place for tourists. One, it sat behind a gate in a community, so only the residents on that cul-de-sac really used the beach.

Joy had rented the tables, the chairs, and the tent. It would go up in the morning by professionals. Her Supper Club friends had said they'd dress and set the tables. Then, Joy would be getting ready at Cass's house, and then...

She'd be married again, at an altar that Scott said he and Harry had been building together.

"It's done," she told Lexie and Morgan, her sons' wives. They both turned to her, and Lexie came forward.

"I'm going to go see it. You're killing me." She grinned as she went past Joy, who didn't stop her from going to see the wedding dress.

"This chocolate fountain is incredible." Morgan indicated it, and it had two types of chocolate already flowing—white and milk. Sage would complain about the lack of dark chocolate on the fondue bar, but Joy didn't mind. She found dark chocolate a bit bitter, and it had to be paired with the exact right thing for her to enjoy it.

She much preferred a semi-sweet or a milk chocolate, and as she'd been prepping for this get-together, everything she'd read online had said to do milk. It flowed easier through the fountain, for one.

Knocking on the front door had her turning, and she watched as woman after woman streamed into her house, filling it—and her—with life, and laughter, and love.

"Okay," Lauren said once Bessie had made it inside and closed the door behind her, sealing out the heat. She clapped her hands a few times. "Dress time."

Joy grinned at all of them, noting that Lexie had snuck back into the room while her friends had arrived. "You sure you don't want to eat first?"

"If I don't see that dress in the next five minutes," Cass said. "I'm going to lose it." She looked one breath away from something bad, but Joy only tipped her head back and laughed.

"All right," she said. "I'll be right back."

"We'll keep the fondue going," Morgan promised.

Joy slipped into the sewing studio, which did house a full-length mirror. She hadn't made a lot of clothing over the years, but she liked seeing the patterns of her fabrics in different ways, and that included using a mirror.

She stepped out of her black shorts and flowery blouse— her standard summer wardrobe. She couldn't believe she'd quit at the library. Her last day had been yesterday, and oh, Joy hoped she wouldn't regret it.

So many changes had come her way in the past year, and as she replaced her regular bra with a strapless one, she reminded herself, "These are good changes, Joy. They're what you want."

In truth, she was getting everything she wanted. A new job on the island where all of her friends lived. A handsome man who adored her.

And this dress...

She stepped into it, straining to reach the zipper and push it up as high as she could. Then she had to reach over her shoulder and try to pull it the rest of the way. Joy got the job done, and she turned toward the mirror to make sure all the layers fluffed out the way she wanted them to.

Her heart squeezed when she realized she hadn't brought in her shoes or earrings. She brushed away the concern. Her friends would see her in all her glory tomorrow.

After rearranging a couple of panels so they layered over one another the right way, Joy left the safety of the room. She took a deep breath and pressed toward the end of the hall, where she knew everyone waited for her.

She'd only taken one step out into the open before a loud, collective gasp filled the air. "Joy," a couple of women said, but she didn't know which ones.

Her own joy filled her so completely that they became face-blind. None of them had to like the dress. *She* loved it, and that was all she cared about. Fine, maybe a small part of her wanted their accolades, their compliments.

"That is the most stunning thing I've ever seen," someone said.

"It's pastel and soft and flowy."

"Walk in it, Joy."

She did as Lauren said, moving slowly, the way she

would as she walked down the aisle. She was not being given away to Scott either, but they'd decided to each come in simultaneously, him bringing his dog Ghost with him, and her bringing her sons and their families. All of them would walk down the aisle together, and they'd become a family.

"I can't see it all fast enough," Sage said. "It's so wonderful."

"It's every color there is," Bea said. "I love the peach."

"What did you do this with?" Cass asked as Joy arrived in front of her. She reached out and touched the fabric that Joy had sculpted over her shoulder to fall down her torso. "It looks like moving water."

"It's chalk," Joy managed to say. "I dyed each of the pieces separately, and then sewed them all together to make the dress as a whole."

"It's stiff," Bessie said. "Liquid starch?"

Joy nodded. "Then I could construct it how I wanted, and it looks like it's moving, but it's not."

"And the wind won't grab it and pull it," Bea said. "It's genius."

"I can't even see the zipper in the back," Lexie said.

"Mom, I want a wedding dress like this," Wyn said, and that got a few of them to laugh.

Joy blinked, and her vision came back to normal. "Not so bad for a Halloween costume, right?"

"You did not use that." Cass rolled her eyes.

"I totally did." Joy bent and lifted up the skirt of the dress. It only fell past her knees anyway, in a ragged hemline of blue, violet, peach, ruby, pink, gold, and pumpkin. "See? There's the Bride of Frankenstein dress."

"You built over it."

"I needed something to be able to put on my body," she said. "And then I sewed every piece to that. I put a liner on it too, so I wasn't getting poked." And the liner made sure no one could see through any holes to her skin beneath.

She looked at everyone, noting the wonder and awe in their faces. "I love it. Do you think Scott will like it?"

"I think he'd have to be blind not to like it," Bea said firmly. "It's definitely the most unique wedding dress I've ever seen."

"I'll have dangly earrings," Joy said, reaching to finger her naked earlobes. "And I'm wearing the most adorable pair of slides. I've dyed them to match the dress."

"What's Scott going to wear in the heat on the beach?" Lauren asked.

Joy grinned at her. "What a great question. I guess we'll find out tomorrow." She faced the fondue bar, with its cheese and chocolate and gravy. "We've got bread and veggies for the cheese. Some fruit too—Morgan says pears are the best, so we got some of those. There's also some proteins, so you can have a ham and cheese sandwich without any bread, or dip your shrimp in a cheese sauce."

Something inside Joy just felt so light. "The chocolate has whatever you want. Marshmallow treats, fruit, pound cake, graham crackers. Go wild." She didn't need to list everything her daughters-in-law had so carefully laid out.

"I didn't want to do broth or oil, but we did a gravy

fondue instead," she said. "We have fully cooked meats for it, and of course you can dip in the veggies too, if you want. Mini meatballs, chicken skewers, and baby potatoes."

"Let's eat!" Lexie said, and Joy backed up while everyone else surged forward. She retreated back to her sewing studio and changed out of her dress, hanging it with love back on the hanger.

"Tomorrow," she murmured, and then she went to join her female loved ones.

"I'M SO NERVOUS, I'M GOING TO WIPE MY SWEATY hands down my dress and smear the chalk." Instead of doing that, Joy walked away from the window in Cass's master bedroom.

"It's fine," Cass herself said. "Everything is set. Nothing has blown over, and in fact, the wind is at a minimum today."

Good thing, Joy thought. Because Cass currently wore a hat fit for the Kentucky Derby. She'd be pressing her hand to her head for the duration of the wedding, Joy was sure.

"Scott's ready," Bea said as she ducked into the room. "Five minutes, Joy."

"Five minutes," she repeated as she faced her friends. Having them all go out and sit in the audience had been a bad idea. How in the world was she going to walk out of this bedroom, through the house, and onto the patio alone?

"You're panicking," Lauren said. "Guys, she's panicking."

Tears filled Joy's eyes, and she closed them to try to do the least amount of damage to her makeup. Lauren reached her first, hugging her tightly as everyone else minced their way over to them.

"I love you all," Joy said through her emotions.

Murmurs of love and camaraderie moved through the group, and Joy took strength from it. From them. "Okay," she said. "I'm okay."

"He's here," Lauren said. "He's ready. Blake said he's glowing." She finally got enough room to step back, and she held onto Joy's shoulders. "You look amazing. You *are* amazing."

Joy nodded, and one by one, her friends and relatives left the room. The last one out was Rowena, Jeff's wife, and she blew Joy a kiss before she ducked through the doorway.

The door drifted closed, and Joy hurried back to the window to watch them all stream across the patio and down the steps to the beach. When it seemed like everyone was in place, Joy turned to leave the bedroom.

Before she could take a single step, someone rapped on the door. Her pulse flew up to the top of her head, and her mouth turned dry.

That could only be one person, and this was not part of their script.

"Scott," she whispered as she moved as fast as her starched dress would allow. When she pulled open the door, her groom stood there.

He wore a navy blue suit that fit his wide shoulders and narrow waist perfectly. His tie was the color of blue cotton candy, and then pink, and then yellow, and then green.

It matched her dress completely, and she started to laugh. "I love you," she said.

Scott had said nothing, his eyes still lazily running down her body. When they rebounded to hers, he wore heat and love and desire and adoration all in his expression at the same time. "Ghost is wearing a tie too," he said, indicating his dog, who sat politely on the end of a white leash. "Look."

"He's adorable," Joy gushed. She turned around fully. "Do you like the dress?"

"Sweetheart, I love this dress. I love this day. I love you."

"I wasn't sure I was going to be able to get out there by myself," she whispered.

"That's why I came to get you." He offered her his arm, and Joy felt like the luckiest and most joyful woman in the world as she linked her hand through his elbow. "So you wouldn't have to do it alone."

She stepped out into the hall with him, and Ghost trotted along on his left side. Her mind blanked, because she was moments away from getting married. *Married.*

Then Scott slid open the door, and everything he did was so calm and so centered. Joy fed off of that, and before she knew it, they stood at the bottom of the steps, about to enter the tent.

At the end of the aisle stood the altar, and Joy sucked in a breath and held it. She'd opted not to carry a bouquet, because she wanted her dress to be the talk of the town, the only addition of color to what was normally a white affair.

The altar had likewise been splashed with color, but this time in the form of flowers. Vines with bright pink and vibrant purple flowers ran up the legs to an all-white, leather top. In that, huge bouquets of flowers had been placed, but she couldn't see any containers or baskets. Only greenery at the bottom gave way to the bright blooms that made Joy's tears renew.

"I love it," she whispered.

"I kind of own a landscaping company," he said out of the corner of his mouth. "Do you really like it?"

She looked up at him, pure love overcoming her again and again. "I absolutely love it. Thank you." She stretched up and brushed her lips across his.

"Hey," someone protested from down the aisle. They hadn't invited the whole town the way Lauren and Blake had. Joy hadn't wanted anything too terribly large, and she only had to walk past about nine rows of chairs before she'd reach the pastor at the altar. "There's no kissing until later."

Joy grinned at Scott, and then at Lauren, who'd rebuked her. They started the march down the aisle to the altar, and Joy told herself not to zone out. Not to go face-blind. To look every person in the eyes, smile at them, and remember that they'd come to celebrate this day with her.

Before she knew it, she stood at the altar, and since she and Scott had wanted a simple ceremony, it didn't take long for the pastor to say, "You can kiss your new wife, Scott."

Scott grabbed onto her, already laughing, and kissed her

with his mouth all curved up. The applause and whooping started, and then Joy turned with Scott toward the crowd. Seeing everyone on their feet, all dressed in their finest, the big, wide, joyful smiles on their faces...

Joy had never been happier, and she and Scott still had the rest of the day—and night—to celebrate their union.

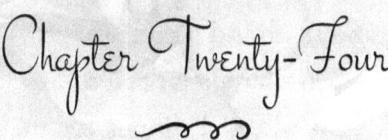

Chapter Twenty-Four

Oliver paced like a caged tiger, wondering why his father and brother hadn't arrived yet. They'd texted an hour ago to say they were driving past Beaufort. And Beaufort was thirty minutes away.

"Where are they?" he growled. He'd ordered dinner, and Bessie was literally on hold until he texted and said his family had arrived. As the clock ticked, Bessie's bedtime approached. The only thing worse would be her here, waiting with him.

Things had been going really well with Bessie, and Oliver had every brick lined up for the Heritage Festival, which started in two days.

Bessie would be baking all day and into the evening tomorrow in preparation for the festival, and that meant if his father and brother didn't show up soon, she wouldn't be able to meet them until the festival.

And that would be like inviting in complete crazy.

"As if we haven't already." He peered through the blinds, but he didn't see any stray vehicles. Oliver snatched his phone from the dining room table where he'd left it, and he stabbed at the screen. He couldn't stand not knowing where his family was, and he found it rude that they'd called to say they were close, when they weren't close.

They knew he'd planned dinner for them. Surely they hadn't stopped for something to eat. "No," he grumbled. "Daddy just lives on his own clock." He wouldn't even notice that the minutes had ticked by. Then he'd wonder why Oliver had his wolverine claws out.

He couldn't really call his brother and chew him out. The ground they walked on was already paper thin, and Oliver took a deep breath. He was not going to ruin this. It was one evening, and Bessie could leave any time she wanted.

He texted her, *I have no idea where they are, but why don't you come over anyway? When they get here, they'll get here.*

Okay, Bessie said. *Be there soon.*

Oliver just wanted someone to show up. He should've known to just live his life, and Daddy and Cam would walk in when they got here. They wouldn't even care that he and Bessie had eaten without them.

Oliver sighed at his phone and set it down again. The doorbell rang in tandem with someone pounding on the door, and Oliver's pulse flew through his veins. He'd only taken one step toward the door when it opened.

Daddy peered in, a wide smile on his face. "This is it," he drawled.

"You've been here before," Oliver said as he continued striding forward. "Come on in." He fastened a smile to his face, and he told himself that he could make the situation awkward or not. He grabbed his daddy in a hug, because he hadn't seen him in a long, long time, and family had become more important to Oliver in the past few months.

He knew that was because of Bessie. Her loved ones meant a great deal to her, and Oliver had learned that he didn't have to be an island in the ocean of life. It didn't make him weak to have others he cared about, to have people he relied on.

"Oh, it's so good to see you." Oliver grinned at his brother, though the cowboy hat was a bit ridiculous. The moment Daddy let him go, Oliver stepped into Cam. "Where have you guys been? You called a while ago."

"We went by the house," Cam said. "And Oliver." He stepped back, his dark eyes shining. "It's great. I don't know how you got that rental for us, but it's great."

"I'm glad," Oliver said. "I had to pull quite a few strings for it, so I'm glad you like it."

Daddy surveyed the house. "This is a nice place, Ollie."

"You've been here before," Oliver said again. "It's the same house."

"Is it?" He scuffed his steel-toed boot against the floor. "Is this the same floor?"

"I don't remember that couch." Cam walked over to it like he'd never seen a black leather couch before.

Oliver pressed his eyes closed and prayed for patience. He'd need a lot of it to make it through tonight, and he had half a day tomorrow before the festival started. He honestly didn't know what Daddy and Cam would do to entertain themselves during those three days, because Oliver had told them he'd be running all day and all night and wouldn't be available.

They couldn't change their trip, though Oliver didn't understand why. They ran a furniture store and could leave any time they wanted. The fact was, leaving Alabama wore Daddy right to the bone, and any change at all would've meant he canceled the trip, not postponed it.

"The couch is new," Oliver admitted. "Listen, Bessie should be here soon."

His father turned toward him, and Oliver felt like he was looking in a mirror twenty-five years into the future. They had the same eyebrows, the same dark eyes, the same strong jaw. Oliver had his mother's nose, and Daddy's hair had started silvering several years ago.

"Tell us about Bessie," he said.

Oliver's jaw tightened. "She's great," he said. "She's a baker. Owns a bakery here on the island. It's still pretty new, so I'd appreciate it if you'd keep the questions to a minimum."

"I'm coming in," Bessie said, and Oliver's pulse ricocheted around his body for the second time in the last five minutes. He spun to face her, and then he lunged toward her when he saw her carrying the food.

"Hey," he said, taking the first bag. "They just showed up," he whispered.

Bessie said nothing, but she wore the same type of smile

Oliver felt gracing his face. He went past his brother, saying, "Give me a second." He hurried into the kitchen and put the food down, then rushed back to Bessie's side.

The silence in the house had never bothered Oliver, but with four of them there, it shouldn't be so silent. With people he knew, there wasn't silence like this.

"Daddy," he said. "This is Bessie Clifton. Bess, this is my daddy, Phil and my brother Cam." He put his arm around her, which felt like the most unnatural thing in the world. His calves ached, and he couldn't quite get a full breath.

"Great to meet you," Bessie said, moving out from underneath his arm. He let it fall back to his side, not quite sure what he was doing. The world felt like it had tilted oddly as Bessie kissed both of Cam's cheeks, asked him if he was married or seeing anyone, and then moved over to Daddy.

Cam's eyes landed on Oliver's as he said, "Yeah, I'm married. Cindy and I have been married for fifteen years."

Oliver heard the subtext—*you haven't told Bessie about us?*

Oliver hadn't, no.

"We have three kids," Cam said next. "Do you have any kids, Bessie?"

"Yes," she said after she'd greeted Daddy. She stayed by his side instead of returning to Oliver's, and he had no idea what to do.

"Should we eat?" Bessie suggested, her eyebrows high and her eyes wide. She turned to go into the kitchen and take out the food Oliver had ordered. She could make small talk and un-bag food, something Oliver had apparently forgotten how to do. "How was the drive? Did you guys do the whole thing today?"

"Nah," Daddy said, really drawing out the word.

"We actually left yesterday," Cam said as he crowded around the table too. They all seemed to fit together, and Oliver couldn't figure out why he didn't. Looking at his daddy, he saw the same thick hair, the same nose, and the same strong jaw. Yet everything about them felt different too. An awkwardness descended upon him every time he spent time with his family, and he'd never felt like he belonged.

"We stopped in Atlanta, because Momma has a candy shop there she loved." He beamed at Bessie, who wore what sure looked like a genuine smile on her face. "We actually toured their factory today," Cam said, shooting a look over to Oliver. "That's what put us here a bit later tonight."

"Yeah, sorry about that," Daddy said. "Ollie says you go to bed pretty early, because of your job."

"I do," Bessie said, and he marveled at how well she'd integrated into them. She didn't seem to see the same things Oliver did, and he wondered how he could look at his family through new eyes.

She looked at him, her expression filled with pleading. "But I can be flexible too. I wouldn't want to be anywhere but here."

He wasn't sure why he couldn't just walk over there and join them. His legs had grown roots down through his toes, and he didn't even recognize himself in his own house.

"What did you get for dinner?" Daddy asked, and the

way he drawled everything out made it seem like he was slow.

Bessie looked at Oliver, her eyebrows sky-high, and he finally understood her pleading. She wanted him to get the heck over there. He hurried in her direction. "Barbecue," he practically yelled as he arrived at the table too.

Bessie actually flinched as she took the lid off one of the Styrofoam containers. "Baked beans," Oliver called as if no one had eyes.

"Mac and cheese," she added in a much quieter voice, sliding another container next to the first. She looked up at Daddy. "Oliver says you won't touch chicken if there's beef to be had."

Daddy started to chuckle, but the sound quickly morphed into a big, belly laugh that filled the house with more sound than it had ever held before. Oliver squared his shoulders, realizing why he'd spoken so loud a moment ago. To keep up with his daddy. To be louder than him. To be as important.

"I do love a good piece of beef," Daddy bellowed into the rafters. "This looks amazing."

"It sure does," Cam said.

Bessie turned and got plates and silverware, which only reminded Oliver of what a terrible host he was, and she moved around his house, around his family, as if she'd been doing so for years.

She did so, because she was so good. She liked them, and they liked her.

The real question was: Why did Bessie like *him*?

Chapter Twenty-Five

B essie did not know the version of her boyfriend sitting next to her. No matter what, he wasn't the same man she'd been dating for the past couple of months. Everything seethed inside her, because Oliver didn't seem like himself at all.

He'd said very little during the meal. He'd only eaten a few bites of food, though everyone had finished about twenty minutes ago. The conversation had wandered from their drive from Birmingham, which was pretty much a straight east shot for them, to the furniture store, to Oliver's momma, to everyone who lived on Oak Tree Lane, where Oliver had grown up.

She had no idea what the topic of conversation would be next, and that unnerved her. The way Oliver sat ramrod straight at her side, his dark eyes hooded and almost narrowed, reminded her of the beast of a man she'd met outside the commercial rental property, in the dark, months ago.

He wore a mask—the same one he'd had on that night outside The Mad Mango. The same mask he'd sported when she and Wyn had gone in to get smoothies and he'd spilled it on her daughter. She wondered if Cam and Phil even knew about Oliver's mask. About the walls and barriers he'd put between him and them.

He'd employed every single one of them, and there was no way they'd get through his defenses. She looked over to him as Cam finished a story about one of his kids. Oliver never talked about his nieces and nephews, his in-laws, or even his siblings. Bessie wasn't sure what to make of it, and she put a soft smile on her face as he tilted his head down to look at her.

"Isn't it about time for you to get to bed, pumpkin?" He settled his arm over her shoulders, which sparked irritation within her.

Pumpkin? Bessie's eyes rounded instantly, and she glanced over to his daddy and brother, but she didn't even reach for her phone to check the time. "I do turn into a pumpkin about eight o'clock." She smiled across the table to Cam, who beamed on back to her. He was warm and caring, and Bessie really liked him.

"We'll get out of your hair," Cam said. He stood and picked up his plate.

"Just leave the dishes," Oliver said as he finally dropped his arm and got to his feet too.

"Yeah," Bessie chimed in, her eyes tracking the two men

as they went into the kitchen. "His housekeepers will take care of everything in the morning." The moment she spoke, she realized her mistake.

Oliver spun back toward her, his eyes dark, dark, dark.

"Yep," Phil agreed. "It's gettin' late, and Cam here likes to unpack his bag the moment he arrives somewhere."

"He's not wrong." Cam put his dishes in the sink and turned toward Oliver. "Love you, Brother." He grabbed onto him in a big bear hug, shocking Bessie. And apparently Oliver, who stood there with his arms pinned to his sides.

Cam grinned at Bessie over Oliver's shoulder. "I'm so glad we're here. You had to cancel your trip last year, and I haven't seen you in two years, and that's too long."

Two years.

Cam stepped back to let Oliver put his dishes in the sink, and he engulfed Bessie in an embrace too. "You keep him honest, now, ya'hear?"

"I have really enjoyed meeting you," she said, really meaning it.

Cam pulled back and smiled at her. "He will—" He got cut off as his father started coughing and didn't stop. He rushed over to him and hit him on the back a couple of times. "He's okay," he said over his shoulder to Oliver. "Just a lingering cough from a cold he had a month or so ago." Cam herded his daddy toward the front door, and Bessie fell to Oliver's side as he approached, and then followed behind a half-step as they followed them out onto the porch.

Oliver put his arm around her shoulders again, sending a measure of discomfort through her as she watched Cam walk with Phil toward their truck. She wasn't sure who normally drove, but Cam took Phil to the passenger side and helped him into the vehicle.

Then he waved as he crossed in front of the truck, and Bessie hated the false smile on her face as she called, "Drive safe."

"I'll see you tomorrow," Oliver added, and they waved Cam into the driver's seat. He backed out of the driveway, and when all she could see were taillights, she shrugged out of Oliver's oppressive embrace.

She looked at him, a fire blazing hot inside her. "I don't like it when you put your arm over my shoulders." He literally never did that, and she wasn't sure what was going on with him. It was like he'd become someone else entirely, and she simply wanted the Oliver Blackhurst she knew to come back.

She went into the house, and Oliver followed her. "I should get home. It's going to be a monstrously long baking day tomorrow."

"You don't have any questions?" He stood between her and the door.

"I have several," she said. "But I think it would be wiser if I asked them at another time, when we're both in a better place."

"You're upset," he said, and he wasn't asking.

She picked up Phil's plate and glass and headed into the kitchen. "I'm not upset," she said. She simply didn't even know who stood in the house with her. Dark, guarded Oliver? Or her handsome, sweet, caring boyfriend who knew all the best places around the island where they could be alone? Where he could show her the beach and the sky and infuse calmness into her?

"I'm sorry I said anything about the housekeepers," she said.

"I'm sorry for all of tonight," he said.

She nodded and faced him. "What was that?"

"I don't know," he admitted. "I'm just...I don't fit with them. I never have, and I don't know how to *be* around them." He took a couple of steps toward her. "I couldn't wait to get out of Alabama. I don't like going back. I just—I feel like no matter what I do, it'll be the wrong thing."

Bessie didn't know what to say to him. This clearly wasn't a simple thing that could be worked out with one conversation and a few days' of visiting. "I'm going to go." She patted her pocket for her keys, but they weren't there. "I think I left my purse in the car." She'd carried in the food, so that made sense.

She wanted to kiss him good-night, but she wasn't sure which version of Oliver she'd get. She stepped into his arms, glad when his hands slid along her waist the way they normally did. She stroked her fingers down his bearded jaw and watched him melt and soften right in front of her.

She sure did like that she could do that to him, and she whispered, "Are you going to survive tomorrow?"

"Yes," he said simply.

"How do you know?"

"Because you're going to be baking from very early to very late," he said. "And you'll survive, so every time I think I won't, I'll think of you. I'll borrow your strength and use it as my own."

"We'll both survive." She did have an astronomically long day tomorrow, and then for the next three of the festival. But she told herself as she kissed the Oliver she knew good-night that she could sleep in only four more days.

"There's someone here for you," Wendy said, barely poking her head around the corner from the front of the shop.

"There is?" Bessie looked down at the dough she'd been putting together for a batch of arepas she'd decided to take to the festival tomorrow. It started just before lunchtime, and she thought perhaps people would buy them for lunch.

"Yep."

"Who is it?" But Wendy had disappeared already back into the front of the shop.

"Could be someone important," Hillie said. "You go on now. It's just dough, and we'll be here all day."

That was the truth, and so Bessie reached for a tea towel and wiped her hands before she left the kitchen. She pushed through the black plastic door and out into the front of the shop. People seemed to teem everywhere, as they'd lined up in the queue markers, and the line then extended toward the door.

Her employees worked behind the display case taking orders, taking money, and then handing over sliced and wrapped bread. The system worked, and the tables out in the shop were full.

It wasn't hard to see the three men standing to the side, all of them looking at her. Oliver, Phil, and Cam. They stood in front of a bookshelf Bessie had put up that held home décor signs about baking and bread, as well as featured their bread of the month—which was an autumn apple that had all the spices and warmth of an apple tart, if apple tarts had golden raisins and maple syrup in them.

"Oliver," she said as she approached him. She wished she'd taken off her apron first, but she figured she could show that she actually baked. She didn't need to impress Cam and Phil, and it wouldn't happen just because she wore a clean apron instead of one with flour all over it.

She moved right into Oliver's arms and kissed him quickly. "What are you three doing here?" She smiled over to his daddy and his brother. "Looks like trouble."

"Cam wanted French toast," Oliver said.

Her eyebrows went up. "Oh? So you need the nine-grain bread."

Oliver smiled at her, and he did seem more relaxed this morning than he'd been last night. "We need the nine-grain bread."

"Ollie says we can't have French toast without it." Cam

"That's what I said," Oliver agreed.

"I'll go get it for you," she said.

"We can just go through the line," Oliver said.

"No, it's fine. I have a bunch in the back."

"But aren't those for the festival?" Oliver met her eyes,

and they had a silent conversation right there in her busy shop. She'd wanted to have this type of wordless, meaningful conversation with a man for a while now, and she ducked away before he could see her emotions.

"Be right back." She went behind the counter and said to Justin, who worked the register, "I need a nine-grain on the managerial account, please."

"You got it," he said, immediately starting to key it in.

"Robbie?" Bessie turned, but the girl had already bustled off to get the loaf of nine-grain from the shelves. She handed it to Bessie with a smile and then moved right back to the register to get the next order.

"Thank you," she said to the pair of them. She took the bread out to Oliver, who handed it to Cam and said, "There you go. It's gonna blow your mind."

"Your place is busy, Bessie," Phil yelled into the fray. "You must be doing well."

"Daddy," Oliver said, plenty of warning in his voice.

"I'm just saying, she's busy." He shook his head. "Ollie doesn't like to talk about money."

"I just don't think it's any of your business how Bessie's doing."

She didn't know what to say. She and Oliver had not talked about money all that much. So little, in fact, that she still owed him for the platinum sponsorship. She'd asked him about it once, because she didn't even know how much it had cost, but he hadn't answered. She could look up the amount online, she supposed, but with everything going on, she hadn't.

"We got the bread," he said. "Let's go."

"Enjoy," she said as they turned to leave.

"We will," Phil boomed to everyone in the store, and Bessie caught the way Oliver semi-rolled his eyes. She smiled and hugged herself as they left, because all she could do now was pray for him that he really would survive today.

The door closed, and she couldn't see them behind the bright, colorful sign Wyn had hung in the top half of it. They were closing the shop for the duration of the Heritage Festival, because then Bessie could simply move her workforce from here over to the park to run the booth.

She didn't have the resources or funds to hire more people the way Oliver had, and she reasoned that he had twelve years of experience on her, and being able to keep her bakery open and staff the Heritage Festival was a goal she could work toward.

But not if she didn't have the bread for the festival. She spun on her heel and went back into the kitchen, because she had a baking to-do list two pages long, and she couldn't be standing out in the front of her shop, daydreaming about her future here at Flour Power, on Hilton Head Island, or with Oliver Blackhurst.

She had bread to bake.

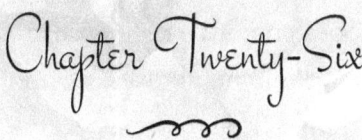

Chapter Twenty-Six

O liver barely made it to the long wooden counters that marked his booth before he dropped the box with six of his blenders in it. His job this morning was to make sure everything had the power it needed to run for the next three days. Then he'd cover all the cords so his employees wouldn't trip and cause a catastrophe, and then he'd work on his menu board.

"This goes in the freezer, right?" Daddy asked as he plopped a heavy box of frozen raspberries next to the blenders. "Is it plugged in and goin'?"

"Leo said it was," Oliver said as he twisted to half-look over his shoulder to the two chest freezers he'd put at the middle-edge of his booth. Bessie had tables set up there already, but they'd been there last night too. "I'm sure they're going. He's headed back to the shop for our final load of ingredients."

Oliver had probably over-planned for this first day of the

festival. The Heritage Festival started on Friday, but the booths didn't open until eleven-thirty. He was never sure how many moms and girls' groups of friends would show up on the initial day, but they did open before lunchtime, and it was hot today. So a smoothie seemed like a good thing to have ready for anyone who showed up looking for a little lunch and something a little cold.

Of course, the booths weren't the only attraction in the park that day. The festival hosted a volleyball tournament that lasted all weekend, live entertainment in the evenings, a fun run, a fireman's breakfast, and plenty of children's activities.

Heck, one year, they'd cordoned off part of the park, filled it with water and fish, and had a "Huck Finn fishing event." Participants could pay a fee, wade into the water with people in their same age group, and "go fishing." Any fishes they managed to get over the edge with their bare hands, they could keep.

Oliver had not participated, of course. He wasn't really the type of man to get wet and go fishing with his hands.

"Yep, they're on," Daddy yelled from behind Oliver, who chose not to answer him.

Tomorrow, Saturday, the festival started at ten o'clock in the morning, and it ran until ten p.m. Families and tourists alike flooded the park, and this year, the Festival Committee had organized a photography contest, and the winners would be set up in the middle of the booth space.

At the end of the day, fireworks filled the sky, and Oliver usually watched them while he packed up his booth with a co-worker. They'd return the next day, but the booths were only open from noon to five on Sunday.

"Morning," Bessie said, and that did get Oliver to turn fully toward her. She put a stack of baskets on her folding tables in the middle, and she wore a pair of jean shorts and a sleeveless shirt that showed off her impressive kneading muscles.

And when she tied an apron around her waist...she was the sexiest woman alive, in Oliver's opinion.

"Good morning," he said to her as he slid his hand along her waist. "I can help you hang your banners after I get my blenders set up."

"Morning, Oliver," Wyn chirped, and he pulled his hand back.

"Hey, Wyn." He leaned down and kissed her cheek.

"Don't worry about the banners," she said. "Douglas is coming to do it."

"Oh, great."

"And Harry's bringing my extra shade that Amy *finally* approved," Bessie said as she started separating her baskets. She'd applied for and gotten another overhang for her butter and jam corner of the booth. She'd wanted Oliver to "work his magic" on the Festival Committee or "pull some platinum sponsorship strings," but he'd only laughed.

That's not how it works, he'd told her. Then he'd pointed her to the right form, and she'd filled it out, turned it in, and gotten it approved.

"So you don't need me at all," he said.

"No," she said. "I totally need you. I want a Surfer Boy the moment the booths open."

He inched closer to her, aware of his brother's arrival and Wyn's nearness. "You want to be my first customer?"

"Yes, sir," she said happily. She didn't wear an ounce of her exhaustion on her face or around her eyes, and Oliver couldn't wait for this festival to end. Then he and Bessie could go back to lazy afternoons spent in the sunshine, kissing and laughing and talking...

He paused, wondering if this was what love felt like. He honestly wasn't sure, and he had nothing to compare it to.

"Ollie," Cam called, breaking into his wild thoughts. "We've got these tablecloths, but they're not fittin', Brother."

"Oh, *brother*," he mumbled under his breath. Then he moved out of Bessie's booth and back to his. He really couldn't be flirting all day. He didn't have time to stand around and contemplate life, the universe, and love.

Make it through the festival, he told himself. There would be time for introspection afterward. He reached for the custom-made table covering, which wasn't really a cloth but a wipeable piece of faux leather.

It had lighthouses and compasses and nautical wheels printed in white over an ocean blue background, and as he pulled it tight, he said, "You have to kind of muscle it into place." He secured one corner and nodded down the length of the counter to Cam. "Do that one."

Oliver continued to boss around his brother until they had all three coverings in place. "They do seem a little smaller this year," he admitted, though he'd measured the counters in the booths, and they weren't any bigger than any other year. That was also his way of saying, *I'm sorry for snapping at you* without having to actually say it.

Leo arrived with several employees, all of them carrying various bags and boxes while the assistant manager towed a wagon behind him. Oliver groaned inwardly at the amount of stuff, because it felt like too much.

He always felt like this, and he always managed to mostly sell through his stock. "Let's pack these freezers, guys," he said. "Coldest things first, then they won't get overworked." He'd lock them at night, and right now was the bulk of the work in bringing in ingredients.

He took the box of mango chunks from a woman named Sarah and put it in the bottom of the freezer. He knew this drill. He'd packed these freezers before. He used the same-sized boxes every year because he knew they fit.

"We've got your water line," someone said, and Oliver straightened from the icy depths of the chest freezer.

"Great," he said in almost a sigh. "Our pump sink is here. Where can I put it?" He started working with the facilities manager, Ben, because he had to rinse out his blenders between every smoothie. There was a precise ratio of ingredients, and he didn't need a clump of protein powder staying in the bottom of one blender only to be mixed in with the next drink.

"We're gonna feed it through the middle here," Ben said, indicating the space between Bessie's tables and Oliver's freezers. Douglas had arrived, and he currently stood on a table while Wyn held up one end of the new Flour Power banners she'd made and ordered.

Bessie loved her daughter with a fierceness Oliver had never known for another person. He had no children, and even if he and Bessie ended up married and together, he knew he wouldn't be her father. The woman was almost twenty-four years old, and she didn't need to be raised. She didn't need a daddy figure in her life.

"...think that will work."

Oliver only caught the tail end of his father's sentence, and he jerked himself back to attention. "What will work?" He glanced around for his daddy, but it took him an extra beat of time to find him down on the ground with Ben.

Hooking up the water link to the sink—which wasn't where Oliver wanted it.

"No," he shouted as if warning someone of a falling tree they needed to escape. "That's not where I want it."

Both men peered up at him, and he frowned mightily at them. "Way down on the end here? My far side people will be walking back and forth. I want it right in the middle."

"The freezers are in the middle, son."

"Then we move one down." Oliver didn't mean to bark, but the clock kept ticking. He should be—and he was—grateful that his father and Cam had come to help set up this morning. It was all hands on deck, and they happened to have boarded the ship last night.

Once everything started, they'd wander the booths, because Cindy loved a good "booth boutique," and Cam would see if there was anything worth buying to take home to her. Truth be told, Daddy loved a good stroll through things, and he'd probably purchase more than Cam.

Daddy frowned at him. "I don't know if it'll reach."

"We need to make it reach as far as we can." Oliver extended his hand toward his father. "Come on, Daddy. You don't need to be down on the ground."

Oliver still hadn't accomplished his powering of the blenders, the covering of the cords, or the menu board. People bustled around the booth, putting out containers with spoons and straws, napkins, and trash receptacles. His eyes met Leo's, and Oliver nodded him toward the trio of huge chalkboards that leaned against the near side of the booth.

"On it," Leo said, though Oliver had wanted to make the menu boards. He'd taken a class on window decoration and visual appeal of menus in his business classes in college, and he had been perfecting his handwriting specifically for menu boards for the past dozen years.

He knew whatever Leo made would be fine, but it wouldn't be what he did. A sense of superiority filled him, and Oliver tamped it back with everything he had.

Daddy finally put his hand in his, and Oliver tried to help him to his feet. But he couldn't lift Daddy as deadweight, and he grunted as his father seemingly put in no effort at all. He started coughing again, and Cam arrived in two seconds flat.

"C'mon, Daddy," he said. "There's not enough air down there." He cast Oliver a look that held apprehension and pure secrecy for half a breath of time. Then it smoothed away into Cam's usual carefree expression, his smile chasing away all shadows of doubt.

But Oliver had seen it. He watched as Cam led Daddy out of the booth by the hand. He'd seen it.

Hadn't he?

"Hey," Bessie said, and his attention got swung in yet another direction. He'd never had a partner at the festival before, and pure chaos raged through his bloodstream. "Is your dad okay?" Her gaze moved to him and Cam too, who'd made it several paces away from their combined booth.

"You know what?" Oliver asked, but he didn't know what to say next. Part of him wanted to confide in her that he was beginning to doubt that his daddy was okay. Part of him wanted to tell her to mind her own business. Part of him wanted to put his head down and get back to work. And yet another part of him wanted to flee this park, this festival, this state until he could work through all of the teeming emotions in his head.

"This is as far as it goes," Ben said, and Oliver looked away from Bessie and back to the task at hand.

Work. That was what Oliver had always turned to in his life. If he worked hard enough, he could save for a car. If he worked hard enough, he'd get a scholarship to the college of his choice. If he worked hard enough, he'd learn what he needed to in order to finally have a successful business.

He rarely acknowledged luck or timing in his business success formula, though he could clearly see it in others. Bessie, for example, had gotten very lucky when she'd been able to partner with him for this festival. His knowledge and experience was surely a huge asset to her. She'd already told him several times how much she'd learned from him through this process.

"Then put it there," he told Ben. "That would be great. Thanks, Ben."

His phone rang before he could return to the blenders, and he couldn't just ignore it. Nicole's name sat there, and he'd put her in charge of the shop for the next three days while Oliver and Leo focused on the booth.

"What's up?" he asked, going for casual but not quite achieving it."

"I've had three people call off this morning already," she said. "There's no way we can open at this point."

Oliver pressed his eyes closed, his mind racing through possibilities. He had brought over a big chunk of people, anticipating needing some extra hands this morning. With his mind being pulled in so many directions, he couldn't even remember the names of the employees he'd assigned to the booth that day.

"Oliver?" Nicole asked.

"One minute," he barked.

"Ollie?" Cam called, and he turned that way.

"Hey, baby," Bessie said, and Oliver found her easing up to him. "Oh, you're on the phone." She backed up a step. "When you have a sec, Harry needs some help with my corner shade." She held up one hand like it could wait, but Oliver didn't want it to wait.

He wanted to drop everything he had going on in his life

and help her. That came with a price, and Oliver had never felt so torn in so many different directions.

Without saying anything to Bessie, he walked over to Cam. "Tell Nicole we'll send her some people." He extended his phone toward his brother, who looked at it like it had become a live snake.

"I need to talk to you about Daddy."

Oliver dropped the phone with the live call on the counter. "I have to—I need a minute." He walked away from his brother, from the booth, from Bessie.

Chapter Twenty-Seven

B essie gaped after Oliver as he stalked away. She knew an angry stride when she saw one, and Oliver was a ten on the Scale of Upset. She met Cam's eyes, and he seemed as shocked as she was.

"Bessie," Harry called, and she spun toward her own booth. He struggled with the poles he'd extended out from the framework of the corner, and he really needed a second pair of hands. Cass had come with him, but she wasn't tall enough. Bessie certainly wasn't.

"Douglas," she said as she passed him. "Can you help Harry?"

Douglas didn't even take a moment to think about it. He dropped the end of the banner and jumped down from the table. He vaulted over the one between him and Harry, his hands quickly shoring up the poles Harry needed him to.

"Thanks," Harry said.

Bessie didn't know how to help. She couldn't get up on

tables or extend her arms past their regular length. "Do these baskets just go along the tables here?" Cass asked, her eyes concerned as she looked at Bessie.

"Yes," Bessie said, trying to make her voice strong. Oliver had called her strong once, and she'd believed him then. Right now, she just wanted to go after him. She looked out into the park, but she didn't see him among the activity of all the other booth owners getting set up. She cast her eyes toward the nearby parking lot, but she couldn't find him there either.

"We'll put bread in them, and I brought signs." She nodded to a box sitting on the ground near her middle tables. She didn't have nearly the amount of set-up as Oliver, as she didn't have to plug anything in. She didn't have to keep ingredients frozen, or rinse anything out. Wyn had made their menu board part of their banner, and she didn't have to do anything there either.

She literally had to put out her baskets, label them, and fill them with bread. She did have two coolers filled with cubed ice and a third with a big block of ice and her compound butters and then bottles of jams.

She'd put those out at the last minute, and she anticipated the tray of ice she planned to put her butters in melting quickly.

"I'll do it," Cass said. "If you want to go find Oliver."

Wyn joined them, and she said, "I can make sure the baskets get labeled properly, Mom."

Bessie shook her head, though she wasn't sure why she

didn't want to go find Oliver. "He won't like that," she said, and that was reason number one.

"He listens to you, Mom," Wyn said.

Cass threw a look over to Harry, but he was still busy with the corner shade. "He's probably just stressed, and Wyn's right. You calm him down."

"He's like ten different people," Bessie whispered. She didn't want to betray him or say anything that would hurt him. "He's..." She sighed as she focused on separating two baskets. "He's in boss mode right now, and I think it's best if we just let him be."

She moved down the table, placing her baskets beside one another. She and Wyn had decided to do two flavors of bread side-by-side, then have a sample station between the next pairing. It went with the theme of partners, and she could "pair up" her breads with appropriate toppings.

The Wildflower Honey Company had been happy to partner with her, and Wyn had done a masterful job bringing them on board. They'd provided jars of honey and jam to go with Bessie's homemade compound butters, and their decorative bottles really beautified her table.

"I want them to have height," she told Cass as she built a pyramid of jams and honeys at the first sample station. "Then, in the front, we'll have one open jar of jam and one of honey, each with a knife in it." She placed those in front of the pyramid. "And then our sample trays of bread in front of that."

She left that space open, seeing it so clearly in her mind. "Oh, the cloths." Bessie turned, and Wyn handed her the blue checkered cloth that they'd chosen to mark their sample stations. They could have one in the middle of each table, and behind them, Bessie would house her check-out spots.

She'd decided to put her card reader on the side facing the rest of the festival, as there was so much more going on than just the local business booths. Of course, it was mobile and could be moved anywhere at any time.

She continued to set up the sample stations, finally putting a big plastic bin in the corner where the extra shade fell. "Thank you, Harry," she said.

He wiped his hand across his forehead. "I think we got it, Bessie. It should withstand the wind."

Douglas, ever the optimist with a smiling face, clapped Harry on the shoulder and re-entered the booth through the gap this time. "The banner is good?"

Wyn turned toward him, and Bessie let her handle it. Her daughter had shown time and again that she could shoulder big burdens, and Bessie was so proud of her. Her emotions stormed through her, especially when she realized how long Oliver had been gone.

Her gaze wandered over to Cam, who stood in the middle of the booth and issued directions. Something told her to get over there and talk to him, and despite the thundering of her heart, she did just that.

"The blenders are all hooked up," he said as if he had to report to her. "I'm having his guys cover the cords, because I know he didn't want anyone to trip."

She looked down at her feet, not realizing she'd stepped up a couple of inches. "He made this floor?"

"I guess he's used it before." Cam sounded absolutely miserable, and he gave her a wary smile. "My daddy isn't well."

Bessie nodded, though the news wasn't exactly welcome or expected. "You haven't told him."

"We thought it best to do it in person, but the festival..." He let the words hang there. "Oliver is so focused, and he doesn't seem to have room for more than one thing at a time. We were going to wait until after the festival."

"So you wouldn't ruin it for him."

Cam nodded, and Bessie's heart expanded and expanded for him. She didn't know what to say, so she just slipped her hand into his and squeezed.

"Daddy just wants to tell him," Cam said. "I keep holding him back, but it's really hard."

"He's focused and headstrong too," Bessie said, realizing where Oliver got his drive and stubbornness from.

"They're like the same person," Cam admitted. "Which is why they've never really gotten along."

"He loves your daddy," Bessie whispered. "In his own way."

"I know," Cam said slowly, albeit not as slowly as his daddy would've. "I know."

Several seconds passed while the last of the floor got laid over the cords and the grass. "Well," Bessie said, not sure what else to say.

"What's going on here?" Oliver asked, his voice harsh and filled with that darkness that Bessie hadn't heard in a long time.

She dropped Cam's hand and turned toward the sound of his voice. "You're back." She stepped into him, but he was unyielding and stiff. She hugged him anyway and said, "I'm sorry I asked for help."

"Stop it," he said.

Bessie hated the tension radiating from him. She hated the defenses he'd erected.

"Floor's in, Brother," Cam said.

"What's wrong with Daddy?" he asked.

His brother simply smiled at him, clapped him on the shoulder, and said, "We'll see you tonight," before he exited the booth.

Oliver and Bessie watched him go, and Bessie had no idea what to do or say next. He glanced down at her, so many knives in his expression. "You two looked cozy."

"Just worried about you," she said, deciding she didn't need to defend herself. He could think whatever he wanted, and when he wasn't in such a heightened emotional state, he'd realize what he'd said and feel bad about it.

"What else can I help you with?" she asked, surveying his booth. "I have more help than I anticipated, so I'm pretty much ready, and I want my partner to be ready too."

Her partner. That word could mean so many different things, and she'd been hoping he'd be a life-long partner with her. A romantic partner. A trusted best friend she could say anything to, who she could vent to after a hard day of baking, the one who would listen to him when he had something on his mind.

She looked up to him, finding the defiance openly on his

face. "You have helped me so much," she said. "If there's something I can do to help you, I would. I absolutely would."

"I hate that I need help."

She smiled at him, finally finding the root of his distress. "I know, baby." She touched her lips to his cheek. "But everyone needs help from time to time, and it doesn't make you weak."

His jaw jumped as he clenched his teeth, and he nodded. "Then I'd love it if you'd help me figure out who to keep here and who to send back to my shop. Nicole called, and we've had some people say they can't make it to work today."

"Of course," Bessie said quietly. "Where's your list?" She knew he'd have one, and Oliver didn't disappoint. He spread it out on the freezer, and they leaned over it together.

Bessie cuddled in close to him, because she could, and he rewarded her by putting one arm around her waist and tucking her against his side as he said, "I lost three people at the shop, and I'm seriously considering sending over Leo, because he can do the work of two people..."

BY THE TIME SIX O'CLOCK CAME, BESSIE WANTED to cry. Today had been six and a half hours on her feet, smiling, talking to strangers, and managing people and product. Tomorrow would be twelve hours of festival, and there was no way she could do it.

Absolutely no way. Wyn likewise looked thrashed, and thankfully, all they had to do was stack their baskets, re-box the honey and jam that hadn't sold, and put butter in a cooler.

"Hey, hey," Grant called as he approached the booth with an industrial-looking wagon. "How'd it go today?" He grinned like they'd surely been partying all day, and Bea was the first to notice that everything wasn't happy-happy.

"Good," Bessie managed to say. "I sold everything but two loaves of bread." The whole wheat would keep until tomorrow. Hillie had been baking all day today, so they'd have product for tomorrow. She'd been planning to go into the bakery and do a few things, but now she wasn't sure if she could.

Maybe she'd just head home and fall into bed, then go into the bakery at three in the morning the way she usually did. The decision fatigue hit her hard in that moment, and as Bea put a Styrofoam container of food on the table in front of her, Bessie's eyes filled with tears.

"Go eat," Bea said. "Grant and I will get this loaded up for you."

"Thank you." Bessie didn't try to hide the pinch in her voice, and neither Bea nor Grant acknowledged it. Grant moved over and took an identical container of food to Oliver, and before she knew it, he'd joined her.

"We have good friends," she said.

"Yes, we do." He sighed as he sat down next to her. "I was not my best self today."

"I feel like sobbing." Her bottom lip trembled as she

318

flipped open the lid on her container. Hawaiian barbecue chicken waited for her, with creamy macaroni salad and a delicious-looking pile of sticky white rice.

Oliver drew her into his chest and his voice rumbled in her ears as he said, "You can cry as much as you want, sunshine."

Bessie's thoughts, which had been zipping all day, solidified. She'd wondered about her relationship with Oliver, and if she could handle the mood swings, the multiple personalities, and the pressure of always knowing exactly what to say and do.

She couldn't do that, she knew. Joy had gotten out of a marriage like that, and Bessie had seen her come back to life.

But when Oliver shielded her from the world and provided such a safe place for her, she couldn't help sliding down that slippery slope toward being in love with him.

She sniffled and pulled out of his embrace. "Are you always going to oscillate who you are when you're around your family?"

Oliver's eyes harbored dark storms. "I don't know," he said.

"What don't you know?"

"Bess." He forked up a bite of his mac salad. "I'm tired."

"You know the answer to this question," she said quietly. "I would like to know it too."

"Why?"

"Because then I can decide if I should keep seeing you or not." The words just flew from her mouth, and Bessie didn't know where they'd come from. She wiped her hand across her forehead, moving her bangs out of the way. She almost felt feverish, as the evening heat wouldn't abate until very early in the morning. Even then, it wouldn't be what Bessie considered cool.

She couldn't look at Oliver, but she knew his body language intimately. He held very still, and the weight of his gaze on the side of her face felt like a couple of tons. "Bess," he said again, this time with disbelief and tenderness.

Bessie didn't want to break-up with him, but he had to understand. "Oliver." Her voice broke, and she knew she shouldn't have this conversation with him while they were both in such a state of exhaustion. Or maybe it was the perfect time to get everything out.

She mixed up a bite of chicken and rice and held it in front of her. Then she looked at Oliver. "I'm falling in love with you," she said. "But in the past couple of days, you've been at least two people I don't know. I don't know how to reconcile that with the kind, handsome, sweet, hardworking man who says, 'Bess,' with that level of emotion in his voice. You've confused me."

To her surprise, he nodded softly. "I know I have."

She didn't want to push him, but she suspected she was the only one who could. "I just want you to answer the question."

"I don't know who I am with them," he whispered. "That's why I act the way I do. Because it's a guessing game for me, and I don't know who I am."

Her heart ached for him, because what a hard thing to

admit. What a hard life to live, to be forty-six years old and not know who you are.

She covered his hand with hers and let her fork drop back to her food, though she desperately needed to eat. "There's the man I really like," she said with a smile. She layered her fingers between his and looked at them, liking how they fit, how they were so different, and yet called the same thing.

"I'm falling for you too, sunshine," he whispered. "I will figure things out, I promise."

She tilted her head up toward his, and he ducked down to create a private pocket for the two of them to look at one another. "I don't want to break-up with you."

"I think I would die if you did."

She nudged him with her elbow. "You would not."

"I would be terribly unhappy." He trailed his lips down the side of her face. "I'm sorry, sunshine. I just need...time to figure things out."

"Your daddy is sick," she whispered as he touched his mouth to her ear. "Cam told me this morning, but I don't have any other details."

He lifted his head. "They're going to meet me at my house in a little bit." He swallowed, and Bessie saw every ounce of vulnerability inside him, and she loved him for it.

"Would you like me to come?" she asked.

Oliver cleared his throat, swallowed, and then cleared his throat again. Oh, she'd done something to unsettle him completely. She grinned up at him. "What did I say?"

"You offered to stand beside me," he said gruffly.

All at once, she realized that Oliver had been a solitary captain in the stormy seas of life for a long time. Sure, he had employees, an assistant manager, even friends. But he wasn't used to working with another person, a partner.

"I wish I could have today as a do-over," he said with a sigh, his emotion contained again.

"I don't," she whispered. "I've learned a lot today. About myself, about this festival, about my bread bakery." She met his eye again and added, "About you." She touched her lips to his for a fraction of a second. "I know you don't want me there tonight, but I'm glad you know I would be there if you did."

"It's not about want," he said with that rugged, raw edge in his voice. "With you, there's nothing I don't want."

Heat filled Bessie, which wasn't all that welcome due to the weather heat-waving around them. "Then it's about you feeling weak if you need me there?"

"It's about me wanting to make sure I don't confuse you any further." He took another bite of his dinner, and Bessie picked up her fork and did the same. They ate with people streaming past them to the concert in the park that night, the silence between them...absolutely perfect.

Chapter Twenty-Eight

*S*age carried a blanket her sister had made out of the old
jeans she'd collected at various yard sales around the
Coastal Bend of Texas. That side went down on the ground,
as denim was sturdier than the thinner fabric on the topside
of the blanket.

A vibrancy buzzed in the air, and Sage drank it all in.
She'd come to the park alone tonight, without telling anyone
except for Thelma. Her Supper Club friends wouldn't text
her sister to find out where Sage was, because they didn't
have plans to get together that evening.

Bessie had been working in her booth all day, and Bea
was taking her dinner. Cass had helped her set up that morning. Lauren would tomorrow, and Thelma on Sunday, and
Sage had volunteered to take lunch tomorrow and help
Bessie break-down her booth on Sunday evening. They'd
honestly all show up then—except for Joy, who was off on
her honeymoon with Scott.

And tonight... Tonight was hers, and she'd been texting with someone else entirely.

Tyler Parker.

They'd agreed to meet at the park, and Sage didn't count meeting someone somewhere as a date. "You can call it what you want," she said to herself with a smile. She'd fallen in front of Ty on the beach a couple of weeks ago. He'd come in to get his hair cut, and then, nothing.

So when he'd texted yesterday to ask her if she'd ever attended the Heritage Festival, their messages had flown back and forth for a while until they'd settled on meeting for the concert in the park.

Sage reasoned it was a fairly safe first meeting, because with the loud music and the big crowd, they couldn't talk too much or be too intimate. She'd still gone shopping for a new outfit, and she wore a pair of dark purple shorts and a cream-colored blouse with smudges of flowers in blue, violet, and pink.

She felt twenty years younger for some reason, and she arrived at the appointed meeting place. Ty wasn't there yet, but Sage didn't panic. He'd said there would be two gates to get into the grassy area where people set up chairs and blankets for the concert. One on the east and one on the west, and they'd agreed to meet at the east gate.

Behind her, a row of food trucks lined the grass, and each one had a line of people waiting to order and others milling about to get their food. The sun had started to set, but plenty of light still hung in the sky, and it wouldn't be cold tonight.

Sage smiled at the passersby, starting to get a tad nervous. She didn't want to pull out her phone and check to see if he'd canceled on her, but she was sure she'd arrived right on time, and that meant Ty was late.

He'd admitted that he ran late to almost everything, and after another breath of debate, she pulled out her phone. "Oh." She wasn't late. Or even on time.

She was early.

"Hey," Ty said in the next moment, and Sage dropped her phone. He laughed as he bent his tall frame to retrieve it, and he looked at it as he handed it back. "I'm not late." He lifted his light hazel eyes to meet hers, and Sage felt the weight of what he'd said way down in her gut.

"Thank you," she murmured, her fingers barely brushing his as she took her phone back. She took a breath, blinked, and then grinned at him.

He smiled back, and they said at the exact same time, "You look nice." A beat of silence hovered between them, and then they laughed together. He wore a pair of khaki shorts that fell all the way to his knee. He'd paired those with a pair of name-brand sneakers and a T-shirt that boasted the South Carolina flag on the front of it.

"Should we find a spot?" He turned toward the grassy area. "Or do you want to get food first?"

"I believe you promised me three things," she said, and he swung his attention back to her.

His blond eyebrows rose, and his hair grew so dang fast he needed another trim already. She loved touching his sandy locks, and she'd even leaned into those broad shoulders on purpose during his last haircut.

"I did?" he asked.

Sage found she sure did like flirting with him. "Yes, sir," she drawled out. "You said we could get dinner here." She lifted one finger to indicate his first promise. "You said the concert would be amazing." Two fingers. "And you said you'd tell me about this particular band—and your involvement with them."

His eyes crinkled as he smiled and chuckled again. "I suppose you're right. I did say all of that." He scanned the row of food trucks. "Food first, then." He carried a couple of stadium chairs, and he reached for her hand. "Is this okay?"

Sage watched her own hand slide into his, and she swore she could see the sparks come to life as they flowed from her wrist, up her arm to her elbow, and then down her back and up to her shoulder.

"Yes," she said, lifting her eyes to his. "You also said you'd tell me how old you are tonight."

"You do seem stuck on that." He flashed her a smile. "Is it going to break the date before it starts?"

"You're holding my hand," Sage said. "I think it's already started."

He squinted like he couldn't see the two or three food trucks closest to him. "I'm fifty-two," he finally said. He cut a look out of the corner of his eye. "I know better than to ask you, but you've sort of made it this sticking point, so."

Ty handled himself with poise and class, and Sage sure

did like that. "I'm forty-nine," she said, relieved to hear he was older than her. "I'll be fifty in February."

He lifted her hand to his lips, his smile blooming and growing right in front of her. "I hope I'm there for the big celebration."

"How do you know I'll have a big celebration?" she teased as they moved past the fried chicken truck to a Mexican one serving burritos and taco salads and churros.

Ty laughed again, actually tipping his head back and sending the sound into the sky. "Because I know your friends. You guys don't even go to the beach without making it a huge event."

She couldn't argue with that, but she said, "I'm a spectator in a lot of those things. It's mostly Bea and Cass who organize everything."

"Hmm," he said and nothing more. "What are you feeling like for dinner?"

"Something I can hold on my lap and eat," she said. "Maybe a sandwich? Chips?" She peered down the row too. "There's a deli—Franklin's?" She looked at him. "Good or no good?"

"They're good," he said, and he took her that way to join the line. "Tell me what you'd get here. Favorite flavor of chips?"

Sage hadn't dated in a long time, and she'd forgotten that they had to start with basic questions. Her throat closed when she realized she'd have to tell him about her previous marriage, her three kids, why she lived with her sister, and literally almost fifty years of her as a person.

She suddenly got overwhelmed, and she shifted the blanket in her hands. That caused her to release his, and her heart pounded at her to end this date—or whatever this was. "Uh," she scanned the menu. "Well, I'm normally a turkey and avocado kind of gal."

"I like roast beef and pastrami."

Sage flashed a smile. "Either plain chips or salt and vinegar."

Ty chuckled. "I like barbecue or those cheddar ones made out of popcorn."

Sage made a face. "No one should eat those. I'm not even sure how they stay in business."

"Probably because I eat a bag every day." He chuckled again, and Sage did like the sound of it. She told herself to calm down. She didn't have to tell him everything today, and she wouldn't learn everything about him in one evening either.

Still, as she looked around and saw couples half her and Ty's age, she couldn't help wondering what she was doing here. They got their sandwiches, and Ty led her to the side of the grassy area where only people sat on blankets, and he spread out her blanket and unfolded the stadium chairs.

She felt like a beached whale as she got down on the ground, immediately regretting not bring a regular chair to sit in like a normal almost-fifty-year-old. At least she had a back to lean against. Again, everyone around them wore shorts that barely covered their behinds, and lots of makeup, and couldn't even be graduated from high school.

Ty didn't seem to notice the discrepancies between them

and those around them as he settled gracefully onto his stadium seat and handed out their sandwiches.

"So, the lead singer was my roommate in college," he said, nodding up to the stage. At least she had a good view of it, and if she went into a panic again, she could focus on the music. It hadn't started yet, but she had food to distract her from her thoughts right now.

"Wow," she said. "I didn't know you needed a college degree to be in a rock band."

"Or a realtor," he said with a smile. He unwrapped his sandwich and added, "I dropped out after a couple of years. Collin did too. He joined a band. I joined a real estate firm."

"And here you are now," she said. "Both on Hilton Head Island." She took a bite of her turkey, provolone, and avocado. The creamy mayo mixed with mustard, and there wasn't anything as good as turkey and mustard. At least in Sage's mind.

"Did you grow up here?" she asked after she swallowed.

He shook his head and wiped his mouth with a napkin. "No," he said. "But in Charleston. I moved here when I determined there was a good market here that was being underserved."

"How long ago was that?"

"Oh, twenty years?" He seemed to be calculating in his head. "Yeah, twenty-one years ago now. Wow. I didn't realize it had been that long." He smiled at her again, and that gesture sent a shockwave through her.

They definitely had chemistry, or at least something

fizzing between them. But as Sage continued to talk to him, she couldn't find one thing they had in common.

The concert started, and that stalled the conversation. He pointed out Collin, though he wasn't hard to notice, what with his black, ripped skinny jeans and the spotlight shining right on him.

When they started to play, the crowd surged and screamed, and because Sage did like pop rock, she enjoyed the song. Ty seemed to as well, and she reasoned that they finally had one thing in common—the pop rock band Death Wish.

That was something...right?

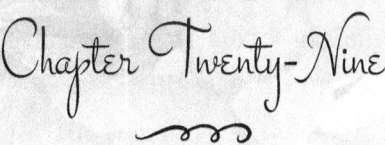

Chapter Twenty-Nine

Oliver pulled into his carport and sighed. He'd lingered too long at the festival, and his daddy's old, well-cared-for red truck already sat in the driveway. He smelled like oranges and strawberries, and he wanted nothing more than a hot shower.

"And Bessie," he murmured. He'd never been in love before, but he'd watched other people make the fall. He knew how he felt, and he knew what he needed to do to make sure they operated on solid ground.

He glanced to the door that led into his kitchen. He had to face his past. Face his daddy. Become his own man inside his family.

"No more running," he told himself. "No more avoidance." It didn't solve anything, and the hollow pit it left behind inside him had been consuming him a bite at a time.

He got out of his SUV and went up the steps to the

door. Oliver walked right through it, calling, "Sorry I'm so late. I wanted to eat with Bessie."

He found his father lounging on his couch, the TV flickering in front of him. Cam rose from the recliner where Oliver sat on the rare occasion he actually used his living room furniture. "Did y'all eat?" he asked.

"We got burgers, yeah." Cam came into the kitchen, pure anxiety radiating from his eyes. Oliver didn't wait for his younger brother to grab onto him. He initiated the embrace, and he held Cam right against his chest.

"I'm so sorry I've been so absent for so long," he said. An apology didn't fix thirty years of absence, but Oliver couldn't go back in time. He had no do-overs to play here. "I've put the burden all on you, and I regret that."

"Don't," Cam said, but the word didn't bark through Oliver's ears. It was a soft-spoken rebuke that his apology wasn't needed. Cam gripped him tightly and didn't let go, so Oliver held very still. "I love my life in Birmingham, at the store. You didn't. You're doing what you were meant to do, and so am I."

He stepped back then and nodded that strong Blackhurst jaw at Oliver. "Okay? Me and you? We're good."

Oliver's tongue sat heavily and thickly in his mouth, so he just nodded too. His eyes wandered to Daddy, who hadn't moved.

"He's sleeping," Cam said, turning to face the living room too. "He's the most stubborn man alive, Ollie." He chuckled and shook his head. "I thought you might give him a run for his money, but nope."

"What's...Bessie said he was sick."

"Yeah." A sigh fell from Cam's mouth. "He's got an ulcer in his esophagus. He can treat it and get it to recede and heal up, and then it comes back. He loves his fried fish and milkshakes." He gazed sadly at their father. "But, I keep tellin' myself that he's his own man. He gets to make his own decisions."

Oliver put the pieces together quickly. "So he won't alter his diet."

"That he will not," Cam drawled. He shrugged a shoulder a moment later. "I guess that's not really fair. He does change what he eats every once in a while, but he can't commit to it long-term."

"Is it fatal?"

"Could be," Cam said. "Just like us loading up in a few days and driving home could be fatal."

Oliver started to relax. "Does he cough up blood?"

"Right now, yep."

He faced his brother, who didn't immediately turn to him. "That's why you hustle him away from me every time he starts coughing."

Cam gave him a sympathetic smile. "He didn't want to tell you at all. Says you've got a life here and he doesn't want to interrupt it."

"That's just stupid," Oliver said. "My life is with his life." As he spoke, his heart rang with truthfulness. "Cam, if he needs me, I want to be there."

His younger brother hung his head. "Neither of us know how to ask you to do that," he said. He looked up, something fierce entering his eyes. Cam never wore this look, as he was a happy-go-lucky teddy bear of a man. No one would ever call him a grump or glare him into silence. He existed on the opposite end of the spectrum than Oliver, and for the first time, Oliver didn't feel like he didn't belong because of it.

"I have people here who can take over for me," Oliver said. "I'm not essential. If you called me right now and told me Daddy needed me, I'd be there as fast as I could."

"I know that. I've told him that."

"So he doesn't believe it." Oliver's heart sunk to the soles of his feet. "I did abandon him and Momma years ago."

"I was so jealous," Cam said. "I wanted to do the same thing you'd done and leave Birmingham."

Oliver couldn't believe what he'd just heard. "You did?"

"I thought you were so brave," he said with another light sigh. "Daddy was already working me at the furniture store, and there you were, blazing your own way."

"I thought everyone thought I'd abandoned them."

"I did, sometimes," Cam said. "But I didn't blame you for it."

"Daddy did."

"Daddy had a vision for how things would go, and he didn't count on a mini-him blowing that up." He shook his head again and turned back to the kitchen. "I will take something to drink."

"I've got all sorts of stuff." He watched as Cam went to the fridge and introduced the light into the darkening kitchen. He pulled out a bottle of something and rejoined Oliver. "You're happy now, right, Cam?"

"Yeah," he said. "I love the store, my life, the city, my wife and family." He brightened as he spoke. "I really do, Ollie. You don't need to worry about me."

"Daddy's still goin' in everyday, isn't he?" Oliver heard the Alabaman twang in his own voice, and he didn't like it. Baby steps, he supposed.

"Every day," Cam confirmed. "He says he doesn't have much to do at home. Sometimes it's only an hour or two, but he sits behind that desk and puts his feet up and bosses everyone around." He grinned like this was great, and Oliver could just picture his daddy doing that. He could still see the office on the second floor of the furniture store in his mind's eye, clear as day.

He could see the whole store from that vantage point, and Oliver had never been able to sneak around with his friends in the furniture store. Back then, Daddy had been all-seeing. All-knowing.

"He's always been a god to me," Oliver said. "I guess I wanted to become that for myself, and I knew I couldn't do it in his presence."

"Yep," Cam said. "That sounds about right." He blew out his breath. "So. Day one at the festival. How did it go? Did you make things right with Bessie?"

"I think so," Oliver said. "I've got a long way to go to deserve her."

"Nah," Cam said. "She loves you already."

"No, she doesn't." Oliver shook his head, instantly frustrated. "Don't say stuff like that." He turned into his brother and hugged him. "I'll sit with him for a few minutes if you want a break."

"You have a twelve-hour shift in your booth tomorrow," Cam argued. "I'll get him outta your hair."

Oliver wanted to stop him from doing that, but he followed behind him as they went into the living room. "Daddy," Cam said as he leaned over him. Oliver sat down next to his father, and the motion jostled him awake, at least a little.

"Daddy," Oliver said. His father's eyes opened all the way, and he focused on Oliver.

"I didn't mean to fall asleep, Ollie."

"It's fine," Oliver said in a quiet voice. He had so many things to say, each word tumbling over the one in front of it. He wanted to say he'd come take over the store anytime, any day of the week, no matter what. He wanted to rage at his daddy for not telling him he wasn't all the way well. He wanted to fold him into a hug and hold on tight, never to let go.

Instead of doing any of that, he said, "I love you."

Daddy's whole demeanor changed, and he was the one to pull Oliver into the hold-tight hug as he said, "I love you too."

Oliver hadn't known how healing those words from his father would be until they'd been uttered. He pressed his eyes closed and captured that moment in his mind, heart, and soul, because he needed to know his daddy loved him.

His heart stitched itself together, and he finally felt like he could use his most vital organ to love someone else. To love himself.

Now, he just needed to figure out his place in his family and how to keep Bessie in his life long enough to show her how prepared he was to love her for the rest of her life.

OLIVER DIDN'T WANT TO SAY GOOD-BYE TO BESSIE in a text, but he couldn't find another way to do it. His pulse pounded behind his eyes as his daddy drove west again, back to Alabama. Oliver had never skipped out on the Heritage Festival, but he'd spent an hour on the phone with Leo last night after his family had left.

He knew it was the right thing to do. He'd miss the fireworks in the park tonight, and he'd been looking forward to enjoying them for once—with Bessie at his side. He hardly recognized himself anymore, and he hoped that was a good thing for his relationship with her.

Hey, sunshine, he texted once the clock struck nine. She'd be arriving at their booths right now, and he'd wanted her to sleep as much as possible this morning, then go about her day as if nothing with him had changed.

I'm currently riding in my daddy's truck as he drives us toward Birmingham. He's got an off-again, on-again esophageal ulcer that's acting up right now, and he needs me for a few days.

I wish I could be there to talk this all through with you, and I hate that I'm not there to help you through the busiest day at the Festival.

He looked up, his eyes having a hard time adjusting from the stillness of his screen to the moving roadway beyond his window. He'd insisted Cam ride up front while he took the backseat, and his stomach wasn't very happy about it.

I miss you already, and I've asked Grant, Harry, Blake, Scott, and Ty to be there for you if you need it today. Please don't work all day. I'll call you tonight if you tell me what time is good for you.

He didn't want to tell her he loved her through a text. He absolutely would not do that. When he said that to a woman for the first time in his life, he wanted to hold her in his arms, gaze into those perfectly blue eyes, and watch how her face lit up.

At least he hoped Bessie's face would light up when he told her he loved her.

He re-read his text, deemed it worthy, and hit send.

Chapter Thirty

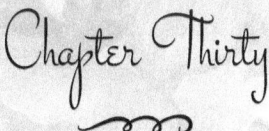

Bessie wandered away from her booth, as she had plenty of help this morning to set it up. Only Oliver was missing, and she'd just gotten a text from him that explained why. She tilted her head back and rolled it back and forth, feeling the pull and stretch in her neck.

She knew nothing about esophageal ulcers—or ulcers in general—just like she didn't know how to comfort Oliver. Or assure him that she'd be fine here. Or tell him that he was the sweetest man in the world for arranging with all of his friends to be there to help her today.

Wyn was going to take the first shift in the booth today, and Bessie would be leaving before the festival opened in just under an hour. She'd slept until six-thirty this morning, and she couldn't help running over to the shop to make sure Hillie had everything she needed to bake all day today.

She'd done a huge batch of the salted honey whole wheat

bread, because she'd had time. She simply wouldn't tell Oliver about that. He'd told her not to go in and bake on her day off, to enjoy sleeping in, but what he didn't understand was that she couldn't sleep in. Even on her days off, she was up by six-thirty at the latest. So she had slept as late as she usually did.

The sky above her shimmered with a blue that reminded her of Oliver, though he was normally dark and stormy from head to toe. A smile creased her face, and she knew exactly what to send to him in response.

I'm so glad you talked to your daddy. You are a good son, and I can't wait to kiss your face when you get back. We can have a do-over on the fireworks and the festival next year.

She sent the message, then turned back to her booth. Harry and Grant wrestled with the corner shade again this morning, while Bea, Lauren, and Wyn worked on setting out the baskets and labels for her bread loaves.

Joy and Scott were still on their honeymoon, and Bessie wasn't surprised at all to get a text from Joy before she made it back to her booth. *Heard about Oliver going to Alabama. Wish we were there to help!*

Nonsense, Bessie said back. *Enjoy the mountains!*

She moved into the booth and slid her hand along her daughter's waist. "I'm going to go take a nap," she said to Wyn, who turned toward her and smiled.

"Great. I'll see you about...three?"

Bessie nodded, the air already hot and still and muggy. "I'll see you then." She quickly went around the booth, thanking her friends and employees for their help.

"Of course," Cass said as she wheeled up a cart full of trays holding loaves of bread. "Now, go." She grinned at Bessie good-naturedly, and Bessie followed her friend's advice.

She went home. She tapped on her heating pad and sank into the soft mattress and the increasing warmth. She swiped on her phone a few times, trying to let her eyelids grow heavier and heavier. A text from Oliver came in, and she smiled before she'd even pulled it down from the top of the screen to read it.

Kiss your face, he'd said. *LOL.*

Getting a laugh from Oliver took a lot, and Bessie let her phone drop to her chest, where she pressed it right over her heart. Then she fell asleep as easily as sinking into a warm bath.

WEDNESDAY MORNING DAWNED BRIGHT AND EARLY for Bessie, as Sage had asked her to go walking with her for the past few days. Apparently, she had a neighbor she usually walked with, but Ed had become jealous after Sage had gone on a date with Ty.

Bessie smiled as she pulled into the parking lot at Sage's apartment building, because Sage hadn't told anyone about the date. In fact, Bessie was the only one in the Supper Club who knew, even now.

Sage had wanted to avoid Ed for a few days, and they'd talked about everything under the sun for the past two mornings—except Ty.

"I'm getting her to talk about him today," Bessie vowed to herself as she collected her phone and got out of the car. She spritzed sunscreen up and down her arms, as the summer sun was already up, because she wouldn't go walking at five-thirty in the morning on her day off. Sage had settled for six-thirty, and she claimed that had worked out for her, because Ed had to go to work early and couldn't wait to walk that late.

Bessie didn't have a dog to bring with her, but Sage met her with Gypsy at the edge of the sidewalk, and they grinned at one another. "Morning, Bessie."

"Hey, Sage." She bent down and patted her big black canine. "Look at you with a bow in your hair. You're so pretty." Gypsy grinned up at her, his giant tail whapping the ground where he sat.

Bessie straightened and stepped into Sage. "I have to go back to the bakery tomorrow."

"I know," Sage said, throwing a look down the sidewalk to another building. "But I think Ed has gotten the hint."

"I thought you liked having a walking partner."

"I do." She stepped off the cement and onto the sand, and Bessie went with her.

Bessie decided to go all-in. "Why don't you ask Ty to go with you? You guys met on the beach. You know he runs here."

"Yeah, he *runs*." Sage shook her head, though her countenance stayed sunny and bright. "I could ask him, and he'd probably slow his pace to a walk for me."

"I'm sure he would," Bessie said with a smile aimed at the sand.

"I don't know." Sage blew out her breath. "The date was fine. Fun, even. But it feels like..." She slowed and said, "Can you go on the other side? Gypsy walks on the left."

"Sure." Bessie made the move and looked expectantly at Sage.

She didn't normally squirm under pressure, but she shot a squinty-eyed look at Bessie. "It felt like we didn't have anything in common but the band."

Bessie wasn't sure what she'd been expecting, but it wasn't that. She took a few seconds and steps to form a response. "Surely you didn't learn everything about him in one date. At a concert."

"No," Sage admitted. "But I'm just not sure I want a second date."

"Has he asked?"

"No." Sage's smile fell completely then, and Bessie gave her the space she always wished her friends would give her. She looked down the beach, enjoying the golden rays, the golden sand, and the golden way she felt so...goldenly good about herself.

"Maybe you ask him," she suggested.

Sage didn't shake her head, but she didn't agree with Bessie either. "I'm just going to wait and see. The man is very busy, and we just went out a few nights ago." Sage looked over to her. "What about Oliver? Is he coming back today?"

Bessie didn't want to talk about Oliver, but she also wasn't with the whole group. "No," she said. "He's decided to stay through the weekend, at least. Then he'll have to fly back, and I'm going to pick him up at the airport."

Sage smiled. "Things are going well with him, aren't they?"

"I thought so," Bessie said.

"They're not?"

"He's...been distant while he's been in Birmingham." Bessie hated sounding so whiny. "I know he's dealing with a lot, and I'm trying not to bother him, but we've actually only talked once. Everything else is a text."

And not very many of those. Bessie had kept her shop closed on Monday following the festival too, and her first day back for the three a.m. bread bakery arrivals started tomorrow. She wasn't dreading it, but she sure had enjoyed getting up later, working around the house, and relaxing on the beach for these past few days—even if Oliver hadn't been with her.

She also wasn't sure what that said about their relationship if she could enjoy herself so fully without him. Doubt threaded through her, and Bessie couldn't get it to leave no matter what she did.

The conversation shifted to Cass and Harry's trip to Jerusalem and when they'd be leaving, Joy and Scott's honeymoon and when they'd be back, and Bea and Grant's daughter and when she'd be moving in.

It felt like everyone had a lot of changes looming on the horizon, but Bessie was stuck.

As she and Sage returned to the cement sidewalk in

between the buildings, she asked, "What do you think I should do about Oliver?"

"Do about him?" Sage tugged on Gypsy's leash to get him to stop. "What does that mean?"

"Should I go to Birmingham and I don't know, offer support? Just show up with lunch or something? I'd like that if I was dealing with something stressful with my momma or daddy." She looked at Sage with wide eyes, needing an answer to this.

Sage searched her face, and Bessie just wanted someone to tell her what to do. The number of decisions she made each day exhausted her, and she hadn't even been baking for the past three days.

"It sounds like you want to go to Birmingham and offer him some support," Sage said slowly. "And you're not getting the communication you want, so you're worried."

"I am, yes," she said. "A little." Not a lot. She trusted Oliver. She just didn't want him to be alone and suffering when she could be there to hold him up. A little. For Bessie could only do a little, and it had been Oliver supporting her this summer.

"Can you leave the bakery?" Sage asked.

"Probably," Bessie said.

"Can you afford to go?"

"It's a six-hour drive," Bessie said.

Sage's face bloomed into a smile. "Then go, Bessie. It's obvious you want to."

She did, and yet, at the same time, she didn't. She hated

these internal battles, because they were with herself, and she always felt like she was going to lose.

Sage drew her into a hug, and Bessie held on tight. "Thanks for walking with me," Sage said.

"Of course." Bessie squeezed her shoulders. "Love you, Sage."

"Love you too, Bessie." They separated, and Bessie drove home. She packed a bag. She got out her phone to text Wyn.

Everything halted.

"There is no way you can go to Birmingham," she said aloud to herself. "You don't even know where he'll be."

Blackhurst Furniture.

That couldn't be too hard to find, could it? A quick search on her phone had the store sitting on her screen in less than a second.

She dropped her phone. She unpacked her bag. She walked the length of her bed, thinking only of Oliver and how he paced in his small office at The Mad Mango.

Running one hand down the back of her neck, she groaned. "What should I do?" She wasn't even sure why she felt like she should go to Alabama. Oliver could be short and terse over text, but when she'd spoken to him on Sunday night, he'd been in good spirits.

"That was three days ago," she said, and that got her repacking her bag. She threw in her phone charger, and instead of slowing down to text Wyn, she rushed out of the house, intending to call her once she left Hilton Head Island.

After all, she was too old to ignore feelings and promptings like this, and she had the very real inclination that Oliver needed her in Birmingham more than Wyn needed her at Flour Power.

Chapter Thirty-One

O liver fitted in another file and pushed the overly-full drawer closed. As he surveyed his daddy's office—Cam's office—at the furniture store, it didn't even look like Oliver had put away a four-drawer filing cabinet's worth of files.

He sighed and sank into the rolling office chair. It probably cost seventy-five bucks at the most, and Oliver didn't understand why they didn't pull one of the good ones off the floor, at least for their own comfort.

The only way he'd been able to get his father to stay home and rest, as well as set some doctor's appointments, was to come to Birmingham and "help out" at the store for a little bit. He and Cam had agreed to tell their daddy that Oliver was consulting with Cam at the store, and therefore, he didn't need to come in.

Thankfully, that had worked. Cam did put in a lot of

hours here at the store, but it was a full-time job to get the office cleaned up, and two to run the furniture store. So Oliver didn't fault Cam for the state of the office, but he didn't have to be happy about it.

He also couldn't sit in this chair for another moment. Oliver got to his feet and hauled the awkwardly-shaped item out of the office and around the corner. Outside, the Alabama heat reminded him of the Hilton Head heat, but he still managed to toss the horrendous chair up over the lip of the Dumpster.

"That thing is heinous," he muttered to himself. He walked through the ugly back area of the furniture store, which looked like a cross between a couch graveyard, a recycling center for cardboard boxes, and worn out Berber carpet.

Out in the front of the store, everything brightened. The displays had been arranged just-so, and the carpets out here got cleaned and replaced often.

He navigated through the living room area, then the bedroom section, to get to the office supply department. A long row of office chairs stood in a line, and Oliver marched all the way to the end of it.

The most expensive one was usually the best one, and Oliver didn't have time to do any research on his phone about the chairs. He simply picked up the last one in the row and started carrying it back to the office. No matter what, it would be better than the thing of plastic and mesh he'd just thrown away.

He'd only been in Birmingham, at the store, for four days, but he'd learned so much about himself as a businessman. Mostly that he was really, really good at what he did at The Mad Mango. He'd taken his failures and learned from them, and he could do some real good here at Blackhurst Furniture.

He wouldn't stay, though. Oliver loved the barrier island off the coast of South Carolina, and he'd dedicated his whole career—all of his successes and failures—to The Mad Mango. It was the business he'd built with his own blood, sweat, and tears, and he wasn't going to leave it all behind to step on Cam's toes.

Back in the office, he sighed as he sat down. "Oh, yeah," he said. "That's so much better." He looked at the various folders and papers and fabric scraps still on the desk. He wondered what would happen if he used both arms to sweep it all to the floor. It would get all messed up, scattered, and he wondered if it would even matter.

When he'd lost his businesses in the past, he'd done just that, and it hadn't mattered.

"Hey," Cam said as he came into the office.

Oliver looked up at him. "You know this should all be in the computer, right?"

Cam blinked at the pages and papers on the desk. "Hey, I can see wood." He came closer and knocked on it. "And yeah, I've got Hollis putting everything in the computer. We're all digital now too."

Oliver sighed, and he didn't want to lecture Cam. He'd

done that enough already, and he really just wanted to dial Bessie and hear her sweet-as-buttermilk-pie voice. He'd hardly spoken to her since he'd texted her on Saturday morning, but he wasn't sure what they were supposed to talk about.

He got up early and made sure Daddy had his coffee. He chatted with the morning employees, went over boring things about furniture and sales and ordering in the newest patio sets with Cam, ordered lunch, checked on his father, and went through all the minute details that it took to run a big business.

It wasn't fun work. It wasn't sexy or exciting. He wasn't enjoying himself, and he didn't want to rehash it all again with Bessie. He wanted to meet up with her after work, smell the sugar and yeast in her hair, on her hands, and take her to the beach. That, or he'd been thinking about having her over to his place, where he'd order dinner and they'd eat on his back deck, the evening shadows bathing her beautiful face in golden sunlight.

Since he couldn't have that, he figured he'd spent his time working out who he was so he could return to Bessie as whole of a man as possible. That was who she wanted—a whole man who knew who he was inside his business, his personal life, his family, and with her.

So he put his head down, and he kept filing. He helped Hollis scan in old papers, and he left the store with Cam. They split in the parking lot, as Oliver was going back to his childhood home where his father still lived to pick up

Daddy. Then they'd head over to Cam's, where his wife was making dinner for everyone that evening.

Oliver had braced himself for the memories of returning to his childhood home. He had to do so every other year when he came to visit—except for last year, of course, when he'd canceled.

Still, every time he made the turn into the neighborhood, he remembered something new. That time he snuck out to meet his friends and go skateboarding on the bridge at midnight. Once, when he'd taken that corner on his bike going at least twenty miles per hour. He grinned at how flat he'd gotten. He'd totally won the race home too.

The old bushes that Daddy had planted close to the house were gone now. As Oliver pulled into the driveway, he could see the house changing over the past forty-six years of his life. He could see the trees and bushes and flowers come and go, the color of the pillars move from white to cream to gray and back to white.

Daddy had always taken care of the house, but Cam had disclosed that he'd finally gotten Daddy to hire a landscaper. Oliver was glad of that, because the last thing he or his brothers needed was their father going into a coughing fit and passing out while he mowed grass he didn't need to be mowing.

He pulled into the driveway, and for the first time he didn't feel like he'd been yoked to a workhorse. He didn't have to sit in his daddy's truck and work up the gumption to go inside. He simply got out of the truck and headed up the front steps.

"Daddy?" he called. "We're goin' to dinner at Cam's tonight, remember?" Yes, he heard the Southern twang in his own voice, and he didn't entirely hate it.

"I'm comin'," Daddy said from somewhere in the back of the house, and Oliver went past the foyer and the staircase that led up to the second floor his father hadn't used in years and years.

Oliver entered the living room at the back of the house just in time to see Daddy trying to push himself off the couch. He couldn't quite do it, and that was when Oliver saw how elderly his father had become.

He'd classified his father as "old" before, but this was something new. Daddy looked worn around the edges, sure. But weakness? Oliver had never thought of his father as weak.

He didn't ask his daddy if he needed help. He simply went over and offered his hand. Daddy put his in Oliver's, and their eyes met. "What's Cindy makin'?" he asked.

"I'm sure it'll be fried chicken," Oliver said. "Isn't she famous for that?" He knew she was, and Daddy smiled as he finally lumbered to his feet. He did have to rely on Oliver a lot, as his bicep and shoulder testified to.

"She sure is," he said. "We goin' now?"

"Cam said to come straight over if we could, yes," Oliver said.

"I just need to use the bathroom." Daddy hobbled down the hall to do that, and Oliver contemplated sending Bessie a quick text.

Dinner with my brother's family tonight. What are you doing?

She didn't answer right away, and Daddy returned faster than Oliver had anticipated he might. The drive to Cam's happened quickly, and then there were shouts and welcomes as Oliver and Daddy walked into the house.

"We're ready," Cindy said, and sure enough, the table sat set and waiting. "Kids, get in here! Uncle Oliver and Grampa are here!"

The back door opened and yelling ensued. Oliver grinned at Cam's oldest, a boy of twelve who loved to take an ATV out into the woods, climb trees, and catch lizards.

"Uncle Oliver, you have to come see this snake we caught."

"All caught snakes will be loosed before bedtime," his mother said, giving her oldest a piercing look. "Carlton, repeat back to me what I just said."

"I'll let 'im go before I go to bed."

"Good boy." She put a platter of fried okra on the table. "Marcia, wash up. Taylor, help Grampa to his chair."

The kids bustled around, doing what their mother asked, and Oliver loved the energy in their home. He'd never been too broken up about not having children, but when he watched Cam reach over Taylor's head to put a pitcher of sweet tea on the table, and then the two of them laugh about something, it did cause a pang of regret to gong loudly in his chest.

He knew exactly where he belonged here, though, and

that was to tell Marcia, "That shirt is amazing. Where did you get it?"

The ten-year-old loved clothes and fashion, and she said, "Mama bought it for me off this sewing show. It's so cute, right?"

"So cute," Oliver said as he took his seat.

"Sit down," Cindy called, and she was a blonde power-house that even Oliver would not dare go up against. He grinned at her as she set the fried chicken in front of him and then took her place next to him.

In the past, he'd have found himself "trapped" between his sister-in-law and his father, but tonight, he knew he was right where he was meant to be.

Even when Cindy said, "So, Oliver. Cam says you're getting the office all cleared up."

"Trying," he said as he took a piece of fried chicken and put it on Daddy's plate. He then loaded one onto his plate too, and he passed the platter on. "I'm just trying to show Cam a different system. Maybe one that won't have him drowning in paper."

"It's goin' great," Cam said. "Have you talked to Bessie? Is she ready to open back up tomorrow?"

All eyes came to him again, and Oliver squirmed a little.

"Bessie?" Cindy asked, glancing between her husband and Oliver. "This is your girlfriend?"

"Yes," Oliver said, giving Cindy a smile and then a more menacing look to his brother. "I know Cam's told you all about her."

"Maybe not all," they said together, and Cindy forked a bite of mashed potatoes into her mouth. "So who is she?"

If he'd known he had to talk about his relationship with Bessie that night, he'd have stayed back in his old bedroom. At the same time, he wasn't embarrassed of dating Bessie. He knew exactly who he was with her—or at least who he wanted to be.

"She owns this great bread bakery on the island," he said.

"They were paired up for the Heritage Festival," Cam said. "Remember I sent you the picture of their shared booth?"

"Oh, sure," Cindy said. "Is it serious?"

Cam's eyebrows went up too, and Oliver wondered how much of this was rehearsed.

"Yeah," he said at the exact same time Daddy did. "He's real serious with her," Daddy added while Oliver gaped at him.

"What?" He picked up the spoon for the okra and took a healthy serving. "You are."

"I know I am," Oliver said. "I guess I just...what made you think I was?"

Daddy very nearly rolled his eyes, but his voice was paternal and gruff as he said, "Just like I knew with Momma. She softens you, and you like it."

Oliver opened his mouth to say something, but he had no idea what. So he just ended up closing it again. Cam grinned, and Cindy sighed. "I think it's great," she said. "I can't wait to meet her."

"Do you think you'll ever bring her here?" Cam asked.

"Yeah," Oliver said slowly. "I think so." He popped a piece of okra into his mouth too. "I do need to be softened sometimes, and yeah, I like it when she does it."

Daddy chuckled, nodding as he did, and while Oliver had never seen the parallels between him and his father, they'd been becoming more evident.

His phone rang, and he pulled it from his pocket. "Oh, this is her," he said, his first inclination to swipe the call away. "I'll call her back later."

"No, no," Cindy said. "Answer it." Her attention got diverted to her younger son as he started arguing with his sister.

Oliver got to his feet and paced into the kitchen before answering Bessie's call. "Hey, sunshine. I'm eating dinner at Cam's tonight." He hoped that was code enough to let her know he couldn't talk for long.

"Oh, well, that explains it."

"Explains what?" As he thought of her, her voice echoing in his head, he realized he was nothing if he didn't have her. As a man, she completed him, and a sense of joy touched his soul. The words *I love you*, threatened to spill from his mouth, but he refused to let them out. Such things shouldn't be said over the phone.

Something sounded on her end of the line, and Oliver tilted his head trying to place the noise. "Where are you right now?"

"Funny you should ask," she said. "I just walked into the best furniture store in Birmingham. Some place called Black-hurst? Have you heard of it?"

He spun away from the sink, his heart pounding. He sucked at the air as he fell back into his chair. All eyes landed on him, and he told himself to speak as slowly as Daddy did. "Are you telling me you're in Birmingham right now?"

Cindy's face lit up like a Christmas tree, only rivaled by the hopeful brightness on her husband's face. And that told Oliver where Bessie fit in his family—and it was right at his side.

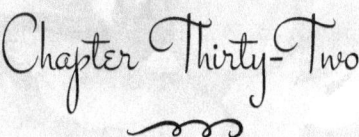

Chapter Thirty-Two

B essie couldn't believe what she was doing, where she was driving. Her palms felt slick with sweat, and yet her hands were icy cold. "It's okay," she said to herself, though she'd infused her voice with plenty of flirtatious vibes only fifteen minutes ago.

She didn't have to guess at which house was Oliver's brother's, because the man she'd driven all day to see sat on the front steps. Her heartbeat positively rioted behind her ribs, and she was eternally glad she had bones and skin to keep it contained.

As she made the slow turn into the driveway, he rose to his feet. She hadn't meant to interrupt his dinner, which he'd said he'd been in the middle of when she'd called. He didn't look too upset, and he somehow managed to walk the distance between the porch and her SUV before she could put it in park and open her door.

He opened the door, and Bessie dutifully rose from the

car. She hadn't grabbed her bag or anything. Her stomach swooped and growled all at the same time, but she managed to meet his eyes. "You're eating dinner early," she said.

She'd hoped to make it to Birmingham before he'd left the furniture store, so they could go to dinner.

"My sister-in-law," he said before he trailed off. He reached out and brushed her fingers with his.

"You went silent," she said, looking down at where their hands connected.

"Not because of you and me," he whispered.

"Then why?"

"Just—" He blew out his breath. "There's nothing going on here. Boring stuff. I can barely make it through the day living it once, so recounting it again with you...I couldn't do it."

"No?" She looked up at him, nearly swooning at his dark good looks. "You think I only want the highlights? The good stuff?"

Oliver's face turned blank, and he clearly hadn't been thinking that.

"Oliver," she said, moving her hands to his chest and leaning into him. "With you, I want it all. The good stuff. The highs. The lows. The in-betweens."

"Bess."

"When you don't call, it makes me worry," she said, her stomach loosening up as all the practiced words she had inside her flowed out. "I wonder if you've had a good day or a bad day, if you're upset or not upset. And I want to know.

I *need* to know, so I can know where you are and how to help you."

His jaw jumped as she spoke, but he didn't interrupt. He put one hand on her hip but didn't pull her closer.

"Maybe *I've* had a bad week so far," she murmured. "Don't you want to know?"

"Yes," he said. "But I figured you'd text me if that was the case." Something washed over his features. "Bessie, are you staying closed tomorrow?"

"No," she said, seeing as he got all the dots to line up.

His hand dropped and he backed up a step. Bessie managed not to fall forward, but she hadn't been expecting him to move away from her. "Are you staying overnight?"

"Yes," she said. "I got a cute little hotel downtown."

"You came here..."

"To see you," she said. She cleared her throat. "Oliver I'm—"

"Don't you dare say it," he said, his voice gruff and full of power. Angry power.

She fell back a step. "You don't even know what I was going to say."

"Yes, I do." He advanced on her now, effectively pinning her against her SUV. The energy pouring from him made her blood heat. "And I won't listen to you tell me you love me. Nope. Not first. *I'm* going to say it first."

Bessie let his words wash over her. They entered her ears and cleared them all out. Love ran through her, then joy as she comprehended what he'd said without saying it. "Say it then," she murmured. "I'm right here, and I drove a long way to hear it."

He swallowed, and oh, she loved that movement in his throat. "You driving all this way just solidified it for me." He sounded like he'd eaten glass for dinner, not whatever his sister-in-law had served. "When I see you, I know exactly what I want. When I hear your voice, I know right where I fit."

Oliver leaned closer and closer until his mouth sat right at her ear. Bessie's muscles stayed tense, but she closed her eyes in bliss. "When I smell this perfume, I know without a doubt that we belong together."

She wrapped her arms around him, planting her palms against his back. "Mm."

"I'm in love with you, Bessie Clifton. I would've driven six hours to see you. I'm here, doing all of this, so I can prove to you that I know who I am inside my family." He finally rewarded her by placing his hands on her waist. The heat they sparked flew up her arms and down her legs at the same time.

"Have you figured that out this week?" she asked.

"Yes," he whispered. "I know who I am now, Bessie, and it's a man who desperately loves you." He pulled back enough for their eyes to meet, and Bessie took her time drinking in the features of his face, the emotions as they ran through his expression.

"It's your—"

"I love you too," she said.

Oliver's face split into a grin, and Bessie thought they

were probably the only two people on the planet who could argue about who would say *I love you* first, then say those beautiful words, and then—

Kiss.

She melted into Oliver's kiss, because there was nothing as magical as kissing the one she loved.

"Ollie," Cam called, and he pulled away with a growl in the back of his throat. "Cindy set another plate for Bessie. When do you think she'll—oh." Cam cut off as Oliver moved out of the way enough that he could see Bessie. "Carry on." He waved quickly and went back inside the house.

"I think maybe we should go in," Bessie said as she glanced around. "This doesn't seem like a neighborhood that minds its own business." In fact, she swore she saw the curtains flutter in the front windows of the house next door.

"I'd like a do-over on a lot of things." He tucked her hand in his, and they started the slow walk toward the front door. "One of which is how little we've talked this week. I'm sorry I haven't been communicative."

"Thank you." Bessie looked up at him, and in the evening sunlight, he sure looked like he wore a golden halo. "I'm sorry I almost said it first."

"Is that what you'd like a do-over on?"

"No," she said, grinning. "Because if I hadn't driven here and started to say...that, you'd still be silent on my phone. I'd still be worried about you, wondering if you're dying a slow death at the hands of your daddy or if you're okay."

They reached the top of the steps, and Oliver paused on the porch. "You're really worried about me like that?"

She saw no reason to fib. "Yes."

A slow, soft smile curved his lips. "Wow."

"Wow—what?"

"It feels nice to be cared about," he said. "Worried over."

"Has no one—?" She cut off, because no, Oliver probably hadn't had a lot of people worrying over him in his life. She faced the front door. "You got your do-over. What should mine be for this week?"

"Looking so amazing in those shorts?" he murmured.

Bessie gaped at him and swatted his chest, surprise flowing through her at his comment. "I was going to say that I've slept so late every morning."

"Mm, you do look amazing in those shorts. This blouse. All of it." He wrapped her up in his arms again, and Bessie sure didn't want to complain.

But they weren't exactly alone, so she said, "Behave yourself," just before he kissed her again. He didn't really behave himself, but Bessie decided this was *his* brother's house and *his* family, and if he wanted to kiss her with so much passion, and so much love, and so much care, who was she to protest?

He pulled away and rested his forehead against hers. "I really do love you, Bessie."

She could feel it in his touch, hear it in his voice. "And I love you, Oliver."

Facing the door, he said, "All right. You wanna meet the rest of Cam's family? Cindy's a killer cook, and she made fried chicken tonight..." He led her into the house, and Bessie hitched her personable smile to her face.

Turned out, she didn't really need it, because Oliver said, "Cindy, this is Bessie Clifton." He gazed at her with stars in his eyes. "She's the woman I'm going to marry."

Chapter Thirty-Three

ix months later:

S Bessie used the corner of the cart to push open the black plastic door separating the back of the shop from the front. She loved the life and vibrancy when they were open, the lines of people, the scent of browned, toasted bread in the air. The sound of chatter and laughter, the amazing sunshine pouring in the big front windows.

But she loved her bread bakery when they were closed too, as they were right now. The sun had just started to peek its head above the eastern horizon, so the light outside reminded her of a flat, matte gray.

They'd open in another thirty minutes, and Bessie started loading the cases with the breads and pitas she and Hillie had made that morning. Her opening employees would be here in mere minutes, and they'd get the chairs off the tables, the floors beneath having been mopped yesterday.

Bessie and Flour Power had been open for eight months

now, and while she'd started to see ups and downs in her revenue, she'd not had a month where she thought she'd have to close yet. She still loved baking as much as she always had, and as she bent to get to her lower racks, she sighed.

"You love Oliver too," she murmured, the words almost made of poison. They'd exchanged *I-love-you's* months ago now. They'd spent three major holidays together—Thanksgiving, Christmas, and Valentine's Day just last week.

He had still not proposed. Not that Bessie wanted a Valentine's Day proposal. That felt kitschy and so not her style. And it wasn't even on Oliver's radar.

She knew she still was. She saw him every day. They talked all the time, and they'd discussed getting married. Perhaps she simply needed to impress on him that she'd like the wedding to happen sooner rather than later.

Behind her, she heard the heavy, metal, back door slam. Probably Justin, who came in to open every day. She really liked him, and Wyn had started talking about making him a salaried employee instead of an hourly one.

Bessie had no problem with it, as long as they could afford it. Wyn handled the books like a champion, and she knew where every penny went. Her classes over the past couple of semesters had really opened her eyes to some things, and she'd implemented some good changes.

In fact, she'd started consulting with Oliver on a few things, and Bessie really liked that her daughter and her boyfriend got along so well. Now, if only she could get him to get down on both knees and ask her to marry him.

The swinging black door opened, and again, Bessie

wasn't alarmed. Justin didn't have a lot to do in the back of the shop, but she still glanced up to greet him.

"Hey—" She cut off when she saw Oliver standing there. She straightened too, though she still had two trays of bread to load into the case. "What are you doing here?"

He smiled that slow, sexy smile that said he knew more than she did, and oh, how Bessie liked it now. She liked it, because she knew he wasn't really saying that at all. He was just trying to hold back the tide of words in his mouth, and he did it with a slow smile.

He swallowed, and the vibe between them shifted in that one moment. Oliver reached the end of her cart, only a few feet between them. "Morning, sunshine."

"Yeah," she said. "It's morning, but it's super early for you." She cocked her head to the side. "What are you doing here?"

He glanced down at her cart, then put his hand on it. He held on tight as he dropped to his knees. "I left something here, but it doesn't look like you've found it yet." After plucking something from the very bottom tray, he looked up at her.

Hope shone in those dark eyes, and he swallowed again. Bessie pulled in a breath, because two swallows in one morning? Him here practically before dawn?

"Bessie Clifton," he said, and she'd known he'd start his proposal with her first and last name. "I'm in love with you. I know I'm going to need a lot of do-overs in the coming years, and months, but I hope none of them will be too terrible. You said you'd go back on your promise not to fall in love with me, and I hope you have." He cracked open a navy blue box to reveal a diamond, and Bessie wondered when he'd bought it and when he'd stashed it there.

Sometimes she doubled up her trays, but she wouldn't have been able to get the one still holding nine-grain bread on it if that box had been on the tray beneath it. He was so sneaky, and that only made her heartbeat rumble louder through her veins.

He looked at the diamond ring too. Then her. "Will you marry me?"

"Yes," she gasped out. She could ask him how he'd staged this later. Right now, she just wanted that ring on her finger and his mouth pressing against hers. She took a couple of stuttering steps toward him, a laugh brewing in her throat. She let it out as she held out her hand and he slid the ring onto the appropriate finger.

The light in the shop seemed to increase, shining directly on the new gem on her hand. "This is beautiful," she murmured. She hadn't worn a diamond ring for a long time, but she really felt like this one suited her.

Her eyes met his, and Bessie lowered herself to the ground too. "I love you, Oliver."

"You were getting impatient with me, admit it," he murmured, his hands already cradling her face.

"A little," she admitted.

"Wyn told me," he said. "I kept thinking I'd like this big plan for it, you know? But nothing was coming, and when she said something about how you didn't like a lot of fanfare, I realized I'd been trying to do something that didn't need to be done."

She smiled softly at him, the moment between them so tender and so sweet. "Can we have smoothies at our wedding?"

He blinked, clearly shocked by the question. Then he thawed as he said, "I've never catered a wedding before, sunshine. I don't think smoothies are quite wedding material."

"Well, for ours, they will be," she said.

"And bread samples," he added.

"We can have a toast and smoothie bar," she whispered as she leaned closer, hoping Justin was running late this morning. Because she wanted to kiss Oliver—her fiancé.

He touched his lips to hers, murmuring, "I love you so much," before he truly kissed her. She kissed him back, this dark cloud who'd lightened for her, shown her how amazing this beach town was, and helped her see that even the most put-together people needed a do-over every once in a while.

"May?" he asked as he pulled away. He got to his feet, and then helped her up too. "Or June? Later?"

"May," she said. "I'm a lot like Joy, and I don't want fancy." She ran her hands up his arms and around to the back of his head. "You've got to check with your family first, I'm guessing."

"Already did." He beamed down at her, and Bessie's joy felt so complete.

"I love you," she whispered.

"Love you back, sunshine," he said just before he kissed her again.

Keep reading for a sneak peek of **THE WATERFRONT WAY,** the next book in this romance and friendship fiction series. It features Sage Grady and her journey toward a second chance romance with a man she thinks is her complete opposite... oh! And they're both in their 50s! It's never too late to fall in love.

I hope you enjoyed Bessie and Oliver, Joy and Scott, Lauren and Blake, Cass and Harrison, and Bea and Grant! **Please leave a review for the book if you did.**

Scan the QR code below to preorder THE WATER FRONT WAY, the next book in the series.

Sneak Peek! The Waterfront Way
Chapter One:

~~~

S age Grady finished with her last appointment of the day and spent a half-hour cleaning up after herself. With the floor at her station pristine, and her tools cleaned and ready for tomorrow's haircuts, Sage left the upscale salon and sank into the driver's seat of her car.

A sigh likewise sank through her, and Sage started the car to get some air moving. It wasn't really too hot yet, as it was still February in Hilton Head, but it wasn't cold either. She just liked having some movement, so she didn't have to inhale the stale, stiff air that had been trapped in the car for the past eight hours.

She wasn't heading back to the apartment tonight, because her Supper Club was meeting to work out their schedule for the rest of the year. With holidays and vacations and people moving in and out, their schedule had been up, down, and around too. Most of them had switched months for one reason or another, and therefore, Cass had texted last week to say they'd just be meeting at a restaurant to go over their schedule for the rest of the year.

It, of course, could still change, and they'd all go with it. Sage felt like she was the one who could step in and accommodate anyone else's changes, for she didn't do anything.

She walked her dog in the morning. She cut hair all day. She went home. Sometimes, when she was feeling particularly rowdy, she'd then change into a swimming suit and go down to the beach or lounge by the pool.

Yeah, Sage was a real party animal.

Her life felt as stale and stiff as the air she wanted to move around, and not for the first time, she missed her hobby farm in Texas. No two days were the same on a farm, and at least she'd had some variety in her life.

She couldn't even imagine life without her five best friends in it, but they'd all moved on without her. Even Bessie was engaged now, and that left Sage as the eleventh wheel whenever they all wanted to get together for a party, a beach day, or a holiday meal.

She'd been told to bring Thelma, her sister, over and over, and that was fine. Of course she'd bring Thelma as her "date," but while she loved and lived with her sister, she was a poor substitute for a man.

Sage finally put the car in reverse and backed out of the spot where she'd parked behind the salon that morning. She had enough time to run into the grocery store and get a few things she and Thelma needed, but she drove on by. "Can't leave milk in the car during dinner," she reasoned.

She arrived at Bakersfield, the chosen restaurant for that

evening, with twenty minutes to spare. After she'd parked in the shade several rows away from the entrance, she pulled out her phone to check it.

Nothing exciting, as usual. A couple of texts from her sister was all, and even her Supper Club thread had been quiet all day. Cass or Bea would probably make them all say something they didn't want to say, and Sage ended up leaning her head back against the rest and closing her eyes.

In quiet moments like these, she let her thoughts roam freely, go wherever they wanted to go. She often thought about starting her own salon, though that idea never stuck around for long. She had a good setup at The Salon Mionic, and she made good money there. Enough to get her and Thelma out of the apartment they rented, but neither of them had wanted to pack up everything they owned very badly.

They were oceanside, and they had all the amenities of great apartment living. True, the space was small. She had to go down several doors to get to the laundromat, which she shared with everyone on her side of the building. But they had sand volleyball courts—not that she played. A pool—which she sat beside but had never been in. A game room she'd walked through once.

She and Thelma mostly worked, then came home. One of them made dinner, and they watched TV at night. Thelma liked to take her walk in the evening, though Sage really didn't know how she could breathe such hot air in the summer. She got up at five-thirty to take Gypsy out, and after the short rough patch with

Ed had been smoothed, she'd resumed walking with him.

His dog never tripped her again, and Sage's thoughts moved to the most taboo of topics—Tyler Parker.

She'd been out with Ty exactly once. She'd cut his hair a few times too, but after the concert in the park during the Heritage Days Festival, she hadn't seen him again. Here and there, briefly, if their friend groups happened to overlap. He was friends with all of the men that had captured the hearts of her Supper Club friends, but he claimed to be too busy for holiday parties or sit-down meals for twelve.

She honestly wasn't sure if they would've been good together or not. One date certainly wasn't long enough to know that, especially as they hadn't been able to talk for a large percentage of it. Still, she remembered the awkwardness and second-guessing that had happened for her, because it sure hadn't seemed like they had much in common.

She thought of Bea and Grant, and they didn't love all of the same things either. Heck, Oliver and Bessie were like night and day, and they'd figured things out. Perhaps Sage just needed to get together with Ty again and see if that fizzing, boiling chemistry between them still existed.

She opened her eyes to check the time, and she realized she was almost late. She grabbed her purse and headed for the entrance of the restaurant.

Inside, she found everyone except Bessie had arrived, and the power blonde who'd opened her own bakery for the first time last year entered only a half-minute later.

"We're all here," Bea said as she stepped over to the hostess station.

The woman there nodded, collected six menus, and said, "Follow me."

Sage generally hung back in times like these. She didn't want to be the first at the table, because then she'd have to make a decision about where to sit. Number two, in a booth situation—which Bakersfield had—she'd have to climb in and slide all the way over, never to get out again. She'd much rather be on the end.

Her wishes came true, and she sat on the end of the horseshoe-shaped booth as she took her menu. "I've never been here before," she said, taking in the appetizers and salads first. The conversation went round about who had, and it turned out only Cass had been here before.

Of course. The prices on this menu weren't cheap, and Cass seemed to have more money than any of them. Whether that was true or not, Sage didn't know. She didn't keep books for her friends.

"The burrata is amazing," Cass said. "So is the calamari."

"Look at that salad," Bea said, leaning closer to Sage. "It has balsamic and ranch dressing." Her blue eyes rounded with wonder. "I think I'm going to get that."

"It looks like a souped-up wedge," Sage said, reading the menu. Candied pecans, bacon, avocado, blue cheese, craisins. "I'm getting that too." Her mouth watered, and anything she ate here would be a far cry better than the granola bar she'd eaten between clients at mid-day.

A waitress arrived, and they put in their drink and appetizer orders. She'd only taken two steps away from the table when Cass said, "All right, ladies. Let's get the hard stuff out of the way."

"We're all really boring now," Lauren said from the middle of the booth. She'd recently cut her dark hair, but it still fell to her shoulders. Sage smiled at the new do, because she'd done it, and she thought it fit Lauren's face so well. She had delicate bone structure and pure beauty in her high cheekbones.

Sage had thinned her hair too, and she looked much more glamorous now—in Sage's opinion.

Lauren caught her looking and said, "Unless Sage has something to tell us," with her eyebrows raised.

Sage laughed and waved her off. "Sage does not."

Bessie's engagement was about a week old, and the whole story had been told over an app that recorded video instead of text. They'd been using that a lot more lately, and while Sage didn't entirely dislike it, she didn't like it either. She couldn't check a quick text at work if it was a thirty-second video others might be able to hear.

And she could face the music, even if none of her friends could. None of them talked for only thirty seconds. Bessie's engagement story had taken about thirty *minutes* to get through from beginning to end.

Then all the reactions...

Sage usually played the videos in her car on the way home from work, or around the apartment if it was her turn to put together dinner. She and Thelma were simple eaters, and neither liked spending too much time in the kitchen, so eating out somewhere fancy like Bakersfield had perks.

"I know it's okay if we swap Supper Club," Cass said. "But I would like to get a schedule ironed out. I feel like if we don't." She paused and looked around the table at the rest of them. "It'll be too easy not to do it."

"I agree," Joy said. "And I want to keep doing it. It's way easier if I have it on my calendar, so other things don't get scheduled over it."

"Mm him," Bea said. "So where are we?"

"February was supposed to be mine," Cass said. "But I swapped with Lauren in November. Things have sort of been off since then."

Sage didn't argue, though she'd been assigned December last year, and she'd fulfilled her commitment just fine, busy holiday season and all.

"Joy, you're usually after me," Cass said. "Can you do next month?"

"Yep." Joy had her phone out, and she started tapping with her thumbs. She looked up. "Do we need to revisit the date?"

"Third Thursday?" Bea asked. "That's always what we've done."

"Yes, but we don't operate under the community center guidelines anymore," Cass said. She looked around again, and Sage didn't care what day of the week Supper Club fell on. Her life could be completely molded around it, even if they decided to make it a lunch club instead of dinner.

"I'm fine with whatever," she said. Bessie and Joy nodded, and Lauren said, "Me too."

"Let's leave it there," Joy said. "I'm in March."

"That puts Bessie in April," Cass said, actually reading from a small piece of paper that looked like it had come from a child's notepad. "Lauren in May, Sage in June, Bea in July, and I'm in August." She looked up, but Bea was already shaking her head.

"Grant and I are going on our National Park road trip all of July," she said. "I won't even be here for Supper Club that month, and I can't host it."

"August?" Cass asked, her lips only pursing for a moment.

"Yeah, I can do August." Cass made the note on her slip of paper and looked up again. "Everyone else good?"

"Yeah," and "Yes," and "Sure," came from the others. Sage simply nodded, and since she'd already chosen what she wanted for dinner, her gaze wandered out into the restaurant. Everything gleamed in the evening light, and Sage sure did like the upscale atmosphere here.

The chatter at the table turned to less serious things than their Supper Club schedule, and to her surprise, no one called for them all to share something that month.

The drinks came; orders got put in; appetizers arrived. Sage laughed with Bea, asked about Shelby, her step-daughter, and listened as Lauren talked about a surgery her cat had to have.

She loved these ladies, and she'd been supping with them for so long, she couldn't imagine not having this monthly occurrence in her life. That was why she'd moved here. It was why she'd given up the variety of the hobby farm and left it all behind.

"Oh, boy," Joy said, and that drew Sage's attention across the table to her. She sat on the end on the other side of the horseshoe, and she met Sage's eye before nodding out into the restaurant.

Sage followed her gaze, wondering what she was looking for. It became obvious when she spotted the deliciously good-looking man in a full suit—slacks, jacket, white shirt, tie, and shiny wingtips.

He smiled at a woman who had dark hair—like Sage— and placed his hand on the small of her back as he pulled out the second chair at a table for two. Then Tyler Parker rounded it and sat across from her, in plain sight of Sage. If he'd look up and to his left the teensiest bit, their eyes would meet.

Her gaze flew back to Joy's. "What's 'oh, boy' about that?"

"It's Ty," Joy hissed, and hissing was never good. It drew the attention of Bessie at Joy's side. And Bea at Sage's.

"What?" they both asked.

"Ty's here," Joy said loudly, practically bellowing the man's name. *That* was "oh, boy."

Sage leaned forward, her eyes narrowing. "Joy."

"Oh, it's Ty," Bea said. "Were you...? Didn't you guys go out?"

"Once," Sage said. "And it's fine. It's not like I never see him." But the truth was, she hadn't seen him again. Not really. Here in there across a crowded room or beach full of people didn't count.

Her heart pumped out extra beats as she looked over to him again. He was too handsome for his own good, especially when he smiled and tipped his chin toward the ceiling as he laughed.

As he brought his head level again, he looked past his date, and his eyes landed on hers. Instant heat roared through Sage as the smile slipped from his face. He was the picture of calm, cool, and collected, as he leaned in and said something to his date.

"Stars in heaven," Joy breathed. "He's getting up."

"He's seen us," Bea whispered.

"Why are you whispering?" Lauren asked. "What's going on?"

Ty indeed had risen to his feet. He buttoned his jacket as the dark-haired woman turned their way. Sage didn't know her, but Bessie said, "Sugar and salt, that's Katherine Tallison."

"Who's Katherine Tallison?" Sage asked, wondering why she'd decided to whisper too. Probably because all six feet of the sandy blond god named Tyler Parker was walking her way, his eyes fastened to hers and no one else's.

Sneak Peek! The Waterfront Way
Chapter Two:

~

T yler Parker wasn't sure why he'd just abandoned Katherine. Maybe because it felt like his body was made of steel and Sage Grady's a very powerful magnet. He was simply drawn to her, and he couldn't resist the pull between them.

Her hair looked like she'd washed it and let it air dry, as it curled softly over her shoulders, and on the one date they'd been on, she said it did that if she let it do whatever it wanted.

Their drinks hadn't come yet, and his mouth felt like he'd been chewing on cotton since he'd picked up Katherine. He glanced around at the drinks and appetizers on the table where Sage sat with her friends, finally able to take his eyes off her.

"Hello, ladies," he said pleasantly. He tucked his hands in his pants pockets, his eyes going right back to where Sage sat on the end. "Sage. It's great to see you again."

All six pairs of eyes focused on him, and Ty felt them weighing him down. Oh, and another female pair behind him. He had no idea what he was thinking, coming over here. He should've ducked his head and texted Sage later.

He missed her, plain and simple, and he recognized those feelings as he stood at the head of the table.

"You too, Ty," she said diplomatically. Her eyes traveled up to his hair. "I see you've found someone else to cut your hair."

That was the worst thing she could've said to him, because then he wanted to tell her why he'd stopped coming to her for a trim. The words sat right there in his throat, but he couldn't get them out. Just like the texts inviting her out to dinner again had sat on his phone, unsent for weeks before he'd finally deleted them.

Something foamed between them, and it wasn't until Bea asked, "Are you seeing Katherine?" that Ty could pry his eyes away from Sage's.

His first inclination was to laugh, but he merely let a smile grace his face. "No," he said. "Sage, could I speak to you for a minute?"

She blinked rapidly, and Ty could understand why. He'd taken her to a concert in the park. Held her hand. On his side of the equation, he'd had a great time. Something wasn't exactly right, but he couldn't pinpoint what that night, and in the months since, he hadn't been able to either.

She hadn't texted him much afterward, and to be honest, he figured she wasn't interested. Fine, if he was being totally honest, he hadn't wanted to press the issue, because he knew he wasn't ready to be dating again.

But it had been a little over six months since the Heritage Festival and their first and only date, and his heart and mind were in a much better place now.

"Go on," Bea hissed at Sage, practically pushing her out of the booth. She stumbled right in front of him, and Ty reached out to steady her. Even at fifty-three years old, he felt like someone had poured popping candy into his bloodstream.

Everything fizzed, and white noise buzzed in his ears. Sage smelled sharp, like her salon, and soft, like the perfume he fantasized about her dabbing behind her ears. He kept his hand on her elbow as he turned his back on Katherine even more.

They walked away from the booth of her friends, and Sage moved her arm enough for Ty to get the hint that he better drop his hand. He did, and when they'd moved away from everyone and stood in front of an empty table, he said, "I'm sorry I never called you after the concert."

Regret pulled through his very core, and now that he wasn't constantly thinking about Gloria and if he'd made the right decision in finally ending things with her, he definitely felt more ready to open the door to another woman.

"I...I wasn't in a good place." He cleared his throat, the sparks racing through him like a meteor shower. He really wanted to try again with Sage, but he wasn't sure he'd get another opportunity with her.

"I appreciate you saying so," she said. "I don't want to keep you from your date."

Ty gaped at her, then let a bit of light laughter come out of his mouth. "Sage," he said. "I'm not on a date with Katherine."

"No?" Her eyebrows went up. "It sure looked like it."

"She's a client." He shifted his feet, suddenly too hot. "Well, a potential client. With a lot of money." He raised his eyebrows too, hoping to get across his point without having to say it.

Sage's face melted into a smile, and she nodded slightly. "Ah, I see. You're wining and dining."

"Something like that," he said.

She reached out and brushed something from his tie. "I didn't get a dinner at a fancy spot when I needed help finding somewhere to live." She smiled and ducked her head at the same time, and Ty wasn't too old to recognize flirting when it came his way.

"I can fix that if you're not seeing anyone."

Sage looked straight at him now, and she simply gazed at him. "Are you in a better place?"

"Yes," he said. "I think I can probably tell you about where I was." He swallowed, though he hoped she hadn't noticed the slight hitch in his voice. "If you'd like to know."

"Ty," a woman said, and he didn't have time to turn fully before Katherine eased into his side. "She's asking for our order." Her eyes landed on Sage too, and Ty suddenly wanted to shield her from the eyes of Katherine Tallison.

"Yes," he said, ducking his head as Katherine slipped her

arm through his. "I'll call you, Sage." He held her eyes for another moment, clearly asking for her permission.

She gave the slightest nod of her head, and that allowed Ty to turn and go back to his table with Katherine. He settled into his seat as he unbuttoned his jacket. "I'm sorry," he said to the waiting waitress. "I'd love the surf and turf, medium rare." His eyes wandered just over Katherine's right shoulder, where he saw Sage settle back onto the end of the bench seat in the booth.

Immediately, her friends leaned in, and she began to talking to them. He didn't particularly like that, but he'd been the one to walk over there and interrupt their dinner. He'd stolen her away for a few minutes.

He couldn't even remember what he'd said to her, and as Katherine cleared her throat, Ty focused on his task for tonight: get her to sign a contract of intent.

"Sorry about that," he said. "She's a friend I haven't seen in a while."

"A friend, hmm?" Katherine wore a look of supreme interest, her right eyebrow higher than her left.

Ty gazed evenly back at her. "Yes, she cuts my hair."

Katherine's eyebrows settled down, and she placed both arms on the table. "Tell me about her."

He shook his head and gave a light laugh. "She's just a friend."

Katherine checked behind her, and Ty took the opportunity to glance over to the table of Sage's Supper Club ladies. "She seems like she has good friends." He hurried to pull his gaze back to his own table as Katherine faced him again. "I'd love my daughter to have friends like that."

"There are a lot of good men and women who live on this island full-time," he said.

"How long have you been here?"

"Over twenty years," he said easily. "I like it in the summer too, when all the tourists are here."

Katherine gave a laugh that screamed false in Ty's ears. He'd worked with a lot of people over the years, and he could read them pretty well. He himself had fake-laughed and falsely smiled through plenty of conversations and situations.

He was honestly tired of it.

Thankfully, the fried calamari Katherine had ordered arrived, and that provided enough of a distraction for her to allow the conversation to die for a moment. It wouldn't matter, because he'd have to come up with the next small-talk topic anyway.

Another glance over to Sage found her looking at him, and when his phone chimed, he plucked it out of his breast pocket. "Oh, this is my mother," he said. "Give me five minutes?"

"Of course, dear," Katherine said.

Ty didn't need to step away from the table for the second time to text his mother back. But he took his phone and turned away from the table, away from the booth where Sage sat, and went back toward the waiting area in the restaurant.

Your daddy got a new dog, she'd said. As Ty tried to formulate a response, a picture of the puppy came in. The tan fluff ball seemed to be smiling at him, and Ty grinned back at this phone.

Wow, he typed out. *I thought he said he was too old to get another puppy.* As he waited for his momma to text him back, he quickly started another text string to Sage.

What's your schedule like this weekend? Are you still walking on the beach in the morning? Would you have time for dinner?

"Can't send her three questions," he told himself. He jammed his thumb on the delete key and watched the words disappear from his screen. He also didn't need to hover in the lobby to text Sage. It wasn't now or never.

So why did it feel like it?

LATER THAT NIGHT, TY STOOD ON THE BALCONY that extended his bedroom closer to the sea and let the night air brush his face. He loved the sound of the waves in the dark, because they roared on whether there was sunlight or not. He couldn't see them, but he sure could hear them just fine.

A feeling of contentment warred with the slip of unrest in his soul. "You got Katherine to sign the letter of intent," he told himself. He should be happy.

He *was* happy.

But at the same time, he was utterly lonely. Sage had not texted him, and in the end, he'd messaged with his mom for a few minutes about his father's dog, and then he'd returned to the table just before dinner had arrived.

He'd managed to charm Katherine enough with stories of the dog, his parents, and the upcoming beach volleyball tournament out on Carter's Cove. A sister island to Hilton Head, Ty did sell some properties there. Not many, as there were no cars allowed on the island. Only golf carts, scooters, or small motorcycles. Everyone had to take a ferry to get there, and most homes stayed in families for generations.

Still, Blake Williams, one of his good friends here on Hilton Head, had asked him to help his ex-wife sell her tiny, two-bedroom home on Carter's Cove last winter, and Ty had done it gladly. She'd relocated to Hilton Head, and Ty had gotten her into a small beach cottage that would serve her needs.

He knew Sage got up early, but he wasn't sure he could go to sleep without following up with their conversation. "You get one question," he muttered to himself. He stayed on the deck and thought through his options.

He could simply invite Sage to dinner. Or ask if he could go walking with her in the morning. He'd kept running with his dogs, but he'd never seen her again.

Outside, his dog nosed his hand, startling him enough to yank it away. "Hey, bud," he said to the golden retriever. "What should I ask her, huh?"

A simple dinner request felt stupid to him. He couldn't take her back to Bakersfield, not right now at least. He couldn't just show up and get a haircut. Could he?

He moaned and leaned against the railing, straining to

see the tips of the waves in the dark. Without a moon, though, such a feat was impossible. "I'm too old for this to be so hard," he muttered to himself. "Come on, Brother."

After the dog trotted back into his bedroom, Ty followed him. He reached for his phone, ready to ask Sage the one question he had for her. His thumbs flew over the screen, and he practically punched send so he wouldn't second- and third-guess himself.

A sigh moved through his whole body as he sank onto the bed. Brother jumped up and joined him and Sherman, the black lab who'd already leaned up against the pillows next to where Ty slept.

"All right," he said as he lay down and reached over to turn off the lamp. "I guess we'll see what she says in the morning."

Preorder THE WATERFRONT WAY now! Scan the QR code to preorder now.

Books in the Hilton Head Romance series

The Love List (Hilton Head Romance, Book 1): Bea turns to her lists when things get confusing and her love list morphs once again... Can she add *fall in love at age 45* to the list and check it off?

The Paradise Plan (Hilton Head Romance, Book 2): When Harrison keeps showing up unannounced at her construction site, sometimes with her favorite pastries, Cass starts to wonder if she should add him to her daily routine... If she does, will her perfectly laid out plans fall short of paradise? Or could she find her new life *and* a new love, all without any plans at all?

The Seaside Strategy (Hilton Head Romance, Book 3): Lauren doesn't want to work for Blake, especially not in strategic investments. She's had enough of the high-profile, corporate life. **Can she strategically insert herself into Blake's life without compromising her seaside strategy and finally get what she really wants...love and a lasting relationship?**

The Beach Blueprint (Hilton Head Romance, Book 4): Joy Bartlett needs a blueprint before she takes a single step in any direction. She loves seeing what she's getting into before committing, and moving 1200 miles from Texas to South Carolina just because half of her Supper Club has doesn't mean she's going to start packing boxes. Can she figure out how to arrange all of the pieces in her life in a way that makes sense? Or will she find herself cut off from everyone who's ever been important to her?

The Tropical Ticket (Hilton Head Romance, Book 5): Bessie Clifton adores baking. With her daughter Wynona by her side, she's turned her passion for the perfect loaf of bread into a dream for a bakery. They move to Hilton Head Island and work to get their shop open with the help of Bessie's five best friends.

It's not just a relocation.

It's a reinvention.

Will Bessie's journey to self-discovery lead her to the love she's always craved?

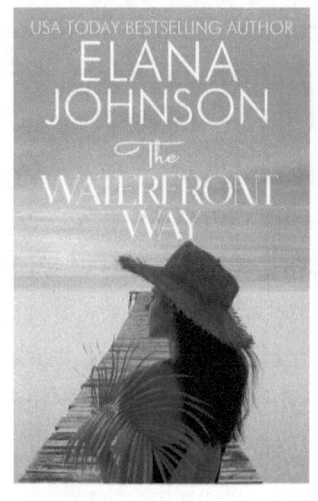

The Waterfront Way (Hilton Head Romance, Book 6): Sage Grady is a master of transformation. She's a seasoned hairstylist who's perfected the art of change, one cut and color at a time. Yet, her own life has started to feel somewhat monotonous, almost like she's stuck in someone else's style—and she needs to shake things up.

It's not a mid-life crisis.

It's a new way of thinking, of living.

Will she find that the path to true love doesn't always follow the path most trod, but might just be discovered through...the waterfront way?

About Elana

Elana Johnson is the USA Today bestselling and Kindle All-Star author of dozens of clean and wholesome contemporary romance novels. She lives in Utah, where she mothers two fur babies, works with her husband full-time, and eats a lot of veggies while writing. Find her on her website at feelgoodfictionbooks.com.